THE CHALLENGE

Dorothy Field

First Edition - July 2018

ISBN 978 0 9570957 1 7

© 2018 M & D Field , ALLOA, FK10 1TF

Inky Little Fingers Ltd.

GL2 8AX

Foreword

Whilst the events and characters described in this book are fictional many have been inspired by the events of European history around the Great War, 1914-1918, and family members involved in that history. Three such family members should be mentioned:

Esther Perkins - the author's maternal grandmother who volunteered as a nurse in WW1. Esther worked in a small hospital in Haslemere. She was just 5ft tall and packed with generosity and laughter.

George Perkins - the author's maternal grandfather who was a gifted accountant. He volunteered to serve in the armed forces in 1914 but his application was turned down because it was felt that he could better serve his country by managing finance and procurement. After 1918, with two associates, he went on to found the Bedfordshire Building Society

Donald Ross - the author's paternal grandfather who, having been born and raised near Dingwall, joined the Lovatt Scouts and then the Seaforh Highlanders. Donald was the Regimental Piper - and had the dubious honour of leading the regiment out of their trenches and over the top armed only with his bagpipes. He survived uninjured until 1916 when he was discharged with a leg injury (a 'Blighty one')

The author gives special thanks to friends
Irene and David Hynd. Irene for untiring support and
commenting on the script at all stages and David for his
careful proof reading

Liza Loader

Chapter One

The elderly Mrs Teague, carrying her sewing bag, was just hobbling her way back home to her shop in Poole High Street, E and C Teague, High Class Provisions, Tea Merchant and Ships' Provisions. It was 9.00pm, a dreary Thursday on a frosty January evening. She had been visiting her friends in the back sitting room of the Albatross Pharmacy. The women, Phemie Ross, Lydia Lovejoy, Caroline Lovejoy, Mrs Negus and others had been having their weekly meeting (Alec Ross, the Scottish pharmacist called it 'The Stitch and Bitch Blether').

In fact, the discussion the women had been engaged in that evening was far more serious, as it involved theft and poverty, just around the corner from the Albatross Pharmacy (Phemie's husband's baptismal name was Albert Ross. He hated it, and had chosen instead to be known as 'Alec'.) For some time, bottles and cans of milk which had been delivered for local residents in the early morning had been going missing. Phemie had become so irritated by both the thefts and inconvenience that she had called round to the local police station to ask the sergeant to investigate. PC Woodeford was instructed to keep an eye on the situation, and on the second morning noticed a young woman acting suspiciously, and questioned her. He discovered that she had two bottles of milk and a can concealed under her coat. Janet Lacey did not deny the thefts and the PC went back home with her and discovered two of the neighbours' stolen milk cans, now empty. Miss Lacey (*she was unmarried*) said she had taken the milk for her children.

Phemie was telling her friends about the court case which she had attended. The woman was mother of three illegitimate children aged four and three years and an eight month baby. They lived with Janet Lacey's mother, an unmarried person who earned ten shillings a week. This was the only money going in to the house, and five shillings had to be paid out in rent, leaving only another five for all of them to live on. PC Woodeford said that when he searched the house, there was not a scrap of food anywhere, and very little else besides. The girl said that she had formerly worked, but ill health had forced her to stay at home.

Superintendent Hack stated in court: 'The baby is only eight months old, and has to be fed. The woman seems physically unfit to work.'

The magistrate, having consulted with colleagues said that the girl would have to be remanded.

Superintendent Hack, who was well known in the town for being a very kind man, appealed for bail, saying that there was the baby of eight months to be considered. The girl, who appeared to be completely bewildered about what was going on around her was bound over to appear again, and the magistrate said he would seek further reports on the family situation. Phemie had discussed the case with her husband and friends. Practical support was given by the neighbours in terms of gifts of food and milk. She attended the second hearing on Saturday. Janet Lacey's mother swore on oath that she was unaware of the milk thefts. Miss Ray of St Thomas's Lodge Orphanage reported that the children were clean and well cared for, but the house was very poor. The magistrate said irritably that it would be far better if Janet Lacey went to the workhouse with the children.

Phemie whispered urgently in the ear of Miss Ray. She spoke to the magistrate who, very surprisingly, discharged the prisoner unconditionally. Phemie and her women friends had decided to provide food regularly for the family on the understanding that no additional babies would be produced. Most people who lived in Poole knew about poverty and its awful consequences, frequently leading to prostitution.

As Mrs Teague walked home from this serious, but satisfying meeting with her friends, she had been observing a respectable looking woman walking from the railway station, carrying a heavy bag. There was something about the woman's walk that looked familiar. By a gas lamp, she paused to say 'Good Evening' to the apparent stranger, and saw, inside the large black bonnet, the face of Liza Loader. She had taken Liza from St Mary's Workhouse many years previously, trained her up to become a good employee and passed her on to her daughter, as a maid. Mrs Teague had been very fond of Liza, and had done her best with her. The silly girl had got herself 'into trouble' with an unknown man and disappeared for a while. She popped up again in Poole a short while later, with her little girl. Living in a hovel near the quay, Liza had rapidly developed her already bad reputation, by taking to drinking, funded by prostitution with sailors in the narrow alleys down at Poole quay. The little girl had vanished, God alone knows where. She shuddered momentarily. This woman was a very bad lot.

Now eighty one, Mrs Teague didn't want to be bothered with the woman. However, as far as she could see in the yellow light of the gas lamp, she was clean, and tidily dressed.

'Liza Loader'! she exclaimed. 'As I live and breathe, it's you, isn't it?'

'Yes Mrs Teague,' she replied very nervously.

'Are you in decent work now my girl?'

The reply was satisfactory. 'I was in work in Wimborne until yesterday. I had given my employer two weeks' notice. I left with a good reference. I so much wanted to come back and find my girl, Marie. It's been twenty years since I gave her away, and I just want to know she's all right. She must be a grown woman now.'

'You got anywhere to stay tonight?'

'No. I was on the train early afternoon, but there's been a big bung up on the line from Wimborne, with a horse and heavy truck blocking the line. The train ran into it, lor, what a mess with the dead horse, splintered truck and all its heavy load and all! Took 'em ages to clear it up, so I'm far too late to find a respectable bed.'

'Come along a-me. I can give you a shake down in the cellar. Ain't much space since Wesley took over the business. Wife 'n babbie'n everything upstairs there now, but you'm welcome to overnight. You look as if you'm being a good gurl now.'

At the shop, still known as 'Teagues' (although it had been given unconditionally to Wesley), the old lady called out for Marion, now her only live in servant to 'put a bite to eat an' a mug a' tea on the table' in her back room. When Liza had cleared her plate, Mrs Teague asked what it was that had caused such a change in her life from drunkenness and prostitution.

'Well, Mistress Teague, you must remember that I grew up in the Workhouse. My mother was locked in the Lunatic Ward, and I never knew my father. I was so grateful when you came to the workhouse and chose me, to train for a better life. You were good to me, and found me a decent position in Parkstone, but I went bad didn't I? Couldn't control misself with men or drink. I went with anyone, just to feel a little bit of love. Some of the men were violent to me, and I have the scars on my face and my body. In the end, I just done it to buy more drink. Sad really.

It was the Methodists what got me right in the end. They were doing a church service on the quay for sailors in the hope of keeping 'em away from naughty girls like me. A nice lady and gentleman told me that Jesus really, really, truly and honestly loved me, and it didn't matter what I'd done. Jesus loved me anyway. They took me 'ome with em, got me cleaned up and nursed me till I was fit for life again. Their house at Longfleet was lovely, an' they took me to the little Longfleet Methodist Chapel with them reglar. Wesley will be pleased to hear that! In the end they done found a good place for me with kind Methodist folks well away in Wimborne. I been working hard and saving for many years now. I feel better 'bout everything. They give me a reference. I just want to find my girl. She must be working herself now!'

Liza said that she had money for finding lodgings and buying food, and would be seeking a further reference from her Methodist friends in Poole. She bedded herself down happily in the cellar, excited to be back nearer (as she thought) to her daughter Marie. First thing in the morning, she consulted Wesley, as now he was the owner and manager of the grocery, thinking it was likely that he and John, the delivery man might be able to make some suggestions of where she could look for 'live in' work. Liza insisted 'the top of the High Street is best, as I don't want to be too near the quay case I be meetin any bad old friends.'

Mrs Teague came wheezing down the stairs with her hair still in its night plait and envelope in her hand. 'I've wrote you another reference. Come straight back yur if you cassn't get nowhere decent to sleep' she said briefly, and shuffled off into the back room in her old slippers muttering 'Cassn't get no peace up thur wi' young George screaming his little 'ed off, teething, God bless the little lad!'

Liza was very fortunate. Wesley and John had suggested one lady, and Mrs Teague another. She was given a 'live in' job at a villa in St Mary's Road, Longfleet by an apparently pleasant lady, who said her household was 'seriously needing help'. She had been most impressed to meet a potential servant with three truly excellent references. It was also just what Liza desired, far away from the quay and all its ale houses and goings on. She wasn't likely to meet anyone she knew.

Marie

Chapter Two

Marie, Liza's illegitimate daughter, (fathered by Harry Lovejoy) had an unusual childhood, and it wasn't until she began to reach adulthood that she began to work out what might have happened. Almost all her childhood memories were based around St Faiths Orphanage in Mount Road, Parkstone. It was part of the Church of England Waifs and Strays Society. The house itself was actually owned by Miss Langley, who acted as Superintendent. She lived with her sister Nina and maid Nellie, in the rooms that had the best view of the gardens.

Her mother had taken her from her disgusting room near Poole Quay to St Faith's Orphanage one winter's afternoon, making her walk as much as she could, but also carrying her quite a lot. She fed and clothed Marie irregularly, and left her at home for hours on end. It was a long walk for a tiny child, and the evening was getting quite dark, and very cold. Marie had to be carried up 'Constitution Hill.' Eventually they reached the big green gates at St Faith's and Marie was dumped in the frosty front garden with a bundle and just left. She screamed until her throat was sore. Evangeline, the Assistant-Under-Matron unlocked the door as quickly as she could, brought the child into the hall and dashed out through the gate to see who had dumped her there. There was nobody to be seen. Miss Langley and her younger sister Miss Nina who were sitting in their parlour, sedately finished the rows of knitting that they had started, and then came out into the hall to enquire 'what is all this dreadful noise about?' They were unimpressed by the filthsome infant standing screaming on their Belgian hall carpet. A poorly written, dirty crumpled luggage label was pinned to her little chest stating *her name is Marie.*

Bella, the nursery maid to the smallest children, ran from the kitchen and scooped Marie up into her arms. Miss Langley decreed that the child must be de-loused, properly washed, and put into a nightdress. She should eat some bread and milk. She further ordered Bella, who slept in a tiny bed in the cupboard under the stairs, that the child would share her bed. Bella set to the cleansing of Marie with great gentleness and kindness. A fair amount of crying was heard coming from under the stairs at intervals during the night.

In the morning, Miss Langley went to inform Sergeant Rawlins at the Ashley Road Police Station that she was inadvertently sheltering an unknown, neglected and abandoned child. Despite police enquiries and several newspaper announcements over a period of two weeks, no-one came forward with any information. Marie slept under the stairs with Bella for a week, then moved upstairs and slept with the other 'teeny-tinies' in their dormitory - pink lino, red bedcovers, and a pottie under every bed. There were about 20 girls, aged 4 and a half to 16 in residence, in two dormitories. The girls passed their days learning, playing, praying, singing, and sewing. Marie slowly settled down in her new environment.

There was a little schoolroom downstairs for the teeny-tinies, with forms with no backs to them, and an upright piano. *'Christ is the Head of this house, the unseen guest at every meal and the silent listener to every conversation'* threatened a large framed notice on the green wall. After lessons Marie particularly enjoyed riding the rocking horse in the corner of the schoolroom. Miss Grainge the school teacher was very severe. Marie, who was probably about three, the youngest child in the house, was behind the class in absolutely everything; speech, social skills and table manners - absolutely none – she ate as if she had never seen food before. Bella was loving and caring to her, and Marie learned surprisingly quickly. Miss Langley and Miss Nina became extremely fond of the child, who should have been sent to the headquarters of the charity in London to be allocated a place in a home for younger children. However, Miss Langley decided that unless claimed by her parents, she would be her ward. A month passed, and Miss Langley, following the charity's rules, arranged to have her christened at a private ceremony in St Peter's church, where she was given 'Faith' as a second name like all the girls at St Faith's home.

Miss Langley consulted her solicitor about adopting Marie Faith Langley, who became a permanent resident at St Faith's, and the older girls set to work with their sewing needles to make some new clothes especially for her, as initially she had been wearing ragged but clean remnants that Bella had found for her. Miss Langley deemed her to be possibly three and a half, but it was hard to tell – most St Faith's girls had suffered from under nourishment in infancy, and were a bit on the small side. She gave Marie the same birthday as her own. Miss Langley had a severe face, but was very understanding of 'her girls'. Her sister, Miss Nina, was frail looking, gentle, simple and rather short, and absolutely loved playing 'rounders' with the older girls. She was an expert player and a good laugh! Roy, Miss Langley's dog, was a great favourite with all the household (but tended to field the rounders ball). Little Marie had an exceptionally good disposition and was so happy in her new home that remarkably she seldom cried again in all the years she was there. Miss Langley, who over a protracted period of time had succeeded in becoming her legal guardian, was very concerned about not 'spoiling' her, or creating any jealousies amongst the other children. The only favour Marie enjoyed in the early years was to dine with Miss Langley and Miss Nina on Sundays.

The charity supporting St Faith's sold the magazine 'Our Waifs and Strays' in local churches. Donations were invited to help cover the heavy expenses incurred at St Faith's, and everyone, including the children had to work really hard to keep the place going. Every child was given a garden plot, but it was hard to grow anything because of the trees around the back garden. The kitchen garden, with better soil and more sun did better, producing some food for the household. When horses were in the area, delivering milk, post, groceries or coal, an older girl would run out with a bucket and shovel to collect any horse droppings for the garden!

Marie loved living in the big grey house, behind the garden walls ornamented with Virginia creeper, which went red in autumn. In spring the red rhododendron beside the front gates flowered and the yellow orange flowers of the broom bushes filled the air with a delicious almond scent. There was even a wooden summer house in the garden for the girls to play in. So tiny a child, having received so little care, Marie couldn't put her feelings and memories of neglect, squalor and hunger into words, so in the beginning, she was a silent, docile and smiling child. She would often pick a flower in the garden and run smiling to the nearest adult with her tiny gift, carefully enunciating 'flower.'

One summer Sunday afternoon, sitting with Miss Langley and Miss Nina in their parlour, Marie was told that she would soon be going to St Peter's School.

'With the *big girls*?' she asked.

On schooldays a small group of St Faith's girls, aged from four and a half to fourteen walked in crocodile formation down North Road in their clodhopper shoes, wearing their summer uniforms - cotton dresses, sewn by the girls themselves and straw boaters. It was a very scary walk, particularly for 'the teeny tinies', with all the trams hurtling down the steep road which stretched from Ashley Road nearly to Poole Park. The big girls walked on the outside, holding the smaller girls' hands. They walked four times a day, as all the St Peter's School children went home for lunch.

It wasn't a nice first day for little Marie at St Peter's. The big classroom was cold and dismal, with just a small fire in the grate. The windows were high up on the walls, only the sky was visible, and a reprimand was likely if she even looked up. Her teacher, Miss Ellis, was passively aggressive which was highly unpleasant, but to be fair, she was contending with a number of small children from large, disorganized families who were not used to sitting down for reasonable periods of time, and didn't have much concentration. Two of the new children cried all day. Marie was unaware that Miss Ellis's job was made harder by the fact that the Vicar had told her not to smack the little children. (*There had been complaints*). It wasn't a very good first day, and was made worse by the fact that the toilets were abysmal – filthy, and outside. Marie was very tired and had a headache when she got back to the Home. She didn't eat much of her evening meal and was sent to bed early. However, she soon began to realize that in comparison with the other children at the school, St Faith's girls were fortunate. They were well clothed, clean and fed. The adults they lived with loved them, and gave all their efforts in helping them to lead good lives.

On Sunday Miss Langley and Marie had a talk about school. Miss Langley asked 'what do you like most about St Faiths?'

'Everyone is very kind to each other.'

'Do you think you could be especially kind to the little boy and girl at St Peter's School who cry all the time? Perhaps they miss their mummies? This might help Miss Ellis too?'

'Yes Miss Langley, I will try,' she said smiling at the dear lady.

Chapter Three

At the beginning of the winter term, any weak chested girls had to be smeared front and back with goose grease, and wore special 'chest protectors', made of flannel, shaped like a bib, back and front. Everyone wore a wool vest, flannelette chemise, then stays or a bodice, and 2 pairs of drawers, 1-2 petticoats, a dress and pinafore. Marie was quite worried that she didn't have any winter school uniform. She wasn't old enough to make her own like the other girls. 'Don't you worry my little lamb' said Miss Nina affectionately, 'I have been making your school uniform for you.' She fetched out a tiny grey flannel gymslip, a white flannel blouse, grey woollen socks, a red cardigan and a scarlet wool cape, bound with black silky thread, with huge buttons.

'You can wear these to school tomorrow.'

'Thank you,' Marie said, with tears of gratitude in her eyes.

Marie hadn't been going to school for very long before a terrible accident occurred during the winter term, whilst she and her friends were walking down North Road. Poole's modern Cambridge blue and white trams were double-deckers with wooden brake blocks and a screw down handbrake. They had electric lights, but their lack of power and braking force made them second class in comparison with the Bournemouth trams. Following a fatal accident on a hill in Bournemouth during the previous year, all Bournemouth trams had been equipped with Westinghouse magnetic track brakes. One icy morning in late December, when the St Faith's girls, wearing their lovely bright red woolly cloaks and clod hopper boots were walking down the steep and slippery hill, a Poole tram, packed to the brim with passengers was coming back from Bournemouth and down North Road when the driver's brakes failed to slow the vehicle, despite the conductress immediately running to the back of the vehicle throwing out sand onto the rails and operating the screw brake. The packed tram left the rails at speed and rolled on its side at the turning to St Peter's Road. Many passengers were injured.

Helen, the oldest, most sensible St Faith's girl, sent the younger girls off to school with Ruth, who was young, but steady. Helen told them to stop off at the Vicarage and ask Canon Dugmore to arrange help, as he was known to have a telephone apparatus. Helen, Josie and Ethel remained and did what they could. The conductress had been thrown clear into the middle of the road and was obviously dead from the massive injuries to her head and body. Helen used her red cloak to cover her. The 'walking wounded' were escorted to the big house called 'Torvaine' by Janet, who was instructed to stay with them. Ethel helped Helen with the driver and two other passengers who were seriously injured. The brave girls tore up their pinafores and petticoats to bind up injuries and make slings, and Canon Dugmore had his carriage sent round to take some of the 'minor injuries' home, where they could be seen to by their own doctor. There were only two seriously injured, and they were conveyed to Cornelia Hospital by Mr. Ernest Paddock the fishmonger, who also drove the Parkstone motor ambulance.

Lady Louise Dugmore, (a housebound invalid) who was a good friend of Miss Langley's, telephoned her, and asked her to walk down and escort the girls back home. They were in no fit state to stay at school. It was an amazing day. Awful in terms of the severity of the accident, but good as only one person died. The tram conductress had been a much loved Sunday School Teacher at the Baptist Church in Poole, and was engaged to be married. Miss Langley and Miss Nina cried with the girls, and said how very, very proud they were of everything the children had done. Canon Dugmore visited that evening WITH A LARGE BOX OF CHOCOLATES for the girls from Lady Louisa, and the girls went to bed, some to sleep, and Helen, Josie and Ethel who had been the most involved with the injured, cried silently in the darkness over several nights, seeing the scenes over and over again. The following day the Poole and Dorset Herald published a picture of the crashed tram, and printed a story about '*the plucky orphans at St Faith's.*' Miss Langley, who had refused to allow the newspaper men to take a picture of her girls, lit the fire in her sitting room with that newspaper. She never wanted to even think of her girls going through such terror again.

At St Peter's School, St Faith's children were known as 'The Home Girls.' They weren't treated particularly well by the teachers and other children, and were teased and bullied in the playground. Girls were not allowed to talk to boys, and never ever accept sweets or gifts from them. The school had separate playgrounds for boys and girls, so there was little chance of fraternization anyway.

Keeping St Faith's open and the girls well-fed was a colossal task for Miss Langley. It would have been impossible without massive help from the people who lived in very large houses in Parkstone. The older girls were regularly sent to knock on the doors of affluent homes to ask if the mistress had any spare fruit and vegetables from their kitchen gardens, and received baskets of carrots, parsnips, onions, potatoes, salad vegetables, pears, apples and hothouse grapes. Sometimes they were given loaves, fruit pies and cakes by the kindly owners. Every year a share of the Harvest Festival gifts were brought to the Home from local churches.

As the nights began to draw in, the girls spent much of their evenings sewing their own clothes. They also worked particularly hard on making a huge variety of little gifts such as pincushions, needle-cases, matchbox holders, woolly scarves, hats and gloves, anti-macassars, handkerchiefs and lace doylies. These were all carefully saved up for St Faith's Sale of Work, a major fund raiser for the home, which was held on the first Saturday of November.

Well before Christmas, 'well to do' ladies began to call round to St Faith's on Saturdays to talk to the girls about what they would like to receive for Christmas. Items such as books, paint boxes, brooches, dollies and sewing boxes were popular. For Christmas Day, the kind ladies ensured that each girl received just one present – the item they most desired. On Marie's first Christmas at St Faith's she remembered three barrels of perfect, hand-wrapped apples being delivered, crates of oranges with the silver paper showing through the slats, boxes of crackers and biscuits and two large cakes with fruit, marzipan and icing. Puddings and fruitcakes were also made in St Faith's kitchen, and St Faith's Christmas pudding contained silver charms: silver coins for wealth, a thimble for a spinster, a boot for travel and a horseshoe for luck (They all had to be given back ready for next Christmas). After Christmas Day, the girls were invited to parties, pantomimes, visits to very smart homes, concert nights, Punch and Judy, and they were even asked out to a lady's house and heard a gramophone. The girls wondered if they were in Heaven already!

One hot summer, when Marie must have been about eleven, one of the Parkstone ladies, Mrs. Barrett, paid for a delightful treat for all the orphanage girls and staff. They took the tram down to the Poole terminus. Marie had a vague sense of something familiar as she walked down the High Street in 'crocodile formation' towards the quay. She felt quite unwell and faint. Miss Nina was very anxious about her. At the quay, she had a feeling of recognition of the smell of the dirty seawater, and heard sounds that were strange but yet familiar. Her little friends were seeing everything for the first time, but she had the weirdest sense of having seen it all before. It passed off as the boat took them away from the quay to Wareham. They had a marvellous day, with a lovely lunch served to them in St Mary's Church hall at Wareham, all pre-arranged by the brilliant Mrs Barrett. Marie found her return to Poole just as odd. Being on the quay had the same strange familiarity about it. That night she had a frightening dream of being tied up to the leg of a table of all things!

As Miss Langley's ward, Marie was not destined to be known as a 'St Faith's Girl' all her life. She had, by the age of seven despite her very poor start in life, an exceptionally active brain. As the years passed, this became ever more obvious. St Peter's School provided education for children until they were fourteen, focusing on reading, writing and arithmetic. The school also taught social discipline – the complete acceptance of the teacher's authority, punctuality and general obedience to adults. On leaving school, the St Peter's youngsters became part of the local low paid working population.

Miss Nina, who rarely made any significant comments raised the matter with her sister very bluntly one evening.
'Should we enter Marie for the new boys and girls Grammar School that is opening at Ashley Cross, as it's just around the corner from St Peter's School?'

Miss Langley had been thinking of exactly the same thing for quite some time, but was concerned about the cost of the fees as both sisters committed a major part of their incomes to St Faith's. In the end, she decided to ask Canon Dugmore for advice.

Sitting in the large sitting room at the luxurious vicarage, which Canon and Lady Louisa Dugmore had built at their own expense, she said:

'I've come about my ward, Marie.'

'She always seems a very fine girl, Miss Langley. I trust that you have not come across any problems? The reports I hear of her from St Peter's school are superlative.'

'There are no problems.'

'Then how can I help you dear lady?'

'Well, the girls I have been helping for many years are of much the same type. With the decent, respectable start they've been given in life, they will have no trouble in getting work as servants in good homes. Marie is different. She is highly intelligent, and if she continues to develop at this rate, she could marry well and use her gifts within the community to be a great blessing to others. Miss Nina and I would like her to go to the grammar school. We are prepared to make sacrifices to pay for the fees and uniform. However, before embarking on such a project, we wanted your third party unbiased opinion.'

'I am in full agreement with you, Miss Langley, such an intellect and excellent disposition should not be wasted.'

'I will pay for the school uniform, shoes, books and any other expenses arising extra to the fees' said Lady Louisa firmly.

Chapter Four

Marie had enjoyed her time at St Peter's school, but it had its limitations, as her brain was quick, and the learning offered was by rote. The school produced well trained boys who would be taking up apprenticeships if they were lucky and girls who would be good servants, wives and mothers. It gave her a good grounding for her move to the Parkstone Grammar School which she simply loved. The new teachers were excellent, kind, and didn't mind the pupils putting up their hands to ask questions. Understanding was as important as memorising. The boys and girls were all very focussed on learning and '*wanting to do well in life*.' The lessons were challenging as the curriculum included mathematics, chemistry, physics, Latin and French. A whole world of learning was opening up before these fortunate young people.

Just before she began attending her new school, Marie received a new surprise. Miss Langley had moved her into a small room in the part of the house she and Miss Nina reserved for themselves. There was just room for a narrow bed, a little desk with drawers and a tiny wardrobe. Previously Marie had been treated much the same as the other girls, in order to avoid any jealousy developing. Now she was to call her 'family' Auntie Fanny and Auntie Nina. It was a wonderful day, as it was also the birthday of Auntie Fanny, who had given Marie the same birthdate. The occasion was celebrated quietly in Miss Langley's rooms.

At the first assembly of the grammar school term in September, Mr Deedham the headmaster reminded all the pupils 'The first aim of grammar school education is to open your minds to the wealth of knowledge that lies before you. Information is important in life, but has no educational value unless you *use* the literary, scientific and technical knowledge placed before you during your school years and learn how to continue to develop it in your daily lives. The staff can only instruct you. It is what you do for yourselves and the questions you ask of yourselves, the teachers and of the materials, both in school textbooks and in practice that will alter the way you think. Thus the questions that you ask and *answer for yourselves* will influence your adult lives.'

At Parkstone Grammar School Marie was not in the 'A' stream. Even in the 'B' stream she was no-where near the 'top' of the class as she had been in primary school. However most of the children in 'A' and 'B' thought that those in 'C' and 'D' were 'thick', despite all of them being in the Grammar School! Notably only the girls in the 'C' and 'D' streams did cookery and only the boys in the 'C' and 'D' streams did wood work. There was certainly a class distinction at the Grammar school, where there had been none at primary school as the expectations of all the children were low.

Miss West was Marie's teacher in year 1B, a kind disciplinarian. There was no cane in the classroom. This had been frequently used as a terror weapon at St Peter's.

'I require each of you to uphold the highest standards of courtesy and honesty' she said. 'Small discourtesies may be punished by me in terms of additional homework, but if there is any serious deviation from the good behaviour that I require from you, you will be sent directly to Mr Deedham.'

So began the autumn term. 'How is school going?' asked Miss Langley one evening after Marie had finished her school 'prep' rather late.

'It's just wonderful! We're studying Arithmetic, Geometry and Algebra, Languages -Latin, French and German, European History, Divinity, Music, English Grammar and Literature and Science for Biology, Chemistry and Physics.'

Miss Langley was most impressed. The school work set required more focussed attention from Marie than had ever been required at St Peter's. She had to work very, very hard at her maths. Biology was her favourite subject, taught by Mr

Barnes. One lunchtime whilst playing with her friends under the oak trees, she found a dead squirrel. They took it to Mr Barnes, who was as usual, eating his sandwiches in the biology lab.

'What a lovely find! Shall we dissect it? Wait, whilst I get the equipment out.' he said, finding a wooden board, a scalpel and pegs. With his help, the girls were able to find exactly what the squirrel kept under his furry coat, now opened down the front, and carefully pegged near the edges of the board.

They looked at everything very carefully, wondering why he had died.

'Oh wow, look at his tiny bladder, still full of squirrel urine.'

'What a beautiful little liver…'

'Is that teeny little thing actually his heart?'

Following the exciting post-mortem examination, Mr Barnes's conclusion was that Mr Squirrel had probably died of old age.

'*We all within life's bending sickle's compass come.*' said Marie reflectively.

'Well done that girl, well done!' Said Mr Barnes. 'Now tell your friends where that came from.'

'It's a Shakespeare sonnet,' said Marie going pink, 'just something I read at home. I can't remember which one it was.'

Thus began, for Marie, a deep interest in how bodies worked, in particular human bodies. By the time she was sixteen, she was reading in the News Chronicle of the establishment of local branches of The Red Cross and St John's Ambulance to raise money and train local volunteers in 'first aid,' but to her sorrow there were no branches in the county of Dorset. Remembering the serious tram accident in North Road a few years previously when St Faith's Girls had excelled themselves, she went over to Mr Paddock's fish shop to ask him how he learned about looking after people who were hurt or ill. He was very busy filleting a basket of local plaice, and put her in *her place*.

'That's nothin' to do with you my maid.' he said disparagingly.

'Hmmp,' she thought to herself, thinking of the children, young people and adults back at her home. One of the teenie-tinies had a glass marble stuck in her windpipe one day. She'd quickly upended her and wacked her back whereupon it shot out and she had helped out when the Home had suffered from an outbreak of Scarlet Fever. She resolved that she would spend some of her precious 'spare time' reading Miss Langley's 'Home Doctor' book.

Marie was sixteen when elderly Miss Bascombe the Latin teacher, who was on morning break 'Playground Duty' suddenly took ill. It was a chilly February morning, and she was standing in the middle of the playground holding a cup and saucer and carefully sipping a very hot cup of tea. Marie had been standing under one of the oak trees daydreaming. She suddenly saw the cup, saucer and contents slither out of Miss Bascombe's hand, and then she fell heavily to the earth. Marie dashed over, could see that she seemed to be choking, and did what seemed best, rolled her on her side and thumped her back. She held her over on her side until Mr Deedham and Miss Mathews arrived to give adult help. Marie then ran across the road to fetch Mr Paddock. By the time she got back, Miss Bascombe was lying on the ground under a woolly rug, with Miss Mathews kneeling beside her. Half her face seemed to be alive, the rest was drooping. Marie felt very scared. Mr Paddock had brought his canvas stretcher, and he and Mr Deedham carried her inside. Mr Paddock nipped back to the fish shop to fetch the ambulance to take Miss Bascombe to the hospital.

Later, Mr Deedham sent for Marie. 'You did exceptionally well Marie.' he said. 'Turning Miss Bascombe over on her side and keeping her there may well have saved her life. How did you know to do that?'

'Well… Mr Barnes has given me a great interest in how animals work, and this has led to me being interested in how the human body functions and first aid, which seems to be becoming popular according to the newspapers. I have been reading things up at home in Miss Langley's 'Home Doctor' book. I was standing under a tree and saw the event unfold before my eyes. I just ran over and put her on her side.'

'Very, very well done Marie.' Mr Paddock said, smiling.

That evening Marie told Auntie Fanny and Auntie Nina what had happened. 'I've been thinking for a long time that I'd like to become a nurse' she confessed. 'I fully understand the expense the training would involve, but Mr Perrett has been trying to persuade me to come and work in his grocery shop. If you would give me permission to do this when I leave school in July, I would be able to save my wages for two years so that I could train as a professional nurse at the new Royal Victoria and West Hants Hospital in Boscombe. How would you both feel about the idea?'

A long discussion followed. Auntie Fanny confessed that she would be very sad indeed if Marie had to work in a shop, however, as a means to an end, the idea had its merits, and she gave her blessing.

Isabel Maude

Chapter Five

In Alloa, Isabel Maude, sister of Phemie, known to her family and friends as Isa, was considering her future. She was already working at Paton's woollen mill, in the carding room. Isa was a 'Carder' in her own right, and knew she would never rise any higher, as all the overseers were men. She was well aware that if she stayed with Paton's her future was deafness from all the factory noise and a bad chest from all the wool 'flyings' in the factory atmosphere.

Isa had never minded particularly about her 'dead end' job. She had her mind on higher things, as she'd always heard God calling her to be a missionary like Mary Slessor. Mary had worked in a mill in Dundee, before accepting God's call to work for Jesus in Nigeria. Isa was in contact with Miss Forrester Paton (the Patons owned just about everything in Alloa due to their successful wool business) via the Young Women's Christian Association Temperance Cafe Miss Paton was funding. She had told Isa 'Piety and good intentions are not enough, you'll need to get yourself a place in the Ladies' Missionary Home I've founded in Glasgow,' and so Isa was saving up so that she could train there as a Medical Missionary. She kept herself really busy, working the usual long hours at the Kilncraigs Mill, attending the Greenbank Mission Church and helping her Ma out whenever she could at the birthing of a bairn, as she expected that women missionaries should know lots about things like that.

Mrs Maude used to say 'Isa, you're no a natural at this like your sister, but ye'll do well enough. Jist keep yer haund in so as tae say.' Looking back, Isa couldn't believe how much she did in a day, or a week. She certainly never had any problem getting to sleep.

In January 1897 Isa, now 34, had a letter from Miss Douglas, Principal of the Lady Missionaries' Training Home in Glasgow, informing her that 'subsequent to your recent interview with Miss Forrester Paton, we have pleasure in informing you that your application to begin training here has been carefully considered by the Committee. Please make arrangements to report here to our Home in Burnbank Gardens on Saturday 1st March to commence your training.'

Isa was that pleased, beaming all over her chubby face. She showed the letter to her Ma, saying 'That's me away soon then, bag and baggage. I doubt I'll be coming back to Alloa except to say hallo to you, Ma.'

'I'm that proud of ye hen,' said Mrs Maude, tears trickling readily from her brimming eyelids. 'You're going to The *Ladies* Missionary Home. So you're to be a *lady* now. That's our family come up a peg the noo then!'

Unfortunately, the letter also contained a long list of things that Isa would have to bring with her in her baggage. She didn't have a trunk, never mind all the things on the list, which included unforeseen items like personal cutlery and crockery, besides a great long list of clothing. Isa had saved enough for her year's training, as of course, she would not be paid, but the list was devastatingly bad news. She knew she would just have to pray about it. Fortunately the following day's post contained a letter of encouragement from Miss Forrester Paton. Right enough, the woman was as rich as Croesus, but she certainly never held back from giving money away.

'Thank you, Lord!' said Isa, clutching an unbelievable *two five pound notes* to her heart. 'This will cover all my needs for training, and help me when I reach Nigeria.'

What a sending away the Patons factory gave her! The proceeds of a collection around the large factory complex yielded a tonnage of small coins from poor people, but as Mr Strachan, the Overseer, said 'Mony a mickle maks a muckle,' (lots of little bits put together, make a lot). Mr Barrow, from the 'Accounts Payable' department, a handsome bachelor who had exhausted himself over the years asking Isa to 'walk out' with him, took charge of it all for her, got the pennies changed into half crowns and made it up, out of his own pocket, to three sovereigns. At the Greenside Mission there was an enthusiastic valedictory service, very passionate hymn singing and the presentation of a further cash gift.

Her mother saw her off at the station on the first of March, a Saturday morning, and they both tried not to sob into their white rag handkerchiefs. 'There's naebody can throw together tatties and mince, and make them taste as good as you do pet, I'm gonnae miss you so much,' she said. The journey was quite an undertaking for Isa, who had been no further than Stirling in her whole life, and was trying not to shake with nervousness. There was a change of train at Stirling and another at Falkirk before she reached Queen Street. She let down a corridor window, and spent most of the journey with her head out of the window, enjoying the rush of air, the countryside and town that they were racing through and the smell of good quality coal burning.

As her trunk had been sent on ahead, and she had absolutely no idea of the size of the city of Glasgow, she decided to walk to the home from the station to save money. She was quickly scared nearly to death from the traffic, with horse drawn vehicles and men pushing large barrows going here, there and everywhere down the most incredibly wide streets. It was very difficult getting directions, as most working class people just knew 'their bit.' Isa, being so naive, hadn't realized either that the Lady Missionary Training Home was in the West End (Best End) of Glasgow, in Burnbank Gardens, just a small distance from the Great Western Road. Isa was muttering (reverently!) *sweet Jesus* when she turned into Burnbank Gardens and *dear Lord, save me*, when she saw the enormous terraced house which was to be her home for the next year. She rang the doorbell. At her home in Alloa, folks would just chap the door loudly and roar your name.

A very nicely dressed housekeeper looking type, who didn't look as if she had ever wielded a scrubbing brush or peeled a tattie, answered the door, and looked at her in a perplexed manner.

'Can I help you Miss?' She enquired in a very refined tone.

Isa was surprisingly, nearly struck dumb. She could sort out any drunk in the street or contemptuous overseer at Paton's mill. She rightly suspected that the very nice lady thought she was some casual and unwanted caller.

After a pause, she found some words. 'I... I'm expected. Er, I'm a new student. My name is Miss Isabel Maude.'
'Ah yes, the other new ladies are here already. My name is Miss Abercrombie. Do come in, and perhaps you would like to freshen up and change? I will show you to your room. You will be sharing with Miss Cameron and Miss McNeil. Then I will show you to the bathroom.'

Isabel felt herself changing from pale with fear to scarlet with embarrassment. She had never *been* into such a house before. She had never *seen* a bathroom before, far less used one. When she was shown to the bathroom, she saw her face in the looking-glass. She was BLACK from all that sticking her head out of the train window. She felt like something the wind had blown in. She was mortified, and wondered how she would face Miss Abercrombie again. She dashed back to the bedroom to unpack her washing things, when she noticed on the chests of drawers belonging to the other two beds what looked like *silver backed hair brushes and perfume bottles*. She wanted to go back home. Now.

She went into the bathroom, washed and prayed for courage. She went downstairs, in her simple, hardwearing clothes, to meet 'the others.' There were fourteen of them. Things got worse when she realized that she was one of a type, not just the only truly working class woman present, but probably the oldest and worse dressed and educated. She started gently humming 'Forth in your name, O Christ I go,' and a lady with a very gentle face, sitting in the corner started singing the words. Another, very young lady moved over to the upright piano, and started playing the melody, and they all started singing the words of the first verse.

'Thank you so much,' said the pianist, whose name was Christine. 'I was feeling so nervous and strained until you came in, and I don't think I was alone in that,' smiling bravely at the others in the room. After that, everything changed, and they all began chatting together and exchanging stories, and things felt a whole lot better. Dinner that night was what Miss Abercrombie called 'a cold collation'. Isa felt very embarrassed when she found out that Miss Abercrombie was actually in overall charge of the Ladies' Missionary Home and its occupants. Furthermore, there was a single maid of all work for domestic assistance in this large household. The tasks of shopping, cooking, cleaning and laundry would be shared by all of the women, under the direction of Miss Abercrombie. This was of no concern at all to Isa, but the very highly educated, more refined persons present went rather pale when Miss Abercrombie mentioned these responsibilities. She also pointed out, between mouthfuls 'missionaries need to be able to do everything for themselves.'

Immediately after the meal they were told to 'consult the notice board outside the kitchen to check your duties. You have been arranged into five teams of three, on a rota for cooking and dishwashing; cleaning and shopping; evening services at Grove Street Institute; soup kitchen at Grove Street. Sheets and towels go to the laundry and washing of clothing is your own responsibility. There are lectures most mornings from 9.30am until 12.00, and practical work in the afternoons will include working in the Western Infirmary, home visits, dispensary and midwifery practical as per the lists on the board.'

Isa went to her shared room that night with her new friends Ailsa and Shona, lay in bed and prayed for most of the night, on the grounds that God would be up anyway. The other two were also tossing and turning. At bedtime, both of them had confessed to worrying about all the household duties they would be expected to participate in. Isa had suggested to them that it would be 'nae bother', as she was well set up to help them. She was secretly hoping that they would help her with the studies that they would all be doing.

So began their daily labours. All members of the household were up at six to begin work. Isa was particularly relieved to be on cooking and dishwashing with Ailsa and Shona for the first week. The vast kitchen was way above the cooking in a couple of pots on the fire at home, but the maid of all work, a cheerful lass in her early twenties called 'Win' had stoked the cooking range as soon as she woke, and put water on to heat. Isa inspected 'the burning fiery furnace', and was well pleased, feeling pleasant anticipation at the thought of getting to 'drive' this monster. The previous evening Isa had found a hay box cooker in a cupboard under the stair, had measured out the ingredients for the morning porridge, and left Win to boil it up and put it in the hay box to finish cooking overnight. Now it just needed a lengthy period on the range to re-boil, and it would be ready to serve.

The 'shopping team' arrived and picked up a list from her, and Ailsa and Shona were clumsily starting vegetable preparation for soup at lunchtime and a stew for the evening. Isa felt that the kitchen operations were starting in a good direction, with Win's excellent help, but was feeling less confident about the three hours 'lessons' that were going to start at 9.30. When the time came, all the students were ready with sharp pencils poised over notebooks, ready to write down every syllable of wisdom that fell from their teacher's blessed lips.

Chapter Six

Isa's first full day as a trainee missionary was a warm day, and there were a few early flowers in the garden. She was full of nervousness and uncertainty, but was beginning to feel that she would be able to cope with all the trials that might be thrown at her. Far from being an impediment to her, she could see that her hard life working in the carding room at Paton's Mill and the necessity to manage every penny that she possessed would be a strength rather than a weakness to her as a missionary.

The morning porridge had turned out well, and was served with bread and marmalade. The other ladies were obviously used to better food, but for Isa, it was just fine. After breakfast, Isa's team had time to put the shopping, which the other team had brought in, away. Isa demonstrated how to re-sharpen the kitchen knives using a steel, and Shona and Ailsa set to chopping the fresh meat for the stew whilst Isa made a gravy, using the left over bits of stock and previous gravy offered by Win, which she thickened with flour, and gave a final stir with Win's 'treacle spoon' which was crusted up with burnt on treacle, and gave a nice brown colouring to her concoction. She and Win could have done everything so much more quickly themselves, but were silently aware of their responsibility to help the other students become competent too. The rest of the day's cooking was of necessity delegated to 'Win the Wonderful', along with her many other tasks.

The first lesson was timetabled as 'Pastor Ewan McKenzie' with the topic 'Holiness'. A plain, pallid man, his face gaunt with suffering, aged about thirty five and leaning heavily on two sticks entered the room, with Miss Abercrombie holding the door open for him. He advanced to the lectern inexorably slowly and painfully. He opened the Bible and read the words 'How beautiful upon the mountains are the feet of him who brings good news, who proclaims peace, who brings glad tidings of good things, who proclaims salvation, who says to Zion, "Your God reigns!"

He beamed. 'Fortunately, I'm not speaking about *my own, perfectly adequate feet* today, but yours, my dear young ladies. You must feel very daunted at the many tasks and dangers that will be set before you as missionaries. I am here to encourage you for an hour every morning, as we look through God's promises.' He took a firm hold of the lectern, and raised one leg a little and showed a heavily booted foot. 'I can assure you, through personal experience, that the grace of God WILL be sufficient for you, today and every day!'

It was a good beginning for days of unremitting toil. On the afternoon of the following day Isa took the underground train, together with Shona, and Ailsa from Kelvinbridge to Hillhead. They were *told* to do this by Miss Abernethy, to try to save their energies a little. They descended the steps to a cold, gas lit cavern which had a peculiar, moist earthy smell about it and stood on an island between two railway tracks. After a little wait, there was an alarming rushing draught, great rattling and banging and a grubby black engine stopped, and they got into a carriage. The train took off again quickly, and shook about violently. The seat Isa was sitting on seemed stable, but the seat back and sides of the coach seemed to be moving independently from side to side. It was most disturbing, but Shona, who was familiar with the system, said 'this is known as the underground shoogle. It's normal, nothing to get alarmed about.'

Isa was most relieved to step out of Hillhead Station, but found herself next in the mayhem of Byres Road. 'It's all right', Shona said confidently, 'We shan't have to cross this road,' and led them up the drive to the immense new Western Infirmary, where they went in the main entrance, and found the door marked 'Miss Weir Assistant Matron'.

Shona knocked. The women were ordered to enter, and were obviously expected. They stood facing Miss Weir, as she sat unsmiling behind her desk. She gave them a few pointers about frequent and thorough hand washing and the absolute necessity of never becoming 'familiar' with either the doctors or the patients and never to let anyone find out their Christian names. They were warned that the patients were a '*very mixed bag.*' The three were all sent off in different directions. Isa was assigned to a Women's Surgical ward. The whole place reeked of very strong disinfectant. The Ward Sister, a very brisk woman greeted her with 'Ah, our trainee missionary helper, and very welcome you are too. We are so busy!' She promptly issued Isa with an overall and a red rubber apron and propelled her towards the ward bathroom, at the ward entrance where she said 'you can help Nurse Balmain.'

There was a terrible commotion coming from inside the room. A very pale, filthy woman was lying on a boarded trolley, and Balmain was struggling to get her heavily bloodstained clothing off her. The woman was screaming 'Ye can't have em! Yous'll sell em for rags!'

Balmain answered patronizingly in 'pan loaf Scottish', 'Of course I won't *deeaar*. I'm just trying to help you. Stop struggling, you're making yourself bleed more. I need to get you undressed, washed and into a clean gown so that doctor can mend you.'

She took no notice, so Isa said 'Keep the heid! See here, hen, if you dinnae help the nurse, she cannae help you. Dae ye want tae bleed to death?'

'Aw right, aw right.'

Isa understood her concern about her raggy clothes. She was clearly a poor woman, and they may have been all that she had to cover herself with. Balmain gave her a pained, 'patient' smile, and carried on trying to undress the woman, saying

'We need to do this quickly, as she's bleeding, but we can't dress her wound properly in the ward until we've decontaminated her. We must try to avoid bringing sepsis into the ward, as it could seriously affect women who've had operations.'

Whilst Balmain continued her none too gentle struggle with the clothing, Isa had noticed that the woman's hair was hoachin' with fleas, and suggested that if they could get her shoulders up to the washbasin, she could wash Mrs McKenzie's hair and fine toothcomb it. Mrs McKenzie had clearly nearly exhausted her strength, and was murmuring that it was her husband who had knifed her in the belly. He had been drunk out of his head. Finally they had her as clean as they could get her. A lot of the dirt was absolutely grimed into her skin, but Balmain was at least satisfied that Mrs McKenzie had no more 'little visitors.'

The two of them put her gently into an 'extra bed' in the crammed ward. Mrs McKenzie's bed was the third in a rank of beds lined head to toe down the middle of the ward, rather like a railway train. It was obvious that the hospital provided no extra staff to care for all these constant 'extras.' A surgeon came to visit, and said he would have to operate on her to stop the bleeding. She nodded weakly, and put a mark on a piece of paper he wanted signed.

The following afternoon, when Isa went back to the hospital, Mrs. McKenzie looked as if she might be dying. A neighbour came to visit her. She said to Isa, 'thank Goad she has no weans. Her man is awfy cruel to her. *He was all she could get.*' Isa was often to hear that phrase when she visited the tenements. A little later Mr. McKenzie came to visit. His very face looked like a breach of the peace. He staggered in, absolutely jaked paralytic, and was so nasty to his wife that the Sister called the porters to have him removed. He was by this time, like a floppy marionette, and they had to put him in a wheelchair to get him to the front door.

After a few weeks of learning what the Sister called 'the rudiments', Isa was drafted into The Receiving Hall. All acute patients arriving at the hospital were dealt with there first, and many of them were sick with rubella, rickets, diphtheria, tuberculosis and venereal diseases. On her first afternoon she encountered Mairi, an unmarried woman with a very high fever, who was bleeding heavily. A female abortionist had tried to 'help her out' (at a price) with a crochet hook a few days previously. She told Isa that she'd lost her virginity to a man who'd said 'Ony chance o'a ham shank?' (sex for money), as she was destitute at the time. Isa quickly understood that very poor women had their own opinions about pre-marriage sex, which was considered normal behaviour in many of the poorer areas of the city, particularly if they were desperate for money, food, clothing or drink at the time. Both men and women at marriage were often sexually experienced, and incest played a part in this too. The doctors were unable to help Mairi, and she died before they could find her a bed in a ward.

Many women were remarkably ignorant about giving birth, and fetched up in the Receiving Hall, complaining of bellyache, to the annoyance of the doctors. Isa was very grateful for the time she'd spent with her midwife mother. On several occasions she'd been the first on the scene of one of these birth 'happenings' in the Hall. Her simple explanation of 'see here hen, it comes oot the same way it went in,' was efficient for the women in their extremity. She preferred dealing with the women.

Bronchitis and pneumonia from the sulphurous smoke belching from the myriad Glasgow domestic and industrial chimneys, worsened by filthy fog from the Clyde resulted in further emergencies. Men, women and children arrived, simply unable to breathe effectively. Then there were the unpredictable drunks, who'd been fighting out in the streets. They could be vile one minute, and the next minute trying to shake hands, or worse still, to hug and kiss Isa. One afternoon Isa was attacked with a knife by a man, off his head with drink, who thought she was his wife. She escaped, very shaken, with a nasty scalp wound which the doctor had to sew up for her. However, it was the state of the children which most distressed her. One afternoon a skinny man ran into the Hall, carrying a bundle of rags, containing a small, very blue child, closely followed by his skinny wife. 'Quick, the wean's swallowed a dummy-tit' he yelled. Isa grabbed the child, flung its rags on the floor, and holding its feet in one hand, suspended it supported against the length of her leg and gave it an almighty whack on the back. Fortunately the dummy tit shot out onto the floor.

'Well done, Miss Maude!' shouted Dr Glen, who had been rushing over to help. The poor little girl was waif-thin, pock marked by disease and filthy dirty. The parents tenderly wrapped little Fiona back in her rags. They explained that neither of them could get work. They were hungry, and were living under the stairs in a nearby tenement close. The dummy tit was being used to pacify Fiona's hunger. Dr Glen gave them sixpence from his own pocket and told them to go to the Gospel Mission Unemployed Relief Committee, who helped with the needs of so many poor, hungry, cold people, and ran two soup kitchens. Sadly, the situation was not unusual. Isa was expecting to see worse when she got her post as a missionary in the tropics.

Day followed on day. The women's training as missionaries was unremitting toil. Isa was quickly grateful that her upbringing and hard working life had well prepared her in terms of physical strength and close contact with working class people for such a testing time. She did all that she could to help the young ladies surrounding her. In fact, her companions impressed her deeply by their determination and ability to learn many practical skills quickly, particularly with kitchen and laundry work. Their 'accomplishments' in terms of being able to play the pianoforte and fast reading and writing were a great help to them in terms of planning their contributions to the mission meetings that all students were expected to get involved in at the Woodside Road Mission. They did however envy Isa's ability to speak to people in slang they could easily understand.

Chapter Seven

The young women were due to finish their course at The Lady Missionary Training Home at the end of February. Isa had completed her allocated stint at the Western Infirmary, and having spent some time at the Grove Street Institute was now spending two days a week with the Glasgow Medical Missionary Society. During the rest of the week, she was doing 'home visits' to the tenements. She and her friends had all been sending cheerful letters home, often written in the bedtime hours, by the light of a guttering candle, with a pencil held in chilblained fingers. One girl had been sent home by Miss Abercrombie in November. She was said to be ill, but they all knew she simply wasn't able to cope with the rigours of the training programme and lack of servants. After a month, Miss Abercrombie announced that Jane Robinson was too ill to come back. Well prior to Christmas, all the trainee missionaries had been writing to the many missionary societies throughout the United Kingdom, offering their services. They felt slightly less concerned than Isa about getting 'fixed up' immediately, and those who hadn't yet been engaged for the missions were planning to return to their homes for a well-earned rest, whilst continuing to make applications for missionary posts.

By mid-February, all Isa's applications for overseas work had met with a blank wall. Miss Forrester Paton paid a visit to encourage all the trainees, and being well acquainted with Isa's circumstances in Alloa, had a private interview with her. She quoted the words of Mary Slessor *'Blessed is the man or woman who is able to serve cheerfully in the second rank — a big test'*. Isa suspected that it meant that she should try to find work locally. Frankly, she simply didn't know what she was going to do, or where her future lay until Pastor Ewan McKenzie suggested unpaid work at the Woodside Road Mission, where Isa was already heavily involved on the medical side, working in the dispensary. She understood the implications: she would have to 'live by faith,' not knowing where the rent money would come from, or even the next meal, but missionaries did not expect to get paid anyway. It took some serious thought on her part, and a lot of prayer, but eventually she agreed to it.

She had a fair bit of her original savings left, and one of her contacts at the Mission, Mollie McMillan was looking for a room-mate in her single end as her friend Janette was leaving and getting married in Dunfermline the following week. Isa went with Mollie on Sunday afternoon to see the room, which was on the first floor of a grey/black tenement in Garscube Road. The close and stone stairs were clean enough, but the landlords had not seen fit to renew the peeling paint on the flat doors. Isa noted the usual splatter of small, smelly weans squatting on the stairs playing. The women had to clamber over the weans to gain entry to what Mollie grandly called 'the flat'. It was normal for tenement mothers to put their children out on the stairs, as it was safer than having them inside the room, with a cooking pot and kettles on an open fire. A baby was created annually by most households. Mothers were often in desperation, trying to find enough rags to cover their weans with, and weans generally lacked shoes. Those children attending school wore black wellie boots. The cludgie *(Glaswegian for toilet)* was shared with everyone, and stood on the landing. It smelled awful, but Mollie remarked encouragingly 'the landlord has recently repaired and re-hung the door'.

When Mollie opened the door to the room, Isa noted that it was luxuriously equipped with a recessed bed, and a hurley bed beneath it, a table, two chairs, gaslight, coat hooks, a shelf for clothes, a dresser, an open grate with a hotplate, a coal box, a sink with a dripping brass tap and a porcelain chanty. It was typical of most Glasgow tenements. Mollie joked 'I killed a flea in my bed this morning, but it was the 10,000 that turned up for the funeral ...'

'Ah'm no used tae onythin special,' Isa said when asked how she felt about the accommodation. 'Ah grew up in much the same, but we had twa rooms. Old Mrs. Mack, who was Maw's friend had the room and Maw, Phemie and me shared. Mrs. Mack wis auld, and could jist dae the cooking. The three of us Maudes all had good jobs, and we managed just fine.'

'Come upstairs and meet Big Rachael. She's expecting to see you, and is a good person to know', said Mollie.

Mollie explained that Rachael worked at a 'man's job' and lived right on the top floor. She had originally worked as a labourer in a Clydebank shipyard, but was now working as a supervisor in a local upholstery and trimming factory. She warned Isa that the other tenement dwellers often perceived Rachael as difficult, and frequently fell out with her, but she had found Rachael to be a right good friend, who enforced some standards of better behaviour on a trio of troublesome male tenement dwellers, who were frightened of her (*their wives were very grateful*). Mollie knocked firmly on Rachael's door as she knew many factory workers had very poor hearing. The door was opened by the largest woman Isa had ever seen in her life. Most working class people were whippet thin and quite short. Isa had never even seen a working class man that big before, certainly not a woman. Rachael was dressed in men's clothes, had a cutty pipe clenched between the teeth at the side of her mouth, and was probably over six feet tall, with a huge, muscular frame.

'Come awa in', she said, beckoning the women in to her flat. Obviously she commanded better pay than other women, as she had *two rooms*. She was clearly very proud of what she called 'ma hoose'. They sat with her in 'the room' as she called her parlour, and she started to chat to Rachael.

'Havnae seen ye fur days.'

'No, I've been awfully busy along at the mission.'

'You wouldnae believe whits been happening at ma wurk this past three weeks.'

'What's that then?'

'Some wumman – they cry her *Miss* Sylvia Pankhurst, is visiting Glasgow. She got permission frae the owners tae come to oor mill. Wanted tae watch us wurkin. Seems she's somethin of an artist, and wanted tae paint the lassies working. The manager didna like her, so he put hur in the mule spinning room – where they spin the yarn ontae spindles. When new lassies begin tae work in there they're a' made sick by the heat and the bad air. It gets gey hot in there, even at this time of year, and Miss Pankhurst fainted in the first oor! I was that cross that she was treated sae bad by the manager, that I spoke to the owner, who telt me tae keep the wee windae open near her. She paints braw pictures, and is gonnae use them tae tell folks how badly women are treated in factories.'

Mollie and Isa looked admiringly at Big Rachael. Isa knew she'd have lost her job at Paton's Mill instantly if she'd gone above the manager's head to the factory owner.

'Fair play tae ye, Rachael,' she said 'fur the way ye acted. 'Ah ken a wee bit aboot the women's' work in their suffrage movement frae ma sister Phemie in Poole, and frae some a' the women I talk tae.'

She wouldn't generally have shared this with many others, but knew immediately that Rachael was a very good person to have as a friend. All three of the women were utterly sick of the way working class women in the city were treated so badly at work, and often, when married, treated by their husbands with no consideration at all. Isa described one of the women on her home visiting list.

'She has three weans. She used tae work in MacAllan's cotton factory, and she got an awfy painful and bent back frae sittin aw day on a backless stool, windin bobbins. By the time she got married, her right hand was painful and twisted. She'll never be fit to work again, and she's no fit tae be bearing children or to manage her hame. Her husband is aye complaining aboot her. She only gets by wi the other women in her tenement helping her. Ah call by and help her when I can. The last time ah wis there, she had twa black eyes. When I see her man sober, I say 'sign The Pledge now, see how your life will change, and try tae build up the attractions of being sober.' He jist gets angry'.

They all knew of the ghastly problems lurking behind some poor tenement doors. Sexual abuse was prevalent between siblings, fathers and daughters, generally fuelled by drink. Life could be absolutely desperate at times for the very poor. The trio decided to go together to a women's suffrage meeting the following Sunday afternoon. Women from all over Glasgow and beyond met round the Doulton Fountain up by the Peoples' Palace at Glasgow Green. Miss Sylvia Pankhurst and her lady Suffragettes were there, demonstrating their numbers, all dressed up in their posh purple, white and green clothes and parading their flags. The initial speeches were sparkling, and many male hecklers who had expected to outshine the women with their sudden flashes of wit were hopelessly out-flashed.

Finally, Miss Pankhurst herself stood up and spoke very clearly and sincerely of the need for changes in society, stressing the changes that could be brought about if women obtained equality in voting, gained more personal liberty, a fairer deal in life and were no longer treated as second class citizens. Isa heard a man saying 'they're rightly named wasps, those wimmin, ye cannae escape them anyhow.'

Miss Pankhurst concluded her short speech by saying 'Ability is sexless. What we suffragettes aspire to be when we are enfranchised is to act as ambassadors of freedom to all women who are oppressed. We claim our right to fight for freedom. It is our privilege and joy in this militant movement, to take some part in the regeneration of humanity. Think of it this way. You have two babies, both very hungry, and both wanting to be fed. One baby is a patient child, and waits indefinitely until its mother is ready to feed it. The other baby is an impatient baby, and cries lustily, screams and kicks and is unpleasant until it is fed. We all know perfectly well which baby is attended to first. That is the whole history of politics. You have to make more noise than anyone else, you have to make yourself more obtrusive than anyone else, and in fact you have to make a noise all the time. I would rather be a rebel than a slave.' When she had finished her speech, she shouted out *'Trust in God, She will provide!!'*

Isa and her friends were very moved by what they heard, which was followed by votes for women songs and a triumphal march of the Women's' leaders, closely followed by a large group of released women prisoners marching down High Street who began singing to the tune of 'Men of Harlech':

> *From the daughters of the nation*
> *Bursts a cry of indignation*
> *Breathes a sigh of consecration*
> *In a sacred cause.*
> *They who share their country's burden*
> *Win no rights, receive no guerdon,* (reward)
> *Only bear the heavy burden*
> *Of unrighteous laws.*
> *Women young and older*
> *Shoulder put to shoulder*
> *In the might of sacred right*
> *Bolder still and bolder.*
> *Let no ancient custom bind you*
> *Let one bond of suffering bind you*
> *Leave unrighteous laws behind you,*
> *Soon you shall be free!*

Initially these proceedings went smoothly, with Miss Pankhurst being guarded by two policemen, and other policemen flanking the parade. However, as the huge procession turned out of London Road and into Argyll Street, many of the women became violent, throwing large stones (which they had concealed in their reticules and about their persons) at shop windows. A crowd of equally unpleasant men in the vanguard of the march, forced their way into the pack of women with the violence of a horde of Zulu warriors. The whole demonstration was a disgrace to British men and women. The policemen at the front of the procession were wonderfully quick, and had to lift Miss Pankhurst and her lieutenants bodily over the heads of the angry mob of men and women, and get them into a room above a nearby shop. Isa and her friends managed to escape up towards Rottenrow and walked home. Being poor, and therefore rarely reading newspapers, the women hadn't realized until that day that there were two main women's suffrage societies.

Isabel and her friends never went as far as to join the Women's Social and Political Union who were known as 'the nasty party' or the 'wasps', as they made a serious nuisance of themselves, and were violent towards property and those who disagreed with them. However they did what they could for the Womens' Freedom League (a breakaway group from the increasingly violent 'Suffragettes'). Many working class women got rather irritated with the middle and upper class socialists who were always carrying on about *the burdens being born by less fortunate women.* They didn't see how life might be made any better by having a vote. In retaliation against the growing women's movements the newspaper cartoonists and other popular publications began to characterize women protesters as ugly, usually with big feet, protruding teeth, hair in a bun and wearing spectacles.

Chapter Eight

Isa managed fairly well whilst she and Mollie shared 'the room' and worked together locally, as they shared expenses, living on the very little that the Grove Street Institute and the poor were able to give them, with occasional contributions from their own families. In mid-1912 however, Mollie went back home to her family, worn out with the daily struggles of working with families of six to eight or even more people living in single rooms in crumbling tenements. These same people, who were themselves desperately poor often gave them pennies or half pennies as love gifts for the things the girls did for them. The home visits, which Isa continued to make, were the Grove Street Mission's attempt to combat poverty, poor housing, crime, filth and disease. She was feeling particularly low, as she had a persistent cough, due to the poor air quality in the streets and of course, within the tenements.

Isa would have felt the loss of her good companion too hard to bear, had it not been that a fortnight later the Grove Street Institute announced that she and two of the other women missionaries, Janette and Wilhelmina (known as 'Net' and 'Wullie') were being awarded a week's holiday in Dunoon during the Glasgow Fair. Their trip was being fully funded by the local Co-Operative Society which had recently founded a Womens' Guild. Many Glasgow families went on holiday for the second and third week of July, so most factories, foundries, shipbuilders and other businesses closed on 'Fair Friday' and thousands of people went on holidays. Preparations began two weeks before, with family trunks being packed with bedlinen, towels, clothes, crockery and cooking equipment ready to stay in 'rooms.' These were picked up by the railway company, and delivered to the holiday address, ready for the family's eager arrival.

Isa, Net and Wullie were dancing and laughing with joy, absolutely thrilled at the thought of making their very first trip 'doon the watter' on the paddle steamer the 'Ivanhoe' from the Broomielaw Wharves, to stay at the Cragieburn Boarding House. The other passengers were in similarly high spirits. Two tidily dressed women in their early twenties were standing at the rail, looking down at the rapidly passing waters of the Clyde. 'So I hear that you and Campbell are getting married after all...?' said one to the other. 'Aye, it just had to be...' answered the other. 'True enough, we had a falling out, but we're going through wi it, as ah've put on sae much weight that ah cannae get ma engagement ring aff.' They laughed uproariously, as did those around them. The trip took a little while, and most passengers had packed sandwiches, which they enjoyed in the sunshine on deck.

On embarking at the terminal at Dunoon, Isa and her two friends were pleased that they didn't have to carry much luggage at all, as they were getting full board. It was a blissful time for the three women, in spite of getting rather sunburned in the first two days. Thereafter, the weather returned to its usual unpredictable Scottish mix. They shared a room, so the companionship was great, the food was far superior in taste, freshness and quantity than anything they had eaten in a very long time and Isa's cough got better.

On return from her holiday, she noticed that the tenement close still smelt of damp, disinfectant, and urine. However she felt a lot healthier than she had in a long while, and went back to work with renewed energy. The very poor, many of whom she was extremely fond of, had missed her, and even some of the rough wino men and general heidbangers greeted her with 'howsitgaunmissawright?' She was very careful with them, though, as they were unpredictable, and would change in a moment. She went to visit a very poor family one day, and after tapping the door, hoping to visit the woman and children who lived there, it was wrenched open unexpectedly by the huge, ugly man of the house with scars and a broken nose, reeking of cheap booze, yelling 'Ye wee bastard ye, dinnae come agin, or I'll tear yir heid aff wi my bare hauns and then I'll throw it tae the rats.' The neighbours called him 'the walking beer cask', as they said he was only missing the wooden slats around him. There was no furniture there. It had all been sold for drink.

Visibly cowering in the far corner of the cold, empty room was his woman, completely toothless at just twenty six, with a black eye and cut lip, her frightened, staring children huddled silently in their rags around her. Hoping that the loathsome man would be out, Isa tried another, more successful visit the following day, bringing a loaf of bread and an ounce of tea with her. Meggie was a good woman, but with six children to feed, and a man she couldn't rely on to help, life was difficult. That said, most family men were clean, honest and hardworking, but the nearly unbearable working conditions, chronically low pay and poor housing got everybody down, and so really it wasn't surprising that some people drank too much. Isa spent her days helping out practically in every way she could, and as she put it *showing the love of Christ.*' Her work remained mostly 'self-supporting', with occasional cash help from the Mission, her sister Phemie and her mother. One day, she planned to visit old Mr McLean (what a misnomer!), who was very poor, and without thinking, bought him a meat pie as a treat. He couldn't chew the hard pie crust as he had no 'wallies' – false teeth, but was very grateful, and managed the meat bits.

When war was declared between Britain and Germany, things started to go downhill dramatically. Isa's cough came back. She had less and less money to cover her expenses. As with most women of her class, she had never been able to afford a coat, and went about in the biting winter weather, wrapped in just a couple of thin shawls. True to her missionary calling, she just kept going with her work. It was unbelievably difficult, particularly during the Glasgow Rent Strike. It was Tuesday the first of January, her day off. She lay in her bed in the little single end until about 9.00am. It was yet another dreich winter day in Glasgow. The fire was going out and she had no money for more coal. However, when she finally pulled herself out of bed she was able to use the last of the hot water in the kettle, which had been sitting on the hob, to make a tepid mug of tea and have a scanty wash. She cut herself a slice of bread from the heel of her stale loaf whilst she considered her dire situation. As a missionary she had chosen to live in the same harsh conditions as those she served. On the previous day she had given her last two shillings, which were to feed her for the rest of the week, to a woman and children who were literally starving, courtesy of the man of the house, a rigger in the shipyards, who regularly drank his wages. She reflected on the fact that today, she would be making her very first visit to the pawnbroker down the street. The only 'spare' item she had was one of her two shawls. She had never owned a coat.

There was a knock at the door, and Mrs Barrow, her neighbour from across the stair, handed her an envelope which had been miss-delivered to her house. It was from Pastor Ewan McKenzie, who knew fine well that it was her day off, cordially inviting her to a light lunch at the Temperance Café in Byres Road. Isa's heart was pounding with joy at such an unexpected treat. She had long harboured romantic feelings for him, which she believed were reciprocated, but of course, both their loyalties were to God's work. On the way to the café, in her shabby clothes, a drunk man yelled at her 'ye'd better pull yourself together hen, the rag man's coming!' She was at the café first, but the pastor arrived about two minutes later in a taxicab. As ever, her heart went out to him, propped on his two walking sticks, dragging his crippled feet. Over lunch, whilst she gazed adoringly into his beautiful face, he told her that he was leaving Glasgow to take up a position in a small church, in an industrial town. The minister of the church had left to serve as a chaplain in the army, and a replacement was desperately needed. 'And indeed, they must be desperate, to take me, and my beautiful feet...' he said.

After they had finished eating, they held hands under the table, the first time they had ever touched each other, and gazed into each other's eyes. Then he reclaimed one of his hands, put it into his waistcoat pocket, and withdrew two sovereigns.

'I nearly forgot to give you this,' he said. 'It's from the Home Mission Committee, who forgot to give you a winter allowance.'

'Thank you', she said, knowing full well that he was lying, as the Committee never gave more than a few shillings, but accepting his love gift anyway. Ewan could afford it. He had a rich family at the back of him, and he could never have done his missionary work without the money for taxicabs and several new pairs of shoes every year, as he quickly wrecked them with his dragging feet.

All too soon his taxicab returned, and he dragged himself slowly to the café door, unable to wave because of his sticks, but giving one last, very sad, thin smile. He hadn't given her his new address, or told her anything about the church he was taking on. She reflected that at least there wasn't any chance of him becoming an army chaplain!

Isa walked back home slowly in the cold, feeling *Holy Inadequate* and purchased two envelopes, a stamp and a few sheets of paper. She wrote her resignation to the Grove Street Institute, with immediate effect, and a letter to her younger sister Phemie in Poole, asking if she could come to stay in Poole for a while, and find some paid work whilst she considered her future. After a trip to the post box, she spent the evening with Big Rachael, who fed her a fine plate of cabbage, tatties and mince, before crying herself to sleep in her single end, in the knowledge that in leaving Scotland she would never again see Ewan McKenzie. She left the next morning, leaving the key to the room with Rachael, and asked her to distribute her few remaining belongings to the poorest neighbouring families. Rachael gave her a brown paper parcel of *meat* sandwiches for her journey, then slices of bread buttered so thickly that when she ate them she could see her teeth marks in it and a mug of tea before she left. Then Isa went to the station, which was simply packed with troops, where she bought a single ticket from Glasgow to Poole, hoping that her letter would be in Phemie's hands before she arrived.

Essie

Chapter Nine

'Hurry up Negus, it's today you're working, not tomorrow', the Ward Sister, Miss Lacey, commented in crisp, icy tones. It was only Essie's second week at the Royal Victoria Hospital, Westbourne, and she had been put to work in Alexandra Ward as a Probationer Nurse to, as Sister Lacey said, 'be broken in.' Essie felt rather like reminding her that she was not a horse, but thought better of it. Sister Lacey had very clearly evolved directly from an amoeba, so she was going to have to put up with her. She simply couldn't let this chance to become a professional lady slip through her fingers so easily.

'There is no ward work that a nurse should deem it beneath her position to know how to do if she is to set the others an example. Get into the sluice room and give those bedpans another scrub Negus,' Sister continued. 'I ought to be able to see my face in them.'

'Her mirror obviously shattered the last time she looked into it, and now she has to use bedpans as a substitute' Essie thought mutinously. It was a horrible job trying to keep the metal items in the sluice room shiny, given the dreadful hard water in the area. She had also been set to clean out the large water tank they called the bedpan sterilizer. Indeed, she was responsible for keeping the sluice room and all its revolting contents clean and tidy, which included sputum cups, and vomit bowls and additionally had to do any other dirty job in the ward that 'those above' cared to throw at her. There was one blessing, her name was Mrs Mattie (Matilda) Riggs, but like the rest of the underlings, she had no title, and was simply 'Riggs', or 'Riggie' if a favour was being wheedled. 'Riggie' was the Ward Orderly, who cleaned, washed the dishes and helped out generally, and was particularly kind to new Probationers. She was strong and fast. Essie's former clerical work had neither provided her with the muscles or the staying power for this new work, so darling Riggie kept an eye on her, and was particularly astute in noticing those moments when she felt like giving up nursing or even wishing that she'd never been born. Beneath all these moments of uncertainty Essie retained the ambition to better herself and become a respected independent middle class woman.

At that time you see, a female was politically classed with infants, idiots and lunatics as being 'naturally incapacitated' and was expected to be so much under the influence of *others* (men of course!) that she could not really have a will of her own. This was why upper and middle class parents went to elaborate lengths to protect the moral and physical welfare of their children. Middle class women were definitely expected to stay at home. There was generally no hope of a profession, although a few had managed to get into nursing. The general view was that as women were known to have smaller brains, they could just about adequately deal with getting married, running a home and having children.

Essie was not really middle class even, as her father was in 'trade.' The family was fortunate, as her father, Samuel Negus was such an excellent craftsman that money was never short in their household. He was a master carpenter and builder, his large firm making furniture and coffins and so was always assured of an income as one of Poole's undertakers. Within the tight family circle he had a monumental, even a gallows sense of humour when it came to dealing with those souls he called 'our dear departed'. His neighbours particularly valued his services because of the compassion with which he attended to the needs of the living, particularly parents who had lost children. Essie was the eldest child, with Jack, Nellie, Mary, Grace and poor Cecil, who died of lockjaw, aged only eleven, in 1911.

She had a very happy childhood, although her parents were strict with all their children. However, don't think that they ever really managed to curb her entirely, as she was naturally a rather naughty person! Her father said it was all because she was rather intelligent *for a woman*. Her brother Jack was sent away to a good school because he was going to follow father into the family business, but as a girl, Essie was educated locally, just until she was fourteen. She learned reading, writing, arithmetic and fine sewing, because father said that she'd probably only get married anyway, so why waste good money on education for a girl. Fortunately she didn't have to help too much at home, as her mother had Mrs Cox, the cook/housekeeper to help her with everything. Father insisted therefore that she took paid work once she left school, so with his help she obtained a position as a clerk at an engineering works on Poole Quay.

Before she became a probationer nurse Essie got involved in the Womens' Freedom League through her music teacher, Mrs Lydia Lovejoy, a very strong woman, who was always complaining about the idiocy of the male dominated world. She was very friendly with Mrs Phemie Ross, the wife of the Albatross Pharmacist. The pharmacy was called The Albatross Pharmacy because of her husband's name, Albert Ross, although he was always known as Alec to his family. He was a very eccentric man, some said he was slightly mad, and the pharmacy name caused a lot of laughs. Essie got very friendly with Agnes and Morag Ross, their daughters, and as part of their peaceful protest against the current position of women, the young women generally dressed in the women's suffrage colours of purple, green and white. Her younger sisters, Nellie, Mary and Grace disapproved, and called the suffrage movement 'The Shrieking Sisterhood.' *(Nellie was waiting, 'in dignified tranquillity until the right man came to claim her!')* Essie's father however, who was a Conservative Alderman on the County Council, kept paying Essie's clothing bills without comment. Neither she nor her friends had anything to do with the militant suffragettes, who were quite terrifying in their violent acts.

In those days, she spent a lot of her spare evenings sitting in the back sitting room at the Albatross Pharmacy, sewing or knitting, talking with Lydia, Phemie, Morag and Agnes about women's potential new place in society when they succeeded in getting the vote. Essie declared her intention of becoming 'a trained nurse.' Phemie, who had been studying the international news, read out 'The Decline of the German Haus Frau.' Apparently German women were becoming more independent every year, and finding other careers than marriage, which the writer commented was 'formerly the only successful establishment in life for a woman.' Apparently the Germans were ahead of the British in this, as with many other things, as over the last twelve years there had been an increase of three million more women working for pay, resulting in twenty seven per cent of German women earning their own livings.

Mr Negus described the group of women as a *'petite coterie of women with independent ideas in Poole'*. 'I'm not against women working', he explained to Essie. 'It will be a comfort to me to know that I won't have to worry about marrying you off, or of you managing to look after yourselves when I'm gone. There are far too many genteel lady paupers eking out fragile incomes. My girls will need to be out of the home doing something positive until they get married. When I am gone, Jack will inherit the business, and there is no chance of you girls becoming master carpenters or undertakers! These are jobs for men.'

At the time of this conversation, her father was lying in bed suffering from a bad bout of influenza. As he was not in a position to walk away from a conversation he didn't want to have with her, Essie started on again about wanting to train as a nurse. Seeking a means to put her off he announced, 'I'm dying, and you don't even care enough to give me a bit of peace to say my prayers'. Quick as a flash, she slipped her hand under his bedclothes.

'No-one dies with warm feet' she replied smartly.

'Joan of Arc did.' he replied. She left him in peace. He did however make moves to help her to achieve her goal, all the while complaining that Essie was giving him earache with her demands to be allowed to train as a nurse.

Mr Negus made his grand announcement to the family on Christmas Day, 1913:

'I have arranged an appointment for Essie on the 4th of January at the Royal Victoria Hospital Westbourne. She will meet with The Lady Superintendent, Miss Airey, with a view to commencing as a Probationer Nurse at the beginning of April'

It was the best Christmas present that Essie had ever had in all her life. She cried with joy. Her little handkerchief was inadequate, and her father gave her his big clean, soft, handkerchief. When she looked at his face, she saw him looking more pleased and proud than she'd ever seen before. She felt respected and important. Looking back, she guessed that all the care and support that she'd given her parents in caring for her brother Cecil, when he died of lockjaw, had been a deciding factor in the efforts father had made on her behalf.

Her meeting with Miss Airey was gruelling. She was a lady of middle years, clearly highly intelligent, and very proud of 'her' hospital, which she stated was well known in Europe for its excellence, and had been visited by delegations of nurses from Holland and Germany in the previous year. Suitable Probationers aged 21-26 were accepted, but '*ladies by birth and education* are preferred as candidates' she said, giving Essie a hard look. 'Membership of the Church of England is also expected, and you need to be physically very strong.'

Essie was quaking in her little black leather boots, but at the end of what Miss Airey described as 'our little talk', she was offered a place on a month's trial subject to a satisfactory Medical Certificate of Health. Her father was not required to pay a premium. (Every carpentry apprentice he took paid a premium). She would have no salary in her first year. If satisfactory and kept on for a second year, she would be paid ten pounds at the end of the final year. She would have to provide her own indoor uniform, but the hospital would provide her outdoor uniform. So, in total she would be on probation for two years, and if she proved satisfactory in her work and passed her examinations, she would be awarded a certificate to work as a 'trained nurse' at the end of these two years.

So, that was how she came to be mutinously scrubbing bedpans in the sluice most mornings. Her new acquaintance, Palmer, with whom she was sharing a room in the Nurses' Home had completed her first year. (*Under no circumstances were nurses allowed to use their Christian names in public.*) Palmer had been promoted to scrubbing out the boiler, kidney dishes, gallipots and basins in the sterilizing room after she'd emptied any nasty contents down Essie's sluice drain. At least the Staff Nurse, Miss Philpott, was very pleasant, and when Sister Lacey wasn't looking, never considered it beneath her dignity to assist others in their labours. The probationers all preferred being 'out on the ward' actually dealing with patients, so that they could learn how to care for them well. Alexandra Ward was for women, but occasional poorly children were admitted as patients.

Simon, or 'Sonny' as he was known, was a delightful little chap of about nine years. He was a cripple from birth, and was admitted with suspected appendicitis. His parents said they couldn't manage to have him back home, and the Crippled Children's' Home down the road said they had no space to take him. He could be very cheeky though. On one occasion, when Sister Lacey said 'It's high time you had a bath young man', and started unstrapping his leg braces, he said:

'I know you're a witch, and you're going to drown me.'

Sister immediately retaliated by saying 'You're a very wicked little boy. Pass me that hairbrush Palmer, I'm going to give this boy a chastisement that he will *never* forget.'

Essie was whispering to Philpott: 'a single big open handed slap would do the trick.'

In the event, Palmer's failure to act promptly and pass the hairbrush gave Sonny the opportunity to make a speedy, deeply abject apology with a plentiful deluge of tears which was accepted. Sister's awful threat achieved its desired purpose and hitting the lad was thus totally unnecessary. Essie began to think that perhaps Sister really did know what she was doing in managing her ward.

Chapter Ten

Perhaps you might like to hear a little more personal detail about Essie's life as a probationer nurse. She lived in the Nurses' Home, a very pleasant red brick house beside the hospital. This was absolutely essential as the nurses worked from 7.30am to 9.30pm with three hours off duty daily and one whole day off duty per month. During their 'off duty' a meal break was due, and lectures were arranged twice a week to fill the rest of the 'off duty' time. For the first couple of weeks she felt physically sick with loneliness and genuine fear of the Sisters and some of the trained nurses who were ferocious and quite sadistic in the way they treated the probationers in particular. Essie had no money at all apart from some very small personal savings. Her father had 'set her up' as he described it with her regular uniform and gave her ten shillings, commenting 'don't spend it all at once!' After that, she had to ask him to give her some of her savings in little bits of cash on her monthly day off, as women didn't normally have bank accounts then. She had to pay for her personal laundry, stamps, writing paper, gloves, hairpins, shampoo, soap, talc, toffees and barley sugar, tea, biscuits and all the other little things a girl needs. She wrote at least two short notes or cards to friends and family every day. If you managed to catch the evening post, it was delivered first post in Poole the following morning. The replies from friends to her notes helped to keep her spirits up.

The days and hours were desperately tiring. She would often get into her attic room, launch herself at her bed, and wake up hours later having slept on her tummy, with her starched cap still uncrushed on her head. However, she and her friend Palmer weren't always that tired, and sometimes entertained other off duty nurses in their room for little parties, particularly when biscuits or cake had been sent from home. Things could get rather uproarious, and sometimes one of the sisters or a trained nurse came to complain that they should make *less* noise in their room. None of the girls ever discovered what an *appropriate* level of noise was! If they had an evening 'do', guests brought their tooth mugs and Essie produced the bottle of sherry that she and Palmer had secreted in their wardrobe. There was no curfew. Exhaustion always ensured prompt bedtimes.

Everyone in 'The Home' was wakened in the morning by the Senior Night Staff Nurse, clanging a fearsome great hand bell, walking through the hall and up to the middle landing and thence to the attics, periodically yelling 'Half past six Nurse!'

Everyone had to yell the reply 'Yes Nurse. Thank you Nurse' even when it was a much deserved day off. Even illness was disregarded. All except those with a day off had to get up in the morning and report on duty. Everyone worked unless they had something infectious or were unable to stand and walk. Actually fainting was regarded as demonstrating a severe lack of moral fibre. Palmer once bravely decided that as an experiment, she and Essie would *not* reply to the morning call as they both had a day off. The Staff Nurse entered their room like a hurricane, snatching the girls' bedclothes off them in two single grabs (obviously a true Fury, a daughter of the mythical Tartarus!).

'Room eleven, stand by your beds! You *will* answer my call. I shall put your names on my report to Miss Airey.'

Essie and Palmer didn't know if this was just a threat, but although they were shaking in their shoes for two days, no summons was ever issued by Miss Airey.

Everyone went to the dining room for breakfast. Porridge was always served. Something fish or meat followed. There was always something fishy on Fridays, such as kippers, fish cakes, smoked haddock, and on other days the nurses had variations on sausages, bacon, eggs boiled or fried and kidneys. Toast and marmalade followed. They ate as much as they could, as they were always hungry from the hard, physical nature of their work. They had to attend meals on time, or risk starving, and this was very difficult as nurses could get 'tied up' on the ward with a task that had to be completed. Essie became quite nervous about mealtimes, as a very tall, well-built staff nurse whose name was Barbara Milburn was having a 'pash' about her. Well, put plainly, she was emotionally obsessed with Essie. Even going out into the gardens on her own was unwise if Barbara was about. She was too immature to be able to tell Barbara that she wasn't interested in *a close friendship*. Essie was very nervous indeed. Her friends were protective of her and colluding with her avoidance tactics, would whisper 'close ranks' if they saw Barbara coming, surrounded Essie and kept moving.

As you can guess, it wasn't too long before Essie had to work with Staff Nurse Barbara Milburn downstairs on the men's ward, Albert Edward. Essie's name had appeared on a list of 'ward changes' outside Miss Airey's office. She was dreading Sunday when the change came into force. Actually, she soon found that she had been making a fuss about nothing. The ward was so busy that everyone was fully occupied caring for a number of very poorly men. Mr Dyer, a dentist and former mayor of Bournemouth had been admitted on Sunday afternoon with delirium tremens, Sister Blythe told her:

'Mr Dyer regularly drank a lot of alcohol. On Friday he knocked Mrs Dyer about and gave her a black eye. She was so heartily sick of his bad behaviour that she poured every remaining drop of alcohol down the drain and locked him in his bedroom for twenty four hours. When she let him out, he was very queer indeed. Keep a sharp eye on him Negus.'

Barbara Milburn told her more. 'Dr Charlesworth was called to Mr Dyer's house and found him in an absolutely filthy state. The Doctor had him brought straight here. The smell off him was enough to choke a black. *'Bodily fluids'* she told Essie in a meaningful tone. 'Ernie (the male ward orderly) and I had a terrible time getting him stripped and bathed before he was clean enough to bring into the ward. He's all right now though, quite content picking imaginary beetles off his counterpane. Mrs Dyer is refusing to come and see him.'

In fact, Mr Dyer was not all right at all. Essie went into the sluice room to do some work, and when she went back into the ward, his bed was empty! Ernie, who had been told to keep watch in the ward was in the kitchen slurping at a hot cup of tea.

'Quick, Mr Dyer's gone' she said, and dashed out into the front hall, terrified that he might get into Miss Airey's room. Fortunately he was on the ward side of the hall.

'Come along, Mr Dyer, I think you need to get back into bed. It's cold out here near that front door' Essie said, taking him gently by the arm.

You would find it difficult to believe the filthy language that screamed out of that man's mouth. Essie backed off, and ducked as he aimed a blow at her. She was dodging and weaving, when she saw Barbara slipping behind him. She restrained him effectively, with her arms under his armpits and a knee in the small of his back. The situation was reversed – Mr Dyer was calling for help now. Dr Jones the houseman, who had been trying to get a few minutes sleep appeared drowsily from his bedroom, which was on that side of the hall. He reappeared with his bed sheet and with Barbara still holding on, he and Ernie managed to effectively pinion Mr Dyer's arms by wrapping the sheet around him. Sister Blythe appeared with a wheelchair, just as Miss Airey descended the stairs saying

'*What is the meaning of this dreadful caterwauling in the front hall? I shall want a complete explanation from you Sister Blythe within the half hour. And you, Dr Jones, put your tie and jacket on immediately. I thought you were a professional man.*'

'That's us told', muttered Barbara confidentially in Essie's ear.

Essie, Barbara, Ernie and Dr Jones managed to get Mr Dyer back into bed, and Sister Blythe brought four strong roller towels from the linen cupboard which the five of them managed to slip knot around his arms and legs and tie onto the bed frame. Dr Jones gave Mr Dyer a very large injection of a stinking drug called paraldehyde. Very quickly Mr Dyer and the ward area around him were stinking of this nasty chemical. Sister Blythe ascertained the facts and went to report to Miss Airey. The result of the meeting was that Miss Airey ordered Staff Nurse Milburn to the office and personally commended her for swift brave action. She was granted an extra half day, to be given at Sister Blythe's convenience. Sister admonished Ernie and Essie for being 'slack' and nothing more was said to Dr Jones for being improperly dressed. Essie settled into her work on Albert Edward Ward, and found that she preferred nursing men to women. Barbara became a good friend, although trained nurses were not expected to keep company with probationers, not even to have a cup of tea in a cafe when off duty. Meeting a young man and having any kind of friendship was impossible for the girls. Nurses were sure to be reported to Miss Airey if anyone saw them with a man. Essie became very impressed with Barbara. She had done her nursing training at St Bartholomew's Hospital in London. She was both pleasant to work with, and a good teacher. Regardless of 'the rules' which strongly discouraged trained nurses and probationers from being close friends, on late winter evenings they often sat together downstairs in the sitting room of the Nurses' Home. On one occasion when they were sitting untidily in armchairs, either side of a roaring fire, reading their books, Essie felt stupidly content. She said to Barbara 'I have made it. I am here. I am on the road to being a professional woman.'

On Essie's monthly day off, the Nurses' Home maid, Flossie brought her a late breakfast in bed at 8.30 am. She would get dressed to go home to Poole, looking very prim, with a plain, high necked blouse with her long serviceable skirt of dark navy with her jacket or overcoat and hat. For warmer days, she had a dress which fastened at the back. Like other women, she wore her hair long, fastened at the sides with little tortoiseshell combs, hairpins and a hairnet over the bun. There was little possibility of one of the other nurses being 'off' at the same time.

As her visits home were so infrequent, she was given a very warm welcome by her parents and sisters and Mrs Cox the housekeeper. Mother would be watching at the window for her coming, and would embrace her at the front door, her usual greeting being

'Gor maid, you'm got thin about.'

To which Essie replied 'Gor Mother, you'm got big about.'

As a Devonshire lady, Essie's mother had never lost her dialect. Like Mistress Caroline Lovejoy, the farmer, who spoke broad Darzet, she much enjoyed this way of speaking in her own home, and as their native speech had many common words they appreciated regular meetings. It was good to be at home. Essie missed dear Cotton, Mrs Cox's son who had recently died from heart disease. She remember her father's words on the day he died 'God tempers the wind to the shorn lamb,' and she believed that he meant that although Cotton was simple minded, God loved him just as much as his mother and the Negus family did. The feelings of sorrow were poignant, as they were all still raw from the loss of their own young Cecil.

Mother was always trying to feed Essie up, and afternoon tea was generally a sumptuous affair with potted meat sandwiches and homemade scones with jam and cream. She had certainly lost a bit of weight with all the hours and strenuous work that she was doing.

'Put that in your belly case you be hungry,' she would say in her broad accent.

Essie was glad that Jason the fisherman, (son of Mr Harry Lovejoy, a wealthy merchant and his wife Lydia, her former piano teacher and dear friend), had stopped coming round to pay his respects to her. He had finally learned that she was in love with the idea of becoming a professional woman and had no thoughts about becoming a wife and ending up with two thousand children like so many other women living in the town. Lydia did call in and was full of excitement. She had at last, after many years of fruitless effort, been offered an opportunity of playing, (just once, as the booked *male* pianist was suddenly ill) with the Bournemouth Symphony Orchestra. The elderly Madam Ford of Thames Street was sewing a fine black silk dress for this debut appearance. Essie would have given her eye teeth to have been able to go to the concert. However, naturally she had to make sacrifices for her vocation.

Chapter Eleven

The Royal Victoria Hospital was an odd place to work. It gave care to others, but did not always provide much care for its own staff. The Hospital Dispenser was taken ill in the dispensary one day. He had an epileptic fit, and was attended to by Miss Airey and Dr Foote, one of the visiting physicians, who was present in the Outpatient Department at the time. The Dispenser recovered enough to get home, and reported for duty again the following morning. When he had a further epileptic fit a month later, he was immediately discharged from service, and a replacement man was employed.

Frank, the Hospital Porter, received similar treatment. He had been in his job nearly twenty years, during which time the hospital had grown in size and was much busier. He asked the Management Committee if they would consider the employment of a boy to help him. He gave as his reasons the facts that he was involved in carrying many hundredweights of coal around the hospital and Nurses' Home to keep everybody warm. He also had to dispose of the ashes and any other rubbish. He kept the hospital drains clear and received all the deliveries and carried them to the appropriate departments. He had to answer the hospital front door bell to callers day and night. He also helped with carrying patients on stretchers up and down the stairs to the Theatre on the middle floor. The Management Committee's response was simple. They gave him a month's notice, (*which they thought was generous*) telling him that they now needed a younger, fitter man and advertised his job in the Poole and Dorset Herald.

For the nurses, as a female workforce, life was tricky when having their monthly indisposition, which they referred to politely between themselves as 'being visited by Aunt Flo'. Sometimes it was sensible for them to avoid lifting heavy patients and get a colleague to help instead. The Sisters showed not a trace of sympathy. Barbara, who had wonderful lady like manners, once made a highly original excuse to Sister Blythe 'The banks of the River Nile are overflowing and running red.'

'Get out of my sight, Milburn', said Sister, and went and helped to lift the patient herself.

If a nurse was feeling 'off colour', *having to eat* was another problem. Miss Airey superintended everything, including the kitchen. She even weighed the meat when it arrived from the butcher, in case he had sold the hospital 'short weight', which apparently happened quite often. At lunchtime, she was there, carving the joint or serving shepherd's pie or whatever, on to the nurses' plates, from which they were expected to eat every morsel. Essie felt it was worse than being at home under mother's eye. On the days when the probationers had Doctors' Lectures, they had to be prompt at lunch and eat quickly, as lateness was not tolerated by the eminent local doctors who gave their teaching services free to the hospital.

Essie was allocated to Night Duty on Albert Edward Ward for most of July, as Mew (yes! That really was her surname) one of the night duty Probationers was taking her annual two weeks holiday. The Ward Sisters enjoyed a monthly day off, but were potentially always 'on duty' as they lived in the hospital building in rooms close to their wards. They could thus emerge at any time of the day or night to check on things. Sister Blythe on Albert Edward Ward was the soul of reasonableness in contrast with Sister Lacey who appeared from the night nurses' comments to suffer from chronic insomnia and frequently got up during the night to check what was going on and change nursing treatments. As, by virtue of being on Night Duty the night nurses would be missing their daytime lunch, it was Essie's responsibility to collect food from the kitchen upstairs and cook it in the ward kitchen for a midnight serving for the three staff in Albert Edward Ward. According to Staff Nurse Gould, who extolled the quality of her cooking 'Mew produces meals I wouldn't serve to a cat!' Everyone got the giggles.

Essie felt sure they ate Mew's meals though. Everyone was always so hungry. She did beef and onion rissoles with mashed potatoes, gravy, carrots and cabbage the first night. Her rice pudding was pronounced by Gould to be 'First rate!'

From that little beginning the three of them got along very well for the rest of the night. The second night was more interesting nursing. A case had been admitted during the afternoon with what were described as 'multiple injuries' following a road accident. He had been nipping across a busy road and was clipped by a cart, lost his balance and a horse stood on his abdomen. Dr Avery, a general practitioner who was experienced in surgery was called in, and operated on the abdominal injuries. Dr Jones administered the chloroform. By the time the night nurses came on duty the poor man was in extreme pain despite being given morphine and was being very sick from the effects of the ether. He was a young schoolmaster. Luckily Essie was cooking a prepared casserole and jacket potatoes that night and the cook had considerately left a cold gooseberry fool out for the staff. It was Essie's job you see, to sit behind the screens with that beautiful young man. Sister Blythe had told the nurses that he was not expected to live. That night nearly made Essie want to give up nursing. She could hardly bear it, as it reminded her so strongly of sitting with her young brother Cecil, when he was dying of lockjaw, and thinking to herself '*Oh, die quickly. Don't go on breathing. Oh, please stop breathing. I can't stand it. You can't stand it. Oh, God give him peace, I can't stand it. I can't.....*'

Sister Blythe materialized out of the darkness and put her hand on her shoulder. 'You've done enough for the time being, go and sit in the kitchen and eat your dinner dear.'By the time Essie went back to his bed, he had reached the calm of utter exhaustion. Sister went away to her own bed, fortified by the knowledge that people rarely die fully conscious. More commonly, they slip into a deeper and deeper sleep. His final passing was painless, and Essie had to get poor Dr Jones out of bed again to certify death. She and Gould washed the body in the semi darkness, slipped it into a shroud and got it on to the trolley to go to the mortuary. It had already been a difficult night, as they had several very sick patients, and were expecting a further death. It sounds bad, but Essie had reached the stage of laughing hysterically. Staff Nurse Gould stayed on the ward whilst Senior Probationer Short went outside with her, using two hurricane lamps to search the bushes. They were looking for the planks to enable them to wheel the trolley down the front steps and onto the drive. Eventually, all was set up, and with Essie at the front and Short at the rear, they manoeuvred the trolley carefully on to the planks. The night was so dark, and the light from the lamps on the path so poor, that one of wheels on the front of the trolley went over the side of the board, and the corpse nearly slipped off the front side of the trolley. The situation was very precarious, and made worse by their giggling. Fortunately the girls were able to hold on to him. They placed the lamps to light their way to the mortuary. Essie started a quiet and deliberately awful, flat singing of a hymn

Through the night of doubt and sorrow
Onward goes the pilgrim band
Singing songs of expectations
Marching to the Promised Land.
Clear before us, through the darkness
Gleams and burns the guiding light.

Eventually, despite their laughter, still working with the light from the hurricane lamps, they managed to get the body safely into the mortuary and lifted it on to the slab. On returning to the ward and reporting their difficulties, Nurse Gould pointed out that the ward had straps for securing bodies to the trolley. Oh dear! Another lesson was learned. Essie felt very upset about the way they had laughed whilst dealing with a patient's body, and confessed to Barbara when she saw her in the morning. She was much re-assured when Barbara said 'it's a common reaction amongst new nurses to extreme stress, particularly where death is concerned. You weren't being disrespectful. Now calm down. It won't happen again now that you understand.'

Things did not however, improve. There was a Doctors' Lecture arranged for 2pm the next day, and regardless of being on night duty, all probationers were expected to attend, in uniform. Flossie called Essie with a cup of tea at an appropriate time. Drooping and yawning with tiredness, she processed her weary way across the garden to the board room on the first floor of the hospital. Normally she enjoyed Dr Avery's lectures. On that day, she was just fagged out. She fought to conceal her yawns. Cautiously she extracted a very strong peppermint from her pocket, and slipped it into her mouth. It had no effect. Palmer, who was sitting directly behind her was poking her periodically with her ruler. Finally, Essie fell off her chair and woke on the floor. Palmer was leaning over her whispering,

'Shut your mouth. You fainted'.

She and Probationer Martin helped her out on to the landing, and she had a cup of tea. It didn't help. Miss Airey appeared and sent her back to bed with a flea in her ear. She heard later that Dr Avery was making most solicitous enquiries about her. Such a nice doctor. The rest of the visiting doctors were pompous pigs.

The girls had to study very hard in their 'spare' time. Night duty was sometimes a good opportunity to study in the small hours, and they did take it in turns to have a little sleep if the ward was quiet, which it often wasn't. It was important to make full notes of all the Doctors' lectures. They had to learn about the causes of illnesses, which of course included the living environment, personal hygiene and general constitution of the person with the illness. They learned the signs of the illness, such as rash, fever, changes in the urine, faeces. They had to observe the symptoms the patient was complaining of. Then they had to learn all about the medical and surgical treatments, and finally how to *nurse* the patient. So really, their training was mainly based on the doctors' knowledge, which they interpreted into the nursing of the case. The British Journal of Nursing set a title for an essay every week. It was a competition for their nurse readers. The winning essay was published two weeks later, and was a really helpful means of learning more about a wide variety of conditions. Titles included 'What points would you observe in nursing a case of heart disease?', 'Venereal Disease' and 'How food and water may act as carriers of disease'.

The Probationers didn't see every kind of disease. Cases of tuberculosis had to go to the Chest Hospital and those with other infectious diseases went to the Isolation Hospital. Paupers were treated in the Workhouse Hospital and poor people were usually ill at home, as were the rich who had plenty of servants. Those who donated money for the hospital's running costs had 'tickets' that they could use to arrange the admission of family, friends and servants. Those without much money or influence were only admitted by permission of the hospital management board, subject to a bed being available. If the sick person's family could afford to pay a doctor to come to their home, the doctor could either attend the patient at home, and even operate on them, or make the arrangements to have the person admitted to the hospital quickly.

Essie finally got used to people dying. Over the years many other nurses confided that when confronted by their first body, they found themselves laughing. It must be one of the mind's defence systems. During particularly bad spells of duty however, all the nurses tended to see a lot of black humour in situations which got worse and worse. It was a way of coping.

Everyone was very concerned when Miss Airey started to look unwell. Sister Blythe told her staff that Miss Airey had given the hospital board two weeks' notice of her application to take a fortnight's leave. Sister Lacey was left in charge of the hospital. All and sundry were quaking in their boots at the thought of two weeks exposure to that rancid temperament. In the event, Miss Airey did not return after two weeks, and was actually absent by the Hospital Board's permission for a further two months. She was said to have been very 'run down.'

Chapter Twelve

By July, Essie was finally getting to grips with her work as a Probationer, and was taking more responsibility. The hospital was better staffed, as with all the rumours of a possibility of a war, two more Probationers had been taken on, and the wards were getting some help from Red Cross volunteers. These volunteers, from the Voluntary Aid Division known as 'VADs', all ladies born and bred, were keen to get involved in things like feeding patients rather than being sent into the sluice as a ward drudge or damp dusting flat surfaces. However, the Sisters and trained nurses were firm with them, making it clear that work such as dressings and all the paraphernalia around this and medicines were definitely the responsibility of trained nurses and probationers, and the VADs would have to start at the bottom and work up. The VAD on Essie's ward, Miss Seagar, kept saying '*eau raally*', and laughing very loudly at inappropriate moments. Sister kept rolling her eyes to heaven and saying sharply '*do give over Miss Seagar*'. Later, in the Nurses' Home, Essie asked Barbara what 'eau raally' meant, thinking it was some kind of French phrase that she hadn't come across before. Barbara nearly wet herself laughing, and told her that Miss Seagar had been saying 'Oh, really!'

It was a good summer, and if there were no lectures during their afternoon time off the Probationers did have the opportunity of a game of tennis on the court outside Albert Edward ward, in their uniforms, or even a gentle perambulation down to Middle Chine in their 'outdoor' uniforms of course. When exhausted, sitting in a deckchair for a doze in the back garden of the Nurses' Home was preferable, but any nurse who got accidentally sunburned was disciplined. They all usually covered themselves carefully anyway, as freckles were a social no-no. Essie wanted to keep herself looking 'nice' as she had developed a deep liking for Dr Jones.

He had a worse job than anyone, as he was available twenty four hours a day and the hospital committee kept saying they had no money to pay a second man. He had a permanently drowsy demeanour. He found Friday and Saturday nights the worst, as drunks would keep turning up at all hours with bleeding scalps for stitching. When he had done with them, often they wouldn't go away, and he had to rope in Ernie or Barbara to help him evict them.

He did, somehow, seem to find time to read his daily newspaper. At the end of July he sat in an armchair in the middle of Albert Edward Ward with his Daily Chronicle newspaper to tell the nurses and patients that Austria had declared war on Serbia, and things were looking so worrying that the King and the Cabinet would be staying in London for meetings over the weekend. Dr Jones read bits aloud. Apparently the Austrian Emperor was justifying the war based on the malevolent attitude of Serbia which had been 'treading a path of open hostility to the Austro-Hungarian Empire for years.' On the 1st of August, he read from his newspaper again, saying that on the previous day Mr Asquith the Prime Minister had been speaking to the House of Commons who were sitting in 'strained silence.' Mr Asquith was reported as saying 'The issues of peace and war are hanging in the balance, and with them the risk of a catastrophe of which it is impossible to measure the dimensions or the effects. I appeal to the patriotism of all parties to postpone controversy in regard to domestic differences.' Dr Jones read on, telling his shocked audience that the Austrians were advancing into Serbia, and the Dominions of Canada and South Africa were rallying to the support of the United Kingdom in the crisis. Germany had entered the war, and the British Government had stated 'If we allow Germany to become victorious, she will become so powerful as to threaten our own existence by occupying Belgium, Holland and possibly Northern France.'

Essie could see tears in Dr Jones's eyes. Many in the ward were openly crying. The staff all did their best, every day, without regard to personal cost to heal the sick and comfort the dying. The sheer vicious uselessness of fighting was only too clear to them. Events rapidly progressed. The British Fleet was ready for action but the British Government continued diplomacy to try to save European peace.

By Sunday the second of August, Germany had declared war on Russia, Luxemburg was invaded, France mobilized all its forces and armies were being mobilized in Sweden, Belgium, Switzerland and Holland. On Tuesday the 4th August Dr Jones came to Albert Edward ward to tell everyone that the War Office had put out a statement that Britain was at war with Germany following the German Government's refusal to respect the neutrality of Belgium. Germany had announced its intentions to march its armies through Belgium to attack France. The King had ordered a complete mobilization of the British Army and thanked the Dominions for their 'loyalty and proffered help.' As the crisis escalated, the hospital board sanctioned the employment of six assistant nurses. Sister Blythe explained that many qualified nurses throughout the country had already signed up with the army. Other hospital and nursing home facilities were being created in Poole and Bournemouth, in the expectation of heavy casualties should an armed conflict ensue. The view of the nursing staff was that 'standards would slip' in the hospital with the employment of people from lower social classes. Theft of hospital equipment would be more likely. The orderlies were already responsible for counting the cutlery every day (patients pinched it if they could), and all vomit bowls, bedpans, gallipots et cetera were counted every week. Sister Blythe finished by reminding staff that 'this hospital is full of very tempting things'.

'I wouldn't mind that young man in bed four' Essie said out of the corner of her mouth to Barbara.

'WHAT did you say Negus?' said Sister.

'I said I wouldn't mind helping at the Front, Sister.'

'Get on with your work Negus' she said in a bored voice, as if she was utterly tired of the antics of a difficult child. Essie felt herself going red, and slunk back to the sluice. She hoped the new Assistant Nurses would take over the rough jobs and leave her free for more interesting work. Very quickly, changes did occur. The hospital lost two Staff Nurses, who went to work in the Mont Dore Hotel, at Bournemouth Square, which was preparing to become a military hospital. Nurses and Probationers were moved around, and Essie found herself with more responsibilities, which included administration of medicines (*into various body cavities...*) and was being taught the art of doing surgical dressings 'from the bottom up' by Barbara. Bottom up meant of course, cutting, folding and general preparation of dressings and sterilization of these in a hot oven and care of scissors and forceps and things. The instruments required boiling up in a large metal vat in The Sterilizing Room. It was cleaner work, but lifting the lid off the sterilizer resulted in a seriously wilted starched cap and a soggy starched apron front. Nurses had to wear a cotton mask whilst preparing the sterile trolleys. Sadly for Essie, the beloved Dr Jones most often appeared when she was looking at her most unattractive, flushed and soggy from labours in the sterilizing room.

In October she was sent back upstairs to work in Alexandra Ward again, with the women, and Miss Lacey as Ward Sister. She was made responsible again, for the Sterilizing Room and its contents. Whilst working in Albert Edward Ward, she had discovered Scruffite, a magical cleaner for removing lime scale from sterilizers. Sister Lacey always insisted that only '*elbow grease*' should be used to clean Alexandra's sterilizer so Essie regularly enlisted Mrs Mattie to go down the fire escape and obtain for her some of Albert Edward's Scruffite in a vomit bowl. Sister was highly impressed with her efforts to produce such a wonderfully clean sterilizer. 'It just goes to show that elbow grease is far better' she said, 'that Scruffite stuff that Sister Blythe swears by just rots the seams of the sterilizer.'

Essie felt herself going rather pink with embarrassment. However, it was not very long before she blotted her copy book. It was a Saturday afternoon, and she had the sterilizer cooling down before she drained it. The window was open, as it was an unexpectedly warm day. Dr Jones came into the room, looking for a sterilized syringe, and stood with her by the window, making some small talk. Outside, just beneath the window, two of the hospital's most pompous visiting local doctors were standing talking. Dr Jones filled a gallipot from the sterilizer, poured warm water down on them, then ducked below the window sill. Things progressed, and culminated with Essie throwing down a medium sized bowl of water. The two of them ducked down very quickly, and were lying giggling on the floor, when Sister found them.

Essie was summoned to see Miss Airey at 9.00am on Monday morning. She commanded an explanation. Essie tried. Miss Airey announced the punishment. Essie was allocated to work in the operating theatre for the first time. The Sister in there, Miss Dean – code name '*Mother*' had a fearsome reputation for eating her 'children'. Essie felt faint and sick at the prospect of working there with '*the child chewer*' and evaluated the possibility of running back home to Poole against braving the lioness's den. Fortunately Barbara confided that she had overheard Miss Airey discussing a staff crisis with Sister Blythe, who had recommended Essie as a 'very sturdy soul', who would probably do well in Theatre. She emphasised that Miss Airey had presented the change to Essie as a punishment, rather than a compliment following her very *bad behaviour with a man*! On the following Monday, Barbara and Palmer marched the terrified Essie up the stairs, pushed her in through the Theatre's double doors, and held them shut, so that she couldn't retract her decision to stay at the hospital.

In the Theatre she was subjected to even greater boiling up of instruments and baking of dressings in the oven. Her cap and apron flopped ever more dramatically in the steamy atmosphere. Miss Dean seemed permanently cross and upbraided her for next to nothing. 'Those are Cheatle forceps, not fairy wands Negus!' she shouted when she saw her clumsily preparing a full surgical trolley for the first time. Eventually Essie seemed to get the hang of things and Miss Dean cut back just a tiny bit on the caustic comments. She loved the work, and didn't feel overawed by the operations. Additionally she saw a lot more of Dr Jones, who administered the ether in emergencies, when the operating doctor couldn't get a colleague to help him. He had a very relaxed approach to anaesthesia, which was a very dangerous craft indeed. Dr Jones lowered his mask and still holding the chloroform inhaler, enjoyed a cup of tea if he was particularly tired or the case took a long time. He patted Essie's hand when he could. She felt that there was something growing between them.

Fortunately, there were no operations, even for emergencies during the night, as the incandescent gas lamp in the Theatre did not give enough light for operating. Anyway, the gas flow in the evenings was often very low, and the lights in the ward would get quite dim, so it wasn't worth the risk. So, the theatre only worked by daylight, and used the gas lamp as well most of the time. Essie didn't miss sleep as a result of the work, but often missed meals if a case 'went over'. When this happened, if Dr Jones was there, he sent Ernie the orderly over the road to the shop for buns. The visiting doctor was of course, able to go home and be fed by his servants, regardless of the hour. Miss Ainslie just saw missing meals as some kind of lack of organizational discipline in the Theatre. Essie began to sympathize with Miss Dean's ratty temperament.

Of course, together with the Theatre Staff Nurse, Essie had to do all the 'backroom' work of threading and preparing needles, cleaning and oiling instruments and cleaning everything else constantly. Dr Jones slipped in occasionally (when he was awake) for a chat when 'Mother' wasn't about. The hospital started to get *really busy* when the Belgian soldiers began to be evacuated to Bournemouth in late August and early September, as the Boscombe Military Hospital (Tents) and the Mont Dore (a Hotel, now temporarily a hospital) couldn't cope with them all. Extra beds were put up down the middle of Albert Edward Ward and in the side wards upstairs.

Dr *Emrys* Jones grew ever sweeter. When he asked Essie to meet him after supper one day, in the *(disused)* old horse's stable at the back of the Nurses' Home, she agreed, even though it was January. She had never been kissed by a young man before, but was immediately addicted to this furtive ecstasy. It aroused sensations within her that she had never been aware of before. He told her that he was signing up with the Army Medical Service, and was leaving at the end of the week to go to Aldershot for training, prior to being sent to France. He asked her if she would write to him whilst he was away, and she readily agreed, wondering how she (and the hospital) would manage without him. Barbara left at much the same time. Her application to join the Queen Alexandra's Imperial Nursing Service had been accepted, as she had been trained at St Bartholomew's Hospital in London, and she would be serving in France. Essie wept to lose two such dear colleagues, and was determined that once her training was complete, assuming the war was still on, she would go to France too.

Jason

Chapter Thirteen

1914 and the years that followed remained a livid wound within many people's memories. The year started with a feeling that a terrible storm cloud was hanging over Europe. Germany under Kaiser Wilhelm the Second was developing a new, ever more confrontational foreign policy. Its navy was progressively strengthened with dreadnought battleships, in an effort to challenge Britain's mastery of the seas. Essie Negus had used the developing international crisis to finally persuade her father to let her go nursing, which made Jason sad, as he'd long cherished hopes of getting married to her, but clearly she didn't share his feelings. He regarded her as an absolutely amazing girl, and he'd been in love with her for a long time.

Things were rapidly changing in Poole regarding women's places in society. Jason's step grandmother, Mistress Caroline Lovejoy had not married until later in her life, partly because his Grandfather, Captain Lovejoy took a long time to ask her, and partly because she so dearly prized her independence from men. Mistress Caroline was the nucleus amongst some of the women Jason knew best, Phemie Ross from The Albatross Pharmacy and her two daughters, Agnes and Morag, his mother Lydia Lovejoy, Mrs Negus and Essie. They were all members of the Church League for Women's Suffrage. Mr Negus went about muttering that he certainly *suffered* domestically from all these women with queer ideas, but Jason thought he was secretly rather proud of them, even though he was a very conservative man. Mr and Mrs Negus were very supportive of Agnes Ross, who decided to follow her mother Phemie's initial profession, and become a midwife in the town.

In January 1914, Jason's older friend, Wesley Clark, owner of Teague's Grocery Store, had been looking for a replacement delivery horse for some time. He knew about horses, did Wesley, and had got wind of the fact that Mistress

Caroline who bred horses as a side-line to her farming had bred a particularly fine gelding that Jason's brother Victor, who worked with her on Blake Hill farm had trained. Mistress Caroline had called this noble beast 'Kitchener' after Lord Kitchener of Khartoum, the famous soldier who succeeded in regaining British control of the Sudan. Victor knew that Mistress Caroline needed to sell Kitchener to help cover the costs of some minor repairs to her house and outbuildings and he persuaded her to invite Wesley over to look at Kitchener.

It was a cold Saturday morning when Wesley and Jason met at Poole railway station. They were wearing coats, mufflers and hats for their expedition. Wesley was saying 'my wife was full of curiosity about my intentions, and was asking if she and baby George could come too. No, I said, it is very cold today, and you wouldn't be interested. I'm just going to see a man about a dog.' I always say that, when I don't want to tell her where I'm going and what I'm doing. It infuriated her!'

In the previous year Mistress Lottie Teague had signed over Teague's Grocery business in its entirety to Wesley in return for a small pension. It was Mistress Teague and her husband Ethelred, who had chosen Wesley from the lads at the Union Workhouse, Longfleet, to work as the delivery boy at their developing business. 'E. and C Teague, high class provisions, Tea merchant and Ships' Provisions', which became one of the most respected shops in Poole. Wesley had begun by wheeling a wooden cart round the town to supply customers and calling at the back doors of grand houses to collect their orders and deliver them promptly. As the business prospered, he progressed to driving a horse drawn cart. He 'lived in' at Teague's from the start. To begin with, he slept in an attic on a straw palliasse. Teagues also chose girls from the workhouse, and trained them for domestic work. They always passed the girls on eventually, when they were ready for domestic service. Wesley said he often used to fret that he would get 'passed on' too, but apparently he was too good to lose. Encouraged in every way, he learned so well that eventually he was replaced as delivery man, by another lad. In the end, Wesley ran the grocery for the elderly Teagues, retaining their philanthropic activities. Mr and Mrs Teague had two grandchildren to leave the shop to, but Mr Michael Curtis and Mrs Lydia Lovejoy were already providing for themselves well, and insisted that Wesley would manage it better, and ought to inherit it outright.

Wesley and Jason walked from Parkstone Station to Blake Hill Farm, to see the horse. The temperature was below freezing as they crunched along the track on frosted grass and opaque grey ice stretched over shallow puddles which shattered under their heavy boots. When they arrived at the farm, Mrs Caroline Lovejoy was in the dairy fidgeting around, unnecessarily supervising Mrs Stone, one of the dairy maids, who with a steady hand was skimming cream off a large shallow dish of milk. Jason was very proud of his grandmother. In her seventies now, her figure was bulky and heavy with farming muscles and her swearing (for necessity only...) was better than anything he'd ever heard from the sailors on Poole Quay.

'Oi, Littl'un! she hollered out across the yard in the general direction of the stables. His brother Victor emerged, tall and muscular. He'd had trouble with his digestion all his years, and Mistress Caroline had done a good job of keeping him reasonably well. She always reckoned it was 'the 'ard work an fresh air at Blake ill wot kep im well,' but Victor had been looking very healthy since his mid-teens when, at her suggestion he'd completely stopped eating bread and cakes and biscuits, and filled himself up with porridge, rice puddings, vegetables, meat, lentils and cheese instead.

'Well, fetch im out in the daylight then! Folks cassn't be expected to make their minds up without seein un proper.'

Eventually Victor re-emerged holding the bridle of a large, handsome, blue-black polished looking horse. 'Kitchener is my friend, Wesley' he said. 'We have to sell him, as frankly, he's far too good to harness to a farm cart. We have other horses that can do that and the ploughing. With his good looks and intelligence, he will be a great advertisement for your business. Customers will love him. He does everything that is asked of him and is thoroughly amiable, as we've never treated him rough. I've never known him to be evil or nasty, and a better friend *you* will never find. He is strong and highly intelligent, the best we've ever bred. I'm sure that Mr. Negus would love him for his undertaking business, but you keep only one horse at a time, and they are always so well looked after, and loved besides. See, you can even ride him,' he said, slipping nimbly on to Kitchener's bare back. 'He's an all-rounder.' The three of them, Victor, Wesley and Kitchener went into the stable to talk money, and Mrs Lovejoy and Jason went into the kitchen for tea and toast by the fire.

Well, in the end, Wesley purchased Kitchener and rode him home to Poole, bareback. Kitchener was much admired around town in his new role as a delivery horse, particularly by Eddie the young delivery driver, as he learned the delivery route after just two circuits. Servants, housewives and little children came out of their back doors to pat and stroke his beautiful mane. Wesley had to warn Eddie very strictly that the customers were, *under no circumstances at all* to feed Kitchener with treats.

Jason continued with his work as a fisherman from his father's boat, The Artemis, and went out with the Poole Lifeboat whenever required. He had been passionate about saving life since accidentally killing a man with a single punch, to save his brother Victor's life during a fight. He obtained the Red Cross Society First Aid Certificate to assist in his work with the lifeboat. Later, continuing feelings about the preciousness of human life led to him joining the Society of Friends, more often known as 'The Quakers.' In late 1913, as rumours of the possibility of a war increased, Jason decided that the Red Cross Male Nursing Certificate might also be very useful. He studied for this with the help of his father, Harry Lovejoy, son of Captain James Lovejoy. Harry had learned a great deal about medicine and surgery whilst at sea with his father. Jason sometimes neglected his fishing, and spent time at The Albatross Pharmacy with Alec and Sandy Ross learning about medicines and regularly helped out on the men's' ward at the Cornelia Hospital in Poole. His efforts were rewarded when he obtained the certificate.

Rumours of a likely war continued. Political, territorial and economic disagreements, particularly over colonial issues led to disagreements between European countries and accelerated an arms race particularly involving Germany, France and Russia, but involving smaller countries as well. A deep feeling of unease had lain for some time over Britain, where shipyards were working flat out to make more Dreadnought battle cruisers. War was actually declared on the 4th August. Britain had expected the Germans to invade France first. In the event, the Germans followed their secret Schlieffen Plan, which used neutral Belgium as a 'back door' to avoid the French fortifications on the Franco-German border. Britain was guaranteeing Belgian neutrality and so the British Expeditionary Force deployed troops in France and Belgium within three days of the declaration of war. This was the culmination of a long period of unease within Britain, and most of the general public thought that the British soldiers would quickly restore order, and would be back home by Christmas.

However, many members of the Society of Friends, who like Jason, had been watching the European crisis develop, had realized from early 1914 that such a war would be far more serious. They were determined that should war break out, they would play a part in trying to save lives. The Friends had set up an International War Relief Committee in the Franco Prussian War of 1870, and now felt that they had 'work to do' in the likely event of Britain becoming involved in a war with Germany, the growing super-power, allied to the Austro-

Hungarian Empire. 'War Fever' was already gripping the country. People were going about the towns shouting *'We don't want to fight, but by jingo if we do, we've got the ships, we've got the men, and we've got the money too.'*

Heartily sickened with the 'jingoistic' atmosphere in the town of Poole, towards the end of August, just before the declaration of war, Jason read an appeal in the Quaker journal *'The Friend'*, for young Friends to volunteer their help and responded immediately. Locally, things carried on in Poole and Bournemouth as usual. Finally, a chat with Wesley, whilst sitting on a bench outside the Poole Arms in the evening sunshine, watching the activity on the quay revealed the following news.

Jason said 'I was in Bournemouth this morning, doing a bit of business for Father. The banks are shut for the time being, so there is a considerable shortage of money. Local people are very worried about the effects of a war on the holiday season. Last week there were plenty of arrivals. Today, being the August Bank Holiday Monday, there were few arrivals on Sunday into the town and fewer today. I went to look at the crowds on the beach, and there were less people on it than at Easter. Paddleboat trips to the Isle of Wight have been cancelled, and the only trip visitors can get is to Weymouth.'

'People are becoming scared' remarked Wesley. 'Already, the richest people are buying up stocks of flour, jam, tinned meats, sugar and whatnot. They're frightened of what will happen. Even poorer people are trying to buy a little extra.'

On Tuesday, 4th August, at 11pm, war was declared. Most people heard about it in the newspapers on the morning of Wednesday 5th August. Everyone was deeply shocked. On the same day, in the afternoon, a temporary Army Recruiting office was set up at the top end of the High Street. Queues of young volunteers waited outside to sign up for three years, or the duration of the war. The government had made an initial call for 100,000 volunteers. The volunteers were given the opportunity to choose which regiment they would join, Many signed up to join the Dorsetshires, but of course a significant number of locals signed up for the navy.

In September Jason heard that he had been accepted for training with the Friends' Ambulance Brigade at the Quaker village of Jordans, in Buckinghamshire. He was part of a group of sixty-three young men, mostly Oxford and Cambridge graduates and not all of them Quakers. He might have felt like a fish out of water as he spent a lot of time in the 'Artemis'. However, his grandfather, Captain Lovejoy was a self-taught Latin and Greek scholar, and the interest was passed down through his family. As a family, the Lovejoys were all 'well read' and well spoken, so he quickly got along well with his new colleagues. He felt satisfied with his commitment to the Religious Society of Friends, who see life as God's gift, and have always supported peace and opposed war. This had all come about as a result of his long personal contemplation of God's ownership of the world, the mysteries of the stars and our interconnectedness, and his feeling that he had no right to judge or harm other people.

At the training camp in Jordans, with sixty other young Friends, Jason began to prepare himself for active service. The intensive programme included first-aid to the wounded, stretcher-drill, basic hygiene and cleanliness, field-cookery and physical training. He soon made a close friend, Timothy, an Oxford University graduate, who was not a Quaker, who stated very clearly 'I am sincerely opposed to the concept of killing my fellow human beings. The so called *enemies* are men like us, and it is crystal clear that our governments intend to use British men in their lethal game of chess.'

Jason replied 'I think the British Government detest us as the more deeply thinking, and possibly highly educated amongst society who are questioning why we should even consider going to war. They are deliberately marginalizing us by refusing to even consider using the resources we are offering them to help the wounded.'

'Yes. It's because our aim is to positively support life, health and peace without any discrimination as to who our patients may be, or what side the British Government is backing' Timothy said.

Victor

Chapter Fourteen

At the outbreak of war the British army had 25,000 horses. They urgently needed to source half a million more. The War Office forcibly procured horses and mules from private homes and farms. In 1914 the British Army owned only 80 motor vehicles so the dependence on horses for transporting goods and supplies was significant. In any case, the conditions on the Western Front were so appalling they were totally unsuitable for motor vehicles.

The impact on farming families was the worst. They in many cases were losing male members from their families *and* their horses, but they were still expected to produce food for the nation. At the end of WW1, it was estimated that eight million horses and countless mules and donkeys had died in service.

By Mid-1915 volunteer numbers were falling fast and the National Registration Act was created. It was a list of all the men fit for military service who were still available. Mistress Caroline wrote to tell Jason about Victor's gentle gay friend, Claude, who, pushed by other lads who were joining up, went to war. Victor missed him terribly. Claude went through all his introductory training. It was very hard for him, and he was constantly ragged for being 'soft'. In the end, his courage, kindness, patience and general goodness won through, and his comrades in the trenches got to like and respect him. He was killed after serving bravely for five months at the front in August 1915.

Claude's mother had walked from Poole to Blake Hill Farm to break the sad the news to Victor and Caroline. Up at Mistress Caroline's farm, life continued as usual. The puddles in the clay soil in one of the fields supported ducks. The greedy little monsters would eat up anything they could find, and would even eat small potatoes. A vast army of Rhode Island Red hens ran around the farmhouse, and the cockerels fought each other. The current victor, called 'Napoleon' paraded around the area aggressively, his large feet clattering over the gravel paths, and he crowed noisily most of the day. He fluffed up his feathers, flapped his wings and strutted around to frighten off friends and strangers, and would see off any dog immediately. He was destined for the pot... Soon... Caroline and Victor made an adequate living, sending a couple of churns of milk down to Poole every day, and Mrs Stone the dairy maid prepared butter and cream to sell in Parkstone shops.

Victor greatly missed the horse, Kitchener, whom he and his step-grandmother, had bred and trained. Whenever he was in Poole, he visited the beautiful black horse, and took him an apple, or some carrots. They were great friends. Mistress Caroline and Victor had bred Kitchener with the intention of persuading Wesley, who was a lifelong friend, to buy him as an asset to the Teague's Grocers. It was however, one of Victor's greatest regrets that he'd had Kitchener gelded for the job he was going to do. Kitchener would have been such a great success financially as he was a most intelligent horse and would have been an excellent stud, but as a delivery horse for Teagues' Grocers, he was better gelded – less to distract him – more docile. For Jason and his grandmother, breeding horses had suddenly become an imperative. Most people had been mildly aware of the possibility of a war for at least the previous two years. In January 1914 without any warning, the military had been going around counting, measuring, inspecting and registering all the horses and mules in the country. It was obvious that many would be needed in the event of a war with Germany. Kitchener and all the other horses at Blake Hill farm were already listed.

The visit from the military meant that there was no possibility of concealing the number of horses on the tiny farm. Victor and Caroline were now frightened of losing their farm horses to the war effort. Fortunately, well prior to the declaration of war, Victor had put Kitchener's mother, Mistress Caroline's brood mare Julie to the same stallion, owned by Miss Foote at Sandbanks. If by a 50:50 chance Julie produced another stallion even nearly as good as Kitchener, Victor planned to breed from him, using other local mares.

In early November, sitting at the kitchen table at Blake Hill Farm, in the light of the oil lamp, Victor had just written a letter to Jason, now in Belgium. Saying goodbye to his brother was a very sad time for Victor. Jason and Victor were as different as chalk and cheese, but they had always been very close throughout their lives.

'Mistress Caroline,' he said, 'I'm thinking of sleeping in the stable with Julie tonight. She's been acting a bit fussy today, and I'm wondering if she will foal overnight, particularly as she's been shitting sloppy and her udder is filling this evening, and beginning to drip sticky yellow.'

'You mind you doan upset er' she replied. 'My Julie is a very private gurl an if you bain't careful she won't drop er foal while you're there.'

'Look, I done alright with Kitchener, so juss leave me be', he said, lighting a lamp to go to the stable, feeling himself to be in an agony of anticipation. 'Julie an me will be juss fine.'

Caroline hobbled off to bed, secretly glad that her grandson was again taking a responsibility that she felt too old to bother with now. She always *acted* grumpily with everyone, to conceal her heart of gold. She was very proud of Victor, as she'd had such a hand in rearing him to be a healthy young man. She loved him dearly, but the only thing that bothered her was his predilection for young men friends rather than girls. It had got him into a lot of trouble with the law in the past, but the only change in his behaviour was that his men friends normally visited him and stayed over at Blake Hill Farm, where she and Victor lived. She didn't care. She'd spent her life watching cows jump on each other, and young bulls trying to mount one another. *'All part of life's untidy big tapestry'* she thought to herself. She'd asked his parents, Lydia and Harry Lovejoy, what they thought about it. However, after the recent court case where Victor had been judged innocent of sodomy, they declined to comment on the situation. She tried to put his tendencies to the back of her mind. *'Doubtless God knows all about it, and He understands. I juss don't wan im in trouble'* she thought to herself. She really liked all his friends, Claude Wareham the drapery assistant, William Rose the hairdresser, George Travers the gardener and John Barringer the blind pianist. None of them had expressed any intentions of going to war except John Barringer, who said he would have joined up if he wasn't blind, as it sounded exciting.

As far as Poole was concerned a great crisis came in late July, when businesses and farms all over the British Isles were visited again by the army's commissioning officers, who negotiated fair prices with the owners, and took away many horses, including Kitchener. It was a very sad time right across the country. Farmers just didn't know how they were going to manage their land with fewer horses. Men and women stood in Poole High Street weeping. They cried for the loss of animals who were like friends to them, and they cried for the loss of the horse as a household amenity, and they cried because they didn't know how they were going to keep their business open with hardly any 'horsepower' left.

At Sandbanks, Miss Foote had lost most of her finest horses. It was said that Wesley couldn't stop crying for a full week after losing Kitchener, and his wife said that he prayed for Kitchener every night, that he would be treated kindly, and be brought back home safely one day. Eddie the delivery boy was now pushing a handcart around the town to make deliveries and to collect some items from Poole Railway station. Owners of the large businesses such as the timber and flour merchants were allowed to keep some horses. At Blake Hill Farm, 'Big Boy', the younger of the two plough horses had been taken. Julie and her foal, a little colt named 'Nutmeg', had been reprieved, as Nutmeg was still suckling from Julie. Stallions were preferred at this time. Food prices started to climb, as people were worried about a possible blockade by the German navy and bought more than they needed, causing shortages. Some food suppliers began to stockpile provisions fearing shortages. This made the situation for poor people very bad indeed. There was a small dairy herd. Mistress Caroline had put a notice in the Evening Echo.

'Wanted, A Man and his Wife, to manage a Dairy of Sixteen Cows; a good character indispensable. Accommodation available. Apply to Mistress Lovejoy, Blake Hill Farm, Poole.' Sadly, there were no replies.

It was at this stage that Victor started discussing with Mistress Caroline whether all the horses and mules that had been taken from the town were going to be cared for properly by the army. 'Didn't people do zummat fur orsses in that thur Balkans war?' she remarked.

'Yes, of course, I remember now' he replied. 'It was called Our Dumb Friends League, wasn't it? They looked after mules as well. We must do something about it!'

Mistress Caroline little realized that she would rue the day that she encouraged Victor to take an interest in the Dumb Friends League. She thought it might comfort him in the loss of Kitchener and Big Boy, but faced with the thought of both innocent animals and people suffering from the violence of war, Victor began to feel very upset. As a fit male with only female help on Parkstone Farm, he felt himself to be indispensable. He certainly had, like Jason, no stomach for fighting, but he wanted to do something positive for the innocent horses.

Encouraged by Mistress Caroline, Victor decided that he would discuss the needs of horses on the battlefields with some of his friends in Poole. They put collection tins labelled 'Blue Cross' beside the 'Red Cross' tins in local businesses to gather small change. Posters were put up around the town:

> **Blue Cross**
> **The society for encouragement of**
> **kindness to animals.**
> **Please contribute for medicines and first**
> **aid help for wounded horses at the Front.**

Many of the people who had lost their own horses to the war in France contributed generously. Initially the donations were small, and not much could be provided from the cash available, so the Blue Cross organization restricted itself to the purchase of small items such as drugs, bandages and dressings, horse salts, medicines, ointments, clippers, antiseptic and humane killers to euthanize horses too ill or wounded for successful treatment. The horse salt was particularly useful as average size horses need about an ounce of salt per day. Very heavily sweating horses can lose a lot of salt in about an hour when working hard, or in hot weather. The horses were absolutely vital to the army's success, to pull supply vehicles, for the cavalry and to pull large guns. Eventually the citizens of Poole and its surrounding villages were sending many veterinary chests to British units. Posters were displayed prominently:

War –torn, wounded and weary
What are you doing for us?
We can't fight, we're not asked to,
But we suffer in helping out brave soldiers to victory
We need help from the public for wounded horses.
We need motor lorries, corn crushers, chaff cutters,
driven by petrol engines.
We need rugs, halters, bandages, humane killers, and
other veterinary requisites, especially the establishment
of a hospital for 1,000 horses.
We are sending out vets, NCOs and soldiers
knowledgeable in first aid for horses.
We need your generous support.
Can you help?

Jason

Chapter Fifteen

The Background to Jason's work

In April 1904, Britain had signed the Entente Cordiale, a formal agreement with France, to end a thousand years of intermittent fighting between the two countries. It was thought that this understanding between the two countries would give France some protection in the event of any further German aggression. (A Franco-Prussian war had been fought in 1870).

On the 16th August, the British Expeditionary Force (BEF) was landing at Le Havre, demonstrating a flurry of friendship towards the local French people. Few could understand each other's language properly, but beer, fags and chocolate provided the currencies of friendship.

By the 20th August the Germans were marching into Brussels to lay siege to Namur Fortress. By the 23rd August, the British were marching towards the town of Mons. In the subsequent battle 1,600 British were killed, wounded or taken prisoner. What became known as 'the race to the sea' started at the end of September and for several weeks the Belgian, British and German armies were on the move, fighting poorly planned battles and incurring vast numbers of casualties.

The first Quaker ambulance team responded to an emergency appeal for help along the border between France and Belgium where masses of untreated casualties were reported to be piling up. Jason and Timothy went out to Belgium together on the 31 October. The hastily assembled First Anglo-Belgian Ambulance Unit was later known as the Friends Ambulance Unit (FAU). The men were led by Phil Baker, who stated 'our aim is to *positively support life, health and peace'*. By this time, a number of doctors and trainee doctors who were described as 'dressers' had also joined them, and formed a group of forty-three drivers and orderlies, three doctors, and eight ambulances who prepared to cross to Dunkirk.

It was a horrific passage. The Friends were only a few miles out to sea on the Invicta, when they came upon Hermes, a torpedoed and sinking cruiser. The crew were already being taken off by small boats from surrounding destroyers. The Friends' ferry drew alongside, and they helped the other crews to rescue the survivors, which took several hours. Jason, who already held a Royal Humane Society medal for lifesaving two men, dived into the water many times, at great danger to his own life, to help survivors into the ship's lifeboats.

'I was terrified that we were going to lose you', Timothy said, massaging his friend's blue and white body with a bit of worn old sail cloth, in an attempt to restore the circulation to his extremities, as the Invicta made full steam ahead to return to England to offload the survivors. It was an awful start to an even worse nightmare. Invicta turned round and again made for Dunkirk immediately the torpedo victims had been safely landed. A further delay occurred when they arrived at Dunkirk, as due to the presence of military supply ships which were offloading, they were kept waiting to dock until 9pm, which was very dangerous, as there were German submarines about and there were German destroyers and light cruisers in the channel.

'Bit of a noxious niff in the air' said Timothy, as to the great relief of all aboard, their ship moored in the harbour.

'Not like anything I've ever smelled before' replied Jason.

Leaving their companions behind to help with offloading the considerable cargo, the already exhausted pair hurried towards the railway sheds where the stench appeared to be residing.

'Armageddon has commenced', said Jason, as a deep rumbling of distant guns began. They entered the first shed cautiously. Timothy, normally an extremely polite young gentleman began to swear loudly and mightily, as they were immediately confronted with about four hundred wounded

Belgian soldiers, lying (*if they were very lucky*) on piles of straw inside the shed. They had been evacuated from the battlefields of Flanders. There were three further sheds. At the back, outside the railway sheds, more men, living and dead, were lying in their hundreds between the tracks. Dressed in their once bright blue battledress tops and bright red trousers, they must have made an easy target for the Germans. Clearly some of the men had been there for days, helpless and untreated, as the filth and stench was indescribable.

In great distress, the pair ran back to the ferry, to find Phil Barker, and to describe what they'd found. Accompanied by a doctor and a dresser, all of them carrying some supplies, they went back to the sheds, and began work until 1.30 am or so. They identified the living, and moved them away from the dead, and using what little they had to hand, and in extremely poor light from hurricane lamps, began to cut away filthy clothing and to clean and bind up wounds. The rotten stench of old blood, sweat, gangrene and sickness was terrible. The hellish noise of human suffering in the surrounding darkness was haunting. Eventually they went back to the Invicta, to try and get some sleep, but were called again at about 4am, to help load some of the Belgian wounded onto the hospital ship HMS Rewa. The wounded were destined for British hospitals. Within the first week, about 3,500 seriously injured Belgians and Germans were evacuated from Dunkirk, but the Friends' work of caring for the wounded who continued to arrive went on.

Eventually Jason found time to write a terse postcard to his parents, Lydia and Harry.

DUNKIRK
Dear all,
Apologies for taking ages to let you know of my safe
arrival.
Have been very busy with Belgian casualties. Am fine and
well.
Love to all, Jason.

[What he didn't say was that the Germans desperately desired Dunkirk for strategic reasons. This port would be the most useful for the future invasion of Britain. British held Dunkirk suffered frequent attacks, as it came within the line of German shell fire. Letters home had to be carefully written to get past the censors, so their writers had to be very careful not to give away any strategic information that could fall into enemy hands.]

Other, slightly longer letters from Jason followed eventually:

DUNKIRK
Dear Mother, Father, Victor,
Still working all hours, receiving the wounded into our
makeshift hospitals in the town. Yesterday, a civilian
hospital was hit by a German shell, and we had to evacuate
the poorly patients to a local cinema.
In my 'off duty' hours, I have learned to drive a motor
ambulance, which is great fun, as is learning about the
mechanics and doing repairs.
Ships bring in daily newspapers, so when we have time to
look at them, we can keep up with news at home.
Love to all, Jason

DUNKIRK

Dear Mother, Father and Victor,

Now that our British Army is engaging fully in the war, in a line extending right across France, I am told that our Friends' Ambulance Brigade is attracting many more volunteers, and we will be spreading our services across the Front Line. At the moment I am working in the wards of local hospitals. Patients are arriving straight from the front, in a filthy state, having been thrown into any available transport. I am expecting to move into ambulance driving and first aiding at the front soon.

I have heard that in occupied areas the Germans are terrifying Belgian citizens with their policy of schrecklichkeit (frightfulness), taking and shooting hostages, burning towns and villages.

Try not to worry about me. I am still your sensible son and brother, and will be very careful.

Love to all, Jason

POOLE

Dear Jason,

Of course we worry about you!!

Do you remember that wild pair of women, Miss Mairi Gooden-Chisholm and Mrs Elsie Knocker (that *divorcee* with a young son)? They were madly fond of motor biking, and were always roaring around our Dorset lanes, adding depth to the ruts. Mrs Knocker in particular, was hardly ever out of the Poole and Dorset Herald. She drove her own car, had her own motor bike, and was always going on motor bike races against men (and often winning). There was a story going about earlier this year that at the end of one race her brakes failed, and she ran into a wall. Mrs Knocker is always *mad to have a go at anything.* The Poole and Dorset Herald did another piece about her when she went as a passenger on a demonstration flight over Merrick Park, and the pilot looped the loop twice above a huge crowd of about 5,000.

Miss Gooden-Chisholm lived with her family in Ferndown, and went to school in Bournemouth. She was mentioned in the Herald last year. Although just seventeen, she rode her own motor bike in the Exeter to London run. She was in the paper again earlier this year. Whilst riding her motor bike she skidded into a local man, breaking his leg. To describe her as 'a bit of a caution is a huge understatement! The two ladies are friends, and since the 25th September, have been in Ostend with Dr Hector Munro and his 'Flying Ambulance Corps,' attending to Belgian Casualties. They took their own motor ambulance over with them. Lady Dorothie Fielding, Helen Gleason and Dr Henry Jellett (a Dublin gynaecologist) are also working with Dr Munro and it is just possible that you may meet with them, when driving your Friends' ambulance.

Mrs Knocker is a trained midwife, so has some medical experience, *in a very different area!* The Bournemouth Daily Echo did a piece about her, 'Dorset Lady at the Front', with extracts from some of her letters to her aunt. Local funds to support the purchase of more ambulances for the war are benefitting greatly from this publicity.

I am sending you more socks, gloves and a muffler, as I have no doubt it is very cold over there.

With much love,

Mother and Father.

Jason

Chapter Sixteen

In March 1915 General French decided to take the village of Neuve Chapelle which formed a German salient (bulge) in the British front line. He also wanted to take Aubers Ridge as a vital observation point which overlooked the plain. He hoped in the longer term to retake Lille.

NEUVE CHAPELLE
March 1915.
Dear Mother, Father,
I've changed my job with the Friends. I'm now a Friends' Stretcher Bearer, working with the army, tending the wounded on the battlefields and bearing them safely back behind our lines.
You are aware now from the newspapers that General French took the village of Neuve Chapelle which formed a German salient (bulge) in our front line. Our armies attacked with four divisions over a two mile front, surprising the Germans. The battle lasted three days, and Neuve Chapelle was taken and held by the British.
Our own work as non-combatants was wretchedly hard. We weren't able to pick up all our Tommies immediately they were wounded as the whole area was under gunfire. I had very little sleep, and my dreams were full of battle noise and pitiful cries. Some Tommies managed to crawl back to our trenches. Following the battle we were working for up to eighteen hours at a time. Some British and German troops were lying on the ground or in shell holes for days after the battle, waiting for our help. The situation was absolutely desperate.
We thank God for our victory, but it is clear that this war will be long and very hard. As the song goes, we will all have to 'pack up our troubles in our old kit bags' and keep smiling!

I met up with Hugh yesterday, he's the regimental bagpiper with the Seaforths 2nd division, and unarmed, led his men in the battle. He is unscathed. What a man!
With love,
Jason

From April to mid May 1915 a second Battle of Ypres was fought to retain the salient. It was another dreadful battle that the Germans were determined to win. The day was curiously silent. The British soldiers standing on the firing steps of the forward edges of the trenches saw a cloud of gas floating on the breeze towards them. It was drifting across in a weird grey/green cloud towards British Hill Sixty. The men standing on the fire step suffered less as the dense chlorine gas settled nearer the ground. On the first day ninety men died from gas before they could be taken to a dressing station, two hundred and seven got to the station, but forty-seven died on arrival and twelve died later after great suffering. It was shocking. The gas made no distinction between friend and foe, and drifted silently with the breeze causing violent irritant to eyes, nose, throat, lungs. In high concentrations it caused deaths.

There was panic in the British lines, with disorientated soldiers running around in the gas clouds in terror, stirring it up and inhaling a lot of the poison. The soldiers who stayed put suffered less than those who ran about, as movement spread the gas. Wounded men, lying on the ground in 'no-man's land' where it was settling were overcome. Those behind the line on stretchers and the men who panicked and moved back with the cloud suffered too. Jason, in a trench at the time of the attack, suspected the gas might be water soluble, doused his large woolly scarf in the trench water tub, and covering his nose and mouth, urged others around him to do the same. Several men further away who could not access water had the presence of mind to urinate into their handkerchiefs and tie them round their faces. Canadian, British, French and Algerian soldiers, despite suffering from the gas attack themselves, moved forwards to fill the gaps left by their comrades. Their courageous efforts stopped the Germans from breaching the Canadian lines inside the salient, preventing the enemy from marching on the city of Ypres. It was from this first gas attack that the mantra below emerged:

'If a whiff of gas you smell,
Bang your gong like bloody hell,
On with your googly, up with your gun –
Ready to meet the bloody Hun'

Ignoring their own exhaustion, Jason and the other stretcher bearer teams went out looking for casualties that evening, despite pockets of green gas lingering in ditches, bomb craters and low lying land. Jason was already developing 'stretcher bearer's hands', calloused and worn despite wearing leather gloves. The heavy wooden stretcher handles split and rotted in the wet, doing a lot of damage to the men's hands, opening the possibility of contracting severe infections in the filthy battlefield. Teams of four bearers also carried between them a heavy pannier full of first aid supplies, bandages, slings, gauze pads, blue morphine tablets, water bottles, cigarettes and blankets. The sodden ground stank of death, with not a blade of grass or living tree to be seen. The bearers were often in the foetid mud above their knees. In other areas they balanced carefully on the edges of many shell craters. Deep in 'no man's land' their first casualty had clearly been sheltering in the mud and filth of a crater for some days, his right leg rancid, the infection rapidly attacking the rest of his body. They gave him a drink of water from their bottle and slipped a morphine tablet under his tongue. He was dying. They left him with a lighted fag in his mouth. Their second casualty was a little whippet of a man that they nearly tripped over in the dark. A short glimmer of light from the moon suggested that he might be about twenty, had only blackened stumps for teeth, and was barely conscious, stinking from gas, dehydrated and with a possible head injury. Now and then he muttered 'take me home. Me ma will take care of me. I want to go home.'

Jason gave the boy a drink from his bottle, and said reassuringly 'You'll get home son,' with a confidence he didn't feel. They strapped the boy to the stretcher for their first 'carry' of the night. It was a dreadful night. There were too many wounded for the bearers to cope with. In the morning, Jason reported himself to the First Aid Post, as he had an infected wound on the forefinger of his right hand. This was very serious, as such an infection in these dire conditions could lead to death. A hot fomentation was applied immediately, and he was sent back down the line to the nearest hospital. A surgeon took a look at it, and he was given an injection of anti-tetanus serum, bathed, given some clean clothes and had his finger re-dressed. His own clothes, unchanged for weeks, were crawling with vermin from the trenches. Exhausted, he was helped on to the next ambulance train as a 'sitter.' It was two days before the train got through to Boulogne, and his finger had become more purulent. Jason was feeling panicky, as he knew this could lead to loss of an arm, or even death. On the boat bound for Southampton, an ancient, retired army doctor lanced the finger as he lay in a bunk. A fine scalpel was used, and the wound cleaned with swabs, methylated spirit and iodine.

'You're a lucky boy' said the old doctor. 'It's high time you went home for a spot of rest.'

At Southampton, Jason was an exhausted 'walking wounded' and was put on a hospital train ultimately bound for Dorchester, but stopping frequently to unload wounded to their home areas. The train drew into Poole Station at 8pm. Several Boy Scouts were present to help the adults with the unloading of the casualties, and a motley collection of large cars and two ambulances were ready to meet the wounded and convey them to the local hospitals. Jason's parents, Harry and Lydia Lovejoy and his friend Wesley were there waiting for him. They had received a letter saying that he would be conveyed home by ambulance train (*which always discreetly discharged the wounded at Poole station at dusk*). They had already spent three evenings at the station, waiting with the volunteers and scouts who helped to unload the trains. They knew Jason was coming, but were unsure of when he would arrive. He was conveyed home with his head on a pillow, lying under a blanket on Wesley's thoughtfully provided handcart – it was quicker than waiting for an ambulance. In the presence of all this kindness and love, Jason was helped into the front door of 'The Poop Deck', his parents' home on the quayside. He was shaking violently, and crying.

His father Captain Harry Lovejoy and brother Victor undressed and washed him. He stank from the trenches he had been living in, and in the gaslight, despite having been bathed a few days previously, they noticed that he still had trench mud between his toes and under his armpits and various vermin in his hair and on his body. Victor put all the clothing in a zinc tub, covered it with water and placed it outside the back door, to be boiled in the washtub in the morning by old Edward, the family's servant.

Fleas and bugs were endemic in the trenches. Being of a seafaring family, the Lovejoys lived in a house called 'The Poop Deck' on Poole Quay, cheek by jowl with fine businesses such as Piplers the Ships' Chandlers, various disreputable pubs, the Seamen's Institute and alleys full of slums. They were no strangers to dealing with these nasty visitors. Jason was sprinkled liberally with Keating's Powder, and his father and Victor quietly sang a little song that Jason was familiar with:

The Keating's Song
Keating's powder does the trick,
Kills all Bugs and Fleas off quick;
Keating he's a jolly brick.
Bravo! Long live Keating!

Keating he's the man who knows
How to bring us sweet repose
When in sleep our eyelids close!
Stop the Fleas from biting!

So, if you would soundly sleep,
Keating's Powder always keep;
Peace and comfort you will reap!
Is not that inviting!

If all folks would use the same,
See each tin bears "Keating's" name,
Fleas would stop their little game
And their midnight meeting.

Victor dozed in an armchair beside his brother all night. Jason's sleep was troubled, as violent dreams frequently woke him, and he didn't realize that he was safe in bed at home. He was mostly asleep for the next three days. The doctor came daily to inspect and dress his finger, which was looking a lot better. Mistress Caroline took the train from Parkstone to visit him, as she was feeling too old and tired to harness the horse and drive her cart to Poole on her own. She stayed beside his bed for most of the day, and managed to spoon plenty of porridge and soup into him. Her dear old eyes were filled with tears at his exhaustion and frailty. On the evening of the third day, Jason woke, dressed and shaved and sat quietly with his parents and brother. He didn't discuss the war at all, or look at any newspapers, and his family noticed how sensitive he was to any noises, jumping at the slightest sound.

'I think he came home just in time' said Harry to his wife, Lydia.

'I don't think he'll stay for long though,' she replied.

The following day, Victor, assiduous in his care for Jason, decided to take him up the High Street, to meet some of the townspeople, particularly their older friend Wesley. The proposed little expedition started badly. Exiting from the front door of 'The Poop Deck', their home at the harbour, there was an exceptionally loud crash. A harbour-side gantry was unloading coal from a ship, and dumping it in the yard of the gas-works. At the sudden noise, Jason immediately put his hands up to both ears and threw himself on to the pavement, rolling over and over to seek the protection of the nearest wall.

'Sorry Vic', he said, still shaking 'it's instinctive after serving on the front'.

'Never mind Jas, come on', said Victor quickly marching his elder brother on to the High Street, thinking it was a better place to be. A loud back-fire from a vehicle's exhaust resulted in Jason diving for cover again.

'Sorry, I thought it was a whizz bang' (high velocity shell) said Jason.

Victor was obliged to take Jason into Teague's Grocers for shelter in their room at the back of the shop, and he stayed there until dusk, when the street was quieter.

Jason went to stay with his Grandmother and brother Victor in the peace of Blake Hill Farm for a period of six weeks. His boss at The Friends' Ambulance Brigade wrote to say not to hurry himself. In truth, his colleagues were absolutely desperate to get him back. However, it was time well spent. His dread of sudden noises slowly vanished in the tranquil surroundings. He still suffered from nightmares, but these gradually lessened. The worst had been when he woke up reliving one of his trench experiences, screaming 'They're dead! They're all bloody dead! They're dead!'

Lydia, his mother, moved into Blake Hill Farm with them. She was now the concert pianist for Dan Godfrey's Bournemouth Symphony Orchestra. Many of the previously all male orchestra were busy with war duties overseas, and at last, women were being allowed to play. Jason's father Harry was at home at The Poop Deck, very busy studying to bring his navigational skills up to date. Formerly the First Officer on his Father's sailing ship, The Daphne, Harry had left the sea following the death of his father, Captain James Lovejoy. He sold The Daphne and split the profits from the last cargo and the ship's sale with Paul Hann, who took over as captain during their last voyage. Harry was trying to get enlisted in the Royal Naval Volunteer Reserve as a navigator, but the fact that he had lost the first and second fingers of his left hand on his final voyage made handling the sextant difficult for him, but not impossible. The possibility of getting the captaincy of one of the local paddle-steamers to use as a minesweeper attracted him.

On the second day of Jason's stay at the farm, something absolutely amazing happened. Victor found an abandoned horse scavenging for food in one of Mistress Caroline's furthest fields. The land drained very poorly in that particular area due to the amount of clay in the ground. The horse looked old, half dead, and very seriously malnourished and dehydrated, with nearly every bone in her poor body clearly visible. Her coat was mangy and covered with scabs and she had curling, overgrown hooves. He suspected the mare had been recently abandoned by gypsies – there were a lot of them in Dorset- and whilst most of them were not bad people, their lifestyle was very messy. The mare was going to drop a foal soon, inadvisable for an old mare in such poor health. The state of her brought tears to his eyes.

He dashed back to the farm and collected Jason, some oats and a bucket of water. The old mare was too poorly to be moved. They gave her food and water, covered her with an old horse blanket, and left her in the field. In their hearts they wished they could have stabled her, but the mange could have infected Julie, her foal Nutmeg and the other farm animals.

Lime sulphur treatment to her coat and a temporary shelter was the best they could do for her.

Jason went back to work with The Friends' Ambulance and was given a different job, working on an ambulance train, evacuating casualties from dressing stations. He was delighted to hear from his brother that the old mare, now called Mary, had produced a foal, George. They were named for the King and Queen. Julie's little colt was called Nutmeg, because of his colour.

Jock and Hugh

Chapter Seventeen

Alec and Phemie Ross also had sons, Jock and Hugh, who signed up to join the army prior to the official outbreak of war. As Jock wrote the letter below to his parents- Alec and Phemie Ross, throughout Europe the weather was bitterly cold – blizzards had raged across Britain, Ireland, Germany, Russia and France. He and his brother Hugh were with their Territorial battalions at Fort George, a very exposed windy and cold place, built after the Jacobite Rebellion. Both men were part of the 51st Highland Division. Fort George is one of the most awesome fortifications in Europe. It was built following the Jacobite Rebellion and the Battle of Culloden (1746) as a secure base for King George II's army. The citadel took twenty two years to complete, and was a very secure base for the British Army.

January 5 1914
Dear Mother and Father,
I'm sorry to disappoint you both, as you are such keen Quaker pacifists, but this is just to let you know that I have joined up as a private with the Seaforth Highlanders (51st Highland Division) to do my duty should it be required in the event of a war. I'm in Preliminary Training 'Camp' at Fort George. It's actually in permanent buildings, so don't worry too much about me in this cold weather. The army are taking on a lot of men at the moment. I felt that I couldn't do otherwise than join up really, having been in the Officer Cadet Corps for all the years Hugh and I spent at Dollar Academy. I feel that I'm about to fulfil my destiny, to defend my country, should it be necessary, from the German forces of evil. I've decided to serve as a private as I don't fancy bossing people about, and have only actually been here in

uniform for four days, but things are shaping up to be quite good fun, I think. My 'eating irons' went 'absent without leave' yesterday. I quickly realized that my knife, fork and spoon had been stolen by one of my companions in arms, who had lost his own. I was very worried, and approached a splendidly uniformed man, wearing a Sam Browne and everything, and explained my predicament. This was my first encounter with a Regimental Sergeant Major, and it was none too pleasant. He yelled at me as if I was a hundred yards away, 'STAND TO ATTENTION WHEN ADDRESSING AN R.S.M.!'

My first reaction was to temporarily forget what it was that I wanted to ask him. Finally, I recovered my courage and told him pathetically 'My eating irons have gone missing.' He gave me an extremely menacing look, and told me very, very quietly that *nobody steals from their comrades in the army son*, and clearly my eating irons had merely been transferred. 'Sonny', he said, 'make sure that you transfer a set of eating irons from any department you like, but GET THEM, and report to my office at 18.00hrs.' The 'transfer' took place, and when I reported back to his office, I thought I detected a wee smile on his face when he dismissed me.

The temporary uniform I've been given is not very good. I can get my chin inside my tunic collar. The sleeves completely cover my hands, my kilt has to be tied around my waist with string, to keep it up, and is so long, it hangs below my knees, but this is an excellent feature given the current weather conditions. My Glengarry is so small that when I stand smartly to attention, it falls off.

Believe me, things can only get better! I will write again as soon as I can.

With love to your dear selves and Agnes, Morag, Sandy and Douglas.
Hugh
P.S. Could you send me some sketch books and pencils please? I'm running out of supplies.

Hugh's letter was followed almost immediately by one from his older brother Jock.

The Ross family in Poole were unsurprised to read Jock's letter, saying that he had been recruited for officer training with the Seaforths.

What the general public did not know at this time, is that The War Office were already making defence plans for a possible German invasion of the East coast of the UK.

January 10 1915
Dear Mother and Father,
Sorry to give you both *another Pacifist disappointment*, but I've just signed up to be an Officer Cadet with the 51st Highland Division. Hugh and I are both in the 2/4th Division, Seaforth Highlanders. Please believe me, as strong and healthy men, used to taking responsibility, we feel that it is our duty to do our part in protecting the British nation, and all that we stand for. Hopefully a stiffening of our armed forces will cause the Kaiser and the other idiots in Germany to hold the peace we all cherish here.

I'm at the Officer Cadets' Training Camp at the moment, for nine weeks of hard work learning basic drill and army routine. I was 'sworn in' yesterday, immediately given an anti-typhoid injection, followed by three days leave –hence the time to write this letter! Apparently the injection can give a lot of side effects, but I feel fine apart from a slightly aching arm. Some of my companions have been quite groggy.

I've been issued with most of my uniform and requirements, but as an officer will still have to buy some things for myself. For example, the army gave me a toothbrush, but not a belt! Thanks to the three days leave, I've been able to give some time and attention to playing my pipes, which is not something I'll be called upon to do as an officer unfortunately. The weather here is dire at the moment, and the sky looks full of snow.

With love to you all,

Jock

Following his initial training as a full time soldier, and with a Glengarry that actually fitted his head, Hugh was sent down to the town of Bedford. The Scottish Territorial Force was mobilized on 4th August 1914, with the first of *sixty seven troop trains from Scotland* arriving at Bedford on 15 August. Bedford's population of 39,000 rose by more than half that summer as a result of the flood of Scottish soldiers who were preparing to reinforce the struggling British Expeditionary Force.

Pre-war military planning had presumed that any attack on Britain by German forces would come via the Schleswig Holstein area, across the North Sea, so the Seaforths were assigned to Bedford, as part of the 'Central Force.' Well before the war the army had arranged transport and billeting with the railway companies, Bedford Corporation and the local police force. The all-kilted Highland Division flooded into Bedford by train. In just forty-eight hours about 17,000 men arrived and were billeted in schools, empty houses, tents in Bedford Park or in the homes of local folk. Local householders gave every available room they had to the Highlanders. Even people who had never before taken lodgers willingly took the Scotsmen into their homes. They were paid 9d per soldier, or 3 shillings per officer, per day, so many poorer families were delighted. The final total of Highlanders in the town was about twenty thousand.

There had been a happy misunderstanding when Hugh and his friends left the train at Bedford station. A porter asked one of the kilted highlanders from Ross-shire where he had come from. The reply was 'Rooshire', and gossip spread that the strange skirted men were 'Rooshians'! The troops were well received by the local people. Many of the Scots, particularly the Cameron Highlanders, spoke Gaelic as their first language, so with the exotic music of the bagpipes and Scottish songs and frenzied dances which generally involved a fair amount of shouting, the Highlanders were regarded as rather wild and uncouth by the more genteel members of local society.

Hugh wrote to tell his parents that his comrades had come across a few cultural difficulties in the town, and enclosed a newspaper clipping as follows:

'Bedford's modern houses-cum-billets offer creature comforts that many of our soldiers have never experienced before; hot and cold running water and gas to burn. There are many men of most excellent character who have come from Scotland, who have never seen a house like any one of these large Bedford residential

properties and who have certainly never been inside one
before. One young soldier, after a long, hot day on army
training in the countryside was washing his socks in a very
small room that had been described by the letting agent as
a 'Gent's Cloak'.

'What do I do when I want some more water, Jock?'
he shouted to his companion in the hall.

'Pull the chain!'

'Christ!' he exclaimed as he watched the departure
of his socks.'

The clipping also noted:

English Colonel to the Highlander sentry, 'Who are
you?'

Sentry to the Colonel, 'Fine Sir, and hoo's yersel?'

In Bedford during August, 1914, the skirl of bagpipes
was heard morning, noon and night. The Officer Commanding
publicly thanked the local people for the many acts of kindness
bestowed on his men. Tragically the Scotsmen, who had mostly
grown up working on the land in remote areas, were completely
unused to infections such as chickenpox and measles that were
common in the town, and there were so many military deaths
from these infections that a large area of Bedford cemetery was
dedicated to these burials.

Hugh was billeted with the Hartup family, and fell in love
instantly with Dorothy, one of the beautiful daughters of the
house who was much younger than him. They 'walked out
together.' Almost immediately, he asked her to marry him. He
was twenty eight, but she was only just seventeen, and her
parents stipulated that it would be a long engagement. The local

girls were fascinated by the exotic Highlanders. Families stood in their doorways and front gardens and gaped at the highlanders, some playing their pipes while others danced eight-some reels in the street to an accompaniment of 'hoochs' and yells. Off duty Scotsmen were everywhere, wallowing in their barbarian role and solemnly assuring their locals hosts that the kilt was their normal civilian clothing. One extremely middle class woman asked Hugh 'don't you wear longer kilts in winter?' 'No,' he replied cheekily, 'we like to keep our knees on display for the ladies.'

During August Bedford swarmed with men in khaki, and little corner shops were making a fortune by staying open all hours to serve cups of tea. The beautiful areas around the river were teeming with off duty soldiers 'walking out' with local girls. Obviously this caused some trouble between local men and the Scots who had taken their English girlfriends. In the evenings church halls filled with people, both local and Scottish who wanted to dance. Those men and local women who had formed steady relationships 'walked out' together along the now crowded river banks. Members of the local Women's League (organized by the *Headmistresses' Association*! in 1914), were present in quite large numbers around the town, patrolling the parks, public halls, cinemas and the perimeters of military camps to enforce the moral behaviour of courting couples. Verbally, these women were terrifyingly fierce, and sometimes they mistakenly intervened to discourage very minor displays of affection between man and wife.

During the winter of 1914–15, it was clear that the first line Territorial battalions, a resource already fully prepared, would be needed almost immediately to bolster the British Expeditionary Force which was struggling to hold back the huge, well prepared German army on the other side of the

English Channel. Bedford's prime central location and good transport links had been carefully chosen as large numbers of men could be efficiently taken by trains to ports on the south east coast, prior to being shipped to France.

Hugh only had two days' notice of his departure. Numerous Scotsmen married their sweethearts before leaving for the war. Registry Offices stayed open for many extra hours. It was a bitter sweet time. Dorothy, her sisters and parents were increasingly tearful.

In early November, with his comrades from the 2/4th Seaforth Highlanders Hugh disembarked at Le Havre. After some further battle training in France, on the 12th December the Seaforths joined the Dehra Dun Brigade in 7th (Meerut) Division on the Western Front as part of the British Expeditionary Force.

Hugh had kept a horrifying secret from Dorothy and his family. He would be an unarmed soldier, and in battle, as a gifted piper, would march out bravely in front of his company, playing his pipes loudly. He would literally be leading his comrades *tactically into the battle*. The sheer cold blooded courage of the piper in front, playing his bloodcurdling tunes was believed by the army to have two effects. The highland troops (and the pipers in particular) were regarded by the enemy as being *terrifyingly wild*, and *exceptionally brave*. Hugh and the other pipers quietly and appropriately expected their dead and wounded rate to be extremely high, *and it was*. In their ignorance, his parents, brother Jock and Dorothy assumed that Hugh was just a Highland foot soldier.

Hugh

Chapter Seventeen

On the 7 November 1914, Hugh and his fellow soldiers landed at Le Havre. He was able to send his first postcard to Dorothy.

'The French people don't understand English, so we Scots have no chance! However, they are very pleased to see us, and we've had gifts of wine and chocolate. I am to be paid an extra penny a day as the regimental piper. Miss you! Hugh xx'

The British Army was *desperate* for re-enforcements. The British Expeditionary Force had suffered 1,600 casualties, killed, wounded and made prisoner at the Battle of Mons. The Germans had 5,000 casualties. They were fortunate to miss out on the training (torture) camp at Etaples. Hugh and his fellow soldiers had to travel a fair distance overland to re-inforce the British front lines. French trains and military buses (taken from London streets and shipped over) took the men most of the way, then it was down to marching, marching, marching. The men sang a lot, as it seemed to help. Their favorite songs were mainly Scottish:

No Awa tae bide Awa
As we were merchin doon the street,
Everyone was cheerin sayin, 'goodbye lads, come home safe,
Thanks for volunteerin'.
We're no awa tae bide awa, we're no awa tae leave ye,

We're no awa tae bide awa, we'll soon come back and see ye.
Hame for Christmas, that's oor plan, big plum puddins eatin.
We'll be back wi medals in oor packs,
We'll leave the Gerries greetin.

Kaiser Bill is feelin ill, Lookin peelie-wallie
Wanderin aboot Berlin, greetin fur his mammy.
Kaiser Bill is feertie cause the Terriers will beat him.
He will run when he hears our guns, we will defeat him!

The Lord is my ShepherdThe

The Lord is my Shepherd in nocht am I wantin'
In the haugh's green girse does He mak me lie doon
While mony puir strangers' are bleatin' and pantin'
By saft-flowin' burnies He leads me at noon.
When aince I had strayed far awa in the bracken,
And daidled till gloamin' cam ower a' the hills,
Nae dribble o' water my sair drooth to slacken,
And dark grow'd the nicht wi' its haars and its chills.
Awa frae the fauld, strayin' fit-sair and weary,
I thocht I had naethin' tae dae but tae dee.
He socht me and fand me in mountain hechts dreary,
He gangs by fell paths which He kens best for me.
And noo, for His name's sake, I'm dune wi' a' fearin'
Though cloods may aft gaither and soughin' win's blaw.
"Hoo this?" or "Hoo that?" -- oh, prevent me frae spearin'
His will is aye best, and I daurna say "Na".
The valley o' death winna fleg me to thread it,
Though awfu the darkness, I weel can foresee.
Wi' His rod and His staff He wull help me to tread it,
Then wull its shadows, sae gruesome, a' flee.
Forfochen in presence o' foes that surround me,
My Shepherd a table wi' denties has spread.
The Thyme and the Myrtle blaw fragrant aroond me,
He brims a fu' cup and poors oil on my head.
Surely guidness an' mercy, despite a' my roamin'
Wull gang wi' me doon tae the brink o' the river.
Ayont it nae mair o' the eerie an' gloamin'
I wull bide in the Hame o' my Faither forever.

The men in the company were exhausted when they arrived, but base camp and daily training was better than the constant marching with heavy packs. They were so grateful to get baths and clean clothes at the divisional HQ. Their blistered feet healed up, their boots felt more comfortable, and they were drilled and instructed ready for the 'Front Line.' They were dreading it.

They went to 'Concert Parties'– composed of a few professional men who had enlisted to fight, and willing amateurs who"blacked up" and sang and played as 'Black and White Minstrels'. One evening the well-known professional concert party, the Co-Optimists and their pianist arrived. The pianist was nicknamed 'Paderewski', after the famous concert pianist-cum-politician. They gave two stupendous outdoor concerts in their ordinary and very mud-stained clothes. They explained to the audience that their kit and properties had been lost and fallen into the hands of the Boche at Esmery Hallon. The concert was a great success both with the British men and also with the French troops who poured into the village. Following this, the Seaforths went to the Divisional baths, then for a '*short arm inspection*' by the Medical Officer, to check for VD. This humiliating check was done frequently, never in private.

Finally, they were told they would be going into battle soon. In the morning they were issued with pencils and postcards, and told to write short notes home in case they did not survive. These would be posted in the event of a soldier's death.

Services were held for catholics and protestants. The Scottish Padre led a very positive service, and gave a short address on the presence of God, particularly at times of doubt and fear. The Bible reading from Exodus 19 was very short, a message delivered by God to Moses, and was completely memorable:

'Ye have seen what I did unto the Egyptians, and how I bore you on eagles' wings, and brought you unto myself. Now therefore, if ye will obey my voice indeed, and keep my covenant, then ye shall be a peculiar treasure unto me above all people: for all the earth is mine.'

At dusk the 227 men of the company who were to relieve their comrades were assembled to march to the front. Morale was generally good, but a few of the men were very panicky and weepy. Hugh, as one of the more mature men, found it better not to engage too closely with the others. Obviously he was frightened, but managed to keep his feelings well under control. They started on French roads. Then they had to be guided by Captain Morrison, walking through narrow and confusing trench systems as darkness fell. It was very cold and mostly silent except for the careful sounds of their feet. The moon shone capriciously, as clouds moved across her face. The pathways that the sappers had excavated were all named. The Seaforths were in the Scottish sector, and the main communication trenches were called 'Avenues', and so they turned into Restalrig Avenue (*Avenues were main trenches – less important trenches were 'Lanes' or 'Alleys' or for Scottish soldiers, 'Walk'*). The men said they were more like rabbit warrens. They were halted by the sandbagged sentry post at the turning into Leith Walk. The moon disappeared and rain enhanced their misery and cold. The officer allowed a brief stop, and they lit their saturated cigarettes. On again. They ducked down as the vivid light of a bursting shell lit the sky above them. They crossed Central Avenue and there were more sodden and much darker ways to come as they entered into Incandescent Trench via Inane Alley. It was all extremely confusing, as the trench maps weren't very clear and the only light was from a match. Captain Morrison who was leading got them lost twice. Then they were there…! Through the darkness, one after the other, they moved into the narrow trench to relieve the exhausted, tired, cold men who had spent a week there. They learned something vital from their Sergeant: 'Keep yur heid doon!' The enemy had experienced sharpshooters, and no 'tin hats' had yet been issued.

Letter from Hugh to his parents;

Dear Father and Mother,
We were wakened at 2.00am and did 96 hours straight off. Yesterday the Germans were wasting their shells on British aeroplanes and it was almost as good as the Bournemouth Regatta – the fireworks and the bangs. They could simply not hit things although shells were bursting all around. I met Lieutenant Whitlock…a St Peter's School old boy. We had a good chat and a smoke. It was just like being at his house again, only there was such a din and smoke going on. I have got used to it now. The worst part of Germans is their snipers. They are always picking off our soldiers – they don't mind who it is.
We had a good night last night. Our observers were picking up the wounded out of the field and trenches and a chap just flashed a light on as I was waiting for my officer (guarding his car). As soon as the light went on, down came the bullets. I got in a ditch and stayed there. I thought of the Ragtime song 'Get out and get under'! The firing lasted about an hour and I was getting uncomfortable as I'd been in about a foot of water and was glad to get out of it. We have captured a lot of German prisoners, and how glad they seem to be out of it. We had new mufflers given to each of us today. Much appreciated as it is so cold being outside in the wet, day and night.
Best wishes,
Hugh

The first battle for Hugh and his mates came in two days—the Defence of Givenchy. The French, hoping to push the Germans back north had asked the British to launch an offensive. This followed British attacks south of Ypres which had all been resisted with heavy British losses. The usual tactic was a brief bombardment (they were very short of shells). These were mostly shrapnel shells which made no impression on German fortified positions. This usually followed by an unsuccessful infantry attack, making little damage to the enemy's barbed wire, trenches and machine gun nests. The British were rationed to forty rounds to each gun. General French planned six small attacks with most of the fighting to be done by the exhausted Indian Corps who had already suffered heavy losses in the defence of Ypres and other attacks along the Belgian frontier. In the terrible winter the underprivileged Indians were suffering the sodden trenches of Flanders, from poor and irregular food and little warm clothing. They were delighted when in early December 1914 the 2/4th Seaforths joined their Dehra Dun Brigade in the 7th (Meerut) Division on the Western Front. The whole division was issued with 'stinkers'- smelly goatskin waistcoats, so the Indians were delighted.

Pusser's navy rum was introduced for men in the trenches that first winter of the war to help them deal with the cold and wet. It was 95 degrees proof, was watered down by the quartermaster and issued twice a day at the front - dawn and dusk, and made the men cough, and their eyes watered. The men were given an additional dose before 'going over the top' (of the trench) into battle. The officers said that the drink brought the men *a glow of light and warmth in their dire surroundings'.*

At home, the newspapers commented: *'The finest thing that ever happened in the trenches was the rum ration. Those who have not spent a night standing or sitting or lying in mud with an east wind blowing and the temperature below freezing will know how helpful it is.'*

Hugh and his mates went to their first battle on the 19th December 1914 at 3.10am, climbing the ladder out of their water-logged trench and going 'over the top' of their trench in heavy sleet to launch a surprise attack. Hugh had been well behind the lines most of the day, nervously tuning his pipes. His bowels were unpredictable, and he vomited once. Fortunately either none of his comrades noticed, or they were discreetly in similar straits. He felt better sitting in the trench, following the rum ration. Waiting for the whistle, he nursed his pipes under a greatcoat, to keep them warm. The sergeant nodded at him, Hugh divested himself from the greatcoat, gently and quietly filled the GHB (Great Highland Bagpipe) with more warm air, a whistle was blown, and Hugh was the first over the top. He took a gargantuan breath and started playing Hielan' Laddie, followed by Cock O'the North. The great music filled the night with reassurance for his fellows and terror for the Germans. He was very, very scared, but just knew that he had to do it. He was keen to give the younger men who were even more frightened than he was, a good lead. The tempo of the music rose. He prayed that he wouldn't get shot down quickly. He was carrying such a huge responsibility to his comrades. The men were terrified, moving into enemy fire. They were relying on him. Notwithstanding the carnage of exploding shells and soldiers crashing down behind him, he played on, and on and on through the German machine gun fire. The men followed him - hearing the pipes gave his comrades courage, but many were cut down by the machine gun fire. The Germans were shocked that anyone would be brave enough to play the pipes in the middle of such a desperate battle. As the regimental piper, Hugh did all this for one extra penny a day. Givenchy was duly defended, at a price.

Hugh

Chapter Eighteen

Hugh and his comrades remained in the Ypres and French Flanders area during the month of December 1914. The war proceeded in this sector on a 'live and let live' basis. Hugh, as a mature, sensible and highly respected soldier felt almost like a nursemaid to his young and frightened companions. *'Get yur heid doon!'* was oft repeated, as there were very good snipers on both sides and new young idiots, who had been warned, sometimes stood on the firestep to look over the trench parapet and got their heads shot off.

They enjoyed singing songs on quiet days to ease the boredom. A particular favourite was:

Keep your head down
Keep your head down Fritzy Boy
Last night in the pale moonlight,
We saw you – we saw you!
Keep your head down Fritzy Boy!

You were mending your broken wire
And we opened rapid fire.
If you want to see your mutter
And your vaterland
Keep your head down Fritzy Boy!

Hold your hands up Fritzy Boy!
Hold your hands up Fritzy Boy!
Just tonight in the pale moonlight
We saw you – we saw you!

Keep your head down Fusilier!
We were laying some more wire
And we nearly opened fire
Keep your head down fusilier!

There were vicious but more subtle enemies within the trench itself – the lice. They were pale fawn little bastards, about the size of grains of rice that swelled when fed. They smelled sour and stale and hid in the seams of clothing, particularly in the mens' vests and kilt pleats. They fed off the men, leaving blotchy red bite marks. They seemed untouchable in their deep woolly trenches- the pleats of the men's kilts, but they didn't like heat! When Angus took off his kilt in desperation and attacked the lice with a lighted candle, it was very nearly a disaster. Initially the heat made them pop and bang like crackers, but then the kilt started smoldering, and he was fortunate to save it. Angus soon found heating a knife in a candle flame and applying it to pleats and seams of his clothing was far safer! The lice won every time. The men would be relieved, go back behind the lines for a clean-up and rest. When they came back, clean all over and in uniforms which had been boil-washed, the lice were waiting for them in the straw the men used to keep their feet warm. They tried to make light of the problem: 'I'll give you a big one for two little ones.'

The rats were a plague too. There were so many unburied bodies on the ground and in craters in 'no man's land' that the rats never went hungry. They got into the trenches as well, great vicious things, as big as cats some of them. You couldn't leave food lying around unless it was in a tin. There was some respite for the men. When the trenches were 'relieved' by fresh troops, there were hot baths and clean uniforms at base. They could get proper sleep, write letters home, go for walks in the fresh air and attend a service with the padre. Just before Christmas 1914, Hugh and his companions went back 'up the line.' 'Same old, same old stinking place' Hugh said to his pal Andrew MacPherson. At the beginning of the war, everyone thought they would be home by Christmas. Both sides were heartily sick of war. Day after day, it was very boring unless there was a 'big push' on, then boredom turned to subdued terror.

Things could get really awful. In the early days, *raw meat* was occasionally sent up to the trenches. They had no means of cooking it. Generally their rations consisted of tins of meat, usually 'Bully (corned) Beef' and vegetables, which the lads heated for themselves over a 'Tommy Cooker', a tin of tallow with a wick in it. They also had 'Maconochie's' food, sliced carrot and turnip in a thin soup, which they warmed up in the tin. Their rations were uniformly terrible. There were occasional HP biscuits. They liked them, but they weren't filling. There were however, some amusing moments. There was a rather 'green' soldier in Hugh's group. At home he was a very keen naturalist and had brought his own binoculars *to observe French birds and other wildlife*! He got extremely upset seeing a pigeon killed by shellfire.

The weather was very wet and cold. Stale despair hung in the very drips of water from the men's waterproofs. Some enthusiasm was generated when a machine gun was delivered to the group. Corporal Brown had been trained to use it, and together with six men got it up and running with military precision.

1) Make a sandbag embankment and site the machine gun.

2) Secure the gun in the ground.

3) Obtain a supply of ammunition and load and secure the belt in the gun.

The next time a German moved in the opposing trench, the gun was used, but missed. Corporal Brown suggested this was because the gun barrel was very cold. A couple of days later, Corporal Brown and one of his mates carried the gun along the zig zag trench, put it on a sandbag and fired at a group of Germans whose heads were visible. The gun was quickly moved back to its original firing position. It became a habit to move the gun about, so that the Germans thought the British had more guns than they did.

Hugh quietly appointed himself to a special task as he had very little to do except relieve the misery of his comrades. A fungal infection that later became known as 'Trench Foot' was rife amongst soldiers who often spent days standing in wet socks and boots with mud and water up to their knees. It started with swollen, numb feet, which rapidly went blue or red. Gangrene set in quickly. Below knee amputation was the only treatment. In good weather and bad, Hugh inspected the feet of his pals, and reported to his hierarchy if a man needed to be moved back for treatment. Eventually the British army found a possible preventive treatment -whale oil. He took it upon himself to make sure that the soldiers around him learned how to thoroughly grease each others' feet every day. The introduction of 'duckboards' helped the lads a bit, but even so, in the wet weather, the trenches were still filled with water. He urged his pals to keep writing home to their mothers, girlfriends, aunties and daughters to ask for more socks, explaining how important it was that every man took his boots off regularly and got his feet properly dry and into a dry pair of socks.

In the quiet front-line sectors of the Western Front a bit of fraternization between the opposing forces developed. In some areas, it showed itself simply as inactivity, with both sides avoiding open hostility. There were often shouted conversations if the gap between trenches was narrow and if the men knew a bit of each other's language. Where Hugh was located, there were even occasional dusk visits from enemy trenches one to another. It came about as both sides' rations were brought up to the front line after dusk, and soldiers on both sides observed a time of peace while they collected and ate their food. Single British and German soldiers sometimes visited each other's trenches to exchange newspapers! This behavior in moderation, was not always challenged by officers.

The men of both sides were heartily sick of fighting. It was three days before Christmas. Private Donald Campbell shouted across no-man's land 'Hey, Fritzy boy!' to the German sergeant who occasionally visited them at night, 'can you help us get rid of some of these bodies?'

Donald wasn't really expecting an answer, but a voice called back 'Yes, Tommy boy. Bring your shovel!'

Donald climbed up the ladder, out of the trench. Several unarmed Germans appeared out of their trench. Then a few Scotsmen emerged. There were smiles, handshakes. As large numbers of soldiers from both sides were present, their officers were nervous about objecting. The Germans and British both set about burying the dead who had been lying in the open for ages. In spite of the freezing cold weather, it was a horrible task, as rats and other wildlife had taken their share of the bodies already seriously damaged in conflict. The British were issued an extra dose of rum to help them in the gruesome task. It took two days. When the work was done, the two sides played football on 'No Man's Land.'

Christmas Eve was cheerless, as the weather suddenly became desperately cold, freezing the ground and the mud in the trenches in which the men were living. Nonetheless, both sides decorated their trenches. The Germans put little candle lamps raised on poles or bayonets at the parapet of their trench which made them clearly visible and vulnerable to getting shot. The British held their fire and heard them sing:

Stille Nacht (Silent Night)
Stille Nacht! Heilige Nacht!
Alles schläft; etnas wacht,
nur das traute heilige Paar.

Holder Knab' im lockigem Haar,
Schlaf in himmlischer Ruh,
Schlaf in himmlischer Ruh!
Stille Nacht! Heilige Nacht!
Gottes Sohn, o wie lacht
Lieb' aus deinem göttlichem Mund,
Da schlägt uns die rettende Stund.
Jesus in deiner Geburt!
Jesus in deiner Geburt!

The Germans were singing Christmas greetings to their enemies. Men on both sides cried when they heard the carol. They pined for home and family and were in dire circumstances. When war started, both sides believed that they would be home to celebrate Christmas. But the men didn't get home for Christmas. Many of them would never return. Just for that moment, peace had broken out. Temporarily. Men of both sides shared Christmas festivities, exchanging their chocolate bars, buttons, badges, and small tins of bully beef and showing each other family photos. On Christmas Day the British and Germans played impromptu football. Captain McGregor and Hauptsturmfuhrer Maier exchanged gifts and reached a mutual agreement to return to formal hostilities in the morning. At 8.30 am on the 26th of December, Captain McGregor fired three pistol shots into the air and stepped onto the British trench bank. Hauptsturmfuhrer Maier stepped up on to the German trench bank. They bowed to each other, and saluted. The Hauptsturmfuhrer disappeared into his trench and fired two shots. The truce was over. This was just one of several temporary truces along the lines. The Generals on both sides issued orders prohibiting fraternization with the enemy, and the war became increasingly bitter.

Weeks and weeks more were endured, and the filth in the trenches got worse. The smell of death was everywhere. You could sense it in the cold moist air, and in the darkness it sometimes embraced an exhausted man. Men detailed to 'look-out' at night spent two hours on the 'fire-step' then had one hour off. The shell bombardments on both sides destroyed the countryside. Vast, featureless quagmires were created. Nothing grew in the soil devastated by the stinking decomposing corpses of the mens' comrades and the immense mud filled shell holes of death. Trees were reduced to blackened ghosts. The most common 'wild life' were the rats, who grew ever fatter and the lice, who as well as causing the men to resort to frantic scratching, also carried Trench Fever. The lice and rats kindly passed it on, biting one man, then another and another. The first symptoms were shooting pains in the shins and a very high fever.

Sergeant Munro was chatting to the men in the trench. He admitted that he'd had no lice on his body so far but was always feared of them. Alasdair, one of the soldiers jokingly said he'd swap one of his big lice for two little 'uns. The Sergeant began to boast that he had a gallon of Lysol in his hut, and regularly sprayed it over his bunk and inside his hut. He'd had some mercury ointment sent to him to further deter lice, and applied it to his leather identity disc and its string. He said it made his neck dirty.

Hugh and the other private soldiers sighed and exchanged glances. Their faces were grey and worn with fatigue, dirty and unshaven for lack of water. Some looked terribly ill. They slept in the trench *with* the lice and rats for a week at a time. They were overdue for relief. The work was exhausting. The machine gunner suddenly started firing at a German working party. About 100 rounds were fired, and then the men hurried to move the gun back to another position.

The officer, Captain Brophy, (the replacement for Captain McGregor, who had been killed,) lived moderately safely in a sandbagged dugout annexe adjoining the trenches and drank a lot of expensive tea. He came round to tell the men that they would be relieved that evening. No-one could raise any joy. They were completely demoralized by the trenches, mud, cold, appalling food and illness. It was like living in a disgusting freezing cold, stinking, wet, ant-heap.

However, on return to basecamp, Hugh was delighted to hear that he had been granted seven days leave. He planned to spend it with his parents at The Albatross Pharmacy, and wrote to invite Dorothy so that they could get married at the local Registry Office. Her parents were invited to stay at the Albatross Pharmacy as well. It took him two and a half gruelling days of constant travelling to get home, and the same to return. On arrival, he just needed to get to sleep and clean himself up. Dorothy pestered him continually asking what war was like and what he had been doing. He was absolutely exhausted and said almost nothing; she got very irritable. Getting married meant joining a large queue with other servicemen at the Registry. He and Dorothy were so stressed that the wedding night duties were completed, but nothing special. Dorothy would be entitled to part of Hugh's army pay, and Hugh felt strangely glad to be going back to the Front.

Before Hugh departed back to the Front, Phemie had a confidential chat with her son. 'I'm quite worried about your brother Jock', she said. He sends letters frequently asking us to send him some very strange pharmacy items.'
Hugh's first thought was hmmm... *French Letters.* So many stupid men were catching venereal disease when they had local leave. Perhaps Jock was wisely protecting himself and others...? However, this was not the case. Phemie came straight to the point. 'He's been asking for face powder and rouge. He wants a lot of male cologne, and has asked for an enema pump apparatus. I've sent him everything he's asked for.'

Jock and Hugh

Chapter Nineteen

Prior to the commencement of hostilities, Jock volunteered as a potential officer together with a surge of other highly principled, well educated 'best types' of young scots men. In Poole, his parents, Phemie and Alec Ross had been delighted at his first appointment as a schoolteacher, became concerned when he and Hugh joined the Lovat Scouts Territorial Force, and were proud and distraught by turn when their two eldest sons joined the regular British Army Seaforth Highlanders as part of the British Expeditionary Force.

Jock spent nine weeks training at Fort George, alongside the other Seaforth volunteers. They were a mixed bag of well-educated upper class and middle classes. The trainee private soldiers went to France. By the time he entered the School of Instruction for the more intense training to become an officer his brother Hugh was already about to serve on 'The Front Line'. Jock was issued with what was described as 'full kit', but still had to buy some essentials such as a toothbrush in the nearest town. The course was harsh and intensive, over a period of twelve weeks, and men deemed unsuitable were sent back to the ranks. He did well in his exams, and the 'chosen ones' - the new officer cadets, were sent to another camp to learn more, where as well as further useful practical knowledge, it was instilled into each officer that *he should both lead and serve his men.*

Jock and some of his friends, who were not 'traditional middle class' but whose families were in 'trade' had to write to their parents asking for money so that they could purchase expensive necessities such as their new uniforms, jackets, kilts, hats and pistols. Jock was sent to Shorncliffe in Kent, to join the 'kiltie soldiers' of his company, and thence to Etaples, the major military staging post for the western front. It had already gained a tarnished reputation for its routine of rigorous military training and iron discipline.

Jock loved his regimental kilt, and was proud to be a soldier. However, he wrote from Etaples to his parents in Poole:

'I love my regiment, the camaraderie, marching with the pipes, tartan kilts and glengarries. This place is beyond vile. The officers and particularly the N.C.O.'s with their canary yellow stripes and their "blood on the bayonet" approach are wicked tyrants. Daily they lead us as lambs to the slaughter, to the sand flats, which they call 'The Bull Ring', and take sadistic pleasure in making us do everything 'at the double' for hours on end, beating us with sticks, yelling insults at us, without fear or favour. We are billeted in tents, fed poorly – I take great exception to this, as I'm taking my men to the Front, and they need to be properly fed so that they can at least start out feeling well. The 'Bull Ring' is like living in hell for two weeks.

Our trainers, NCOs known as 'canaries' because of their yellow sergeants stripes, are here to 'inculcate' us, violently impressing fighting upon us. We have to bayonet charge sandbags, supposed to represent German soldiers until we reach the point of exhaustion, as bayoneting is said to create 'blood-spirit'. One of my men said 'We had murder in our hearts against the bloody canaries who were yelling at us as we bayoneted their bloody sacks today', and went on that 'we felt furious when we were sworn at, chased, hit and prodded, downhill, uphill, running, stumbling, while still the bloody canaries yelled insults at us and hit us.' Some of our men believed that it was all being done to make us glad to escape to better conditions at the front. Getting to and from the Bull Ring, and the training period takes up the whole day. Our living conditions are poor. In the mens' mess two slices of bully beef, two biscuits and an onion is the main meal of the day. They, and I, feel utterly demoralized.

We know what is expected of us in battle, but the unnecessary violence, darkness and utter loathsomeness of this dirty, stinking place is beyond belief. Our custodians treat us like caged wild beasts. The expressions on the faces of our soldier volunteers have changed, their faces look empty and dead. I cannot help them. I am treated just as badly.'

Jock's letter never arrived in Poole. Presumably it was censored. Eventually he was promoted, and was now a fully-fledged Lieutenant with battle experience. He and Hugh arranged to meet up at a Y.M.C.A. motor kitchen behind the British lines in late June 1916, just before the Battle of the Somme. It had been over a year since they had seen each other. Jock embraced his brother. 'Not made corporal yet then?' he said teasingly.

'Far too busy with the pipes the noo' answered Hugh, whose Scottish accent had coarsened over the time he had spent in the trenches. 'I've nae mair ambition than helping ma officer and soldier brothers tae move forward bravely. The sound of the pipes aye makes a big difference when we're attacking. Of course, we all feel frichtened, but the thing tae dae is tae rise above it, and the music seems tae really help. Hoo are things wi ye, *Lieutenant* Jock Ross?'

'Well, much the same as you, Hugh. Like you, I also lead my men into battle and our men bravely follow. Not like the Jerries. Their officers make their soldats (privates) go over the top of the trench first. Their officer is *behind them*, and will shoot anyone who tries to turn back.'

'Yeh, awfy no nice as the Weegie soldiers say. Anyway, you got a girlfriend? Maw says you're aye askin for cologne and perfumed soap and stuff. Are ye chasin' the wimmen? I heard you got the enema pump as well. Maw's awfy worried about your constipation. She thought sending Carters Little Liver Pills might be cheaper and easier.'

Jock went very red and replied slowly. 'As for the perfumed soap, it's to try to wash off the trench stink from my body. Similarly with the cologne, I'm trying to cover the stink by applying it to the front of my uniform. You ever get the shits before you go over the top Hugh? I'm sure you do. We see many of our men lose control of their bowels in the conflict. It's a demonstration of utter terror. I'm their officer. *I have to pretend to be brave all the time,* even though I'm not. The men look up to me. Before we're due to go over the top, I go to my dugout and cleanse my bowels thoroughly with the enema pump. Then I stand in the trench and calmly have a shave with my cut-throat razor. One man holds my mirror, and the other soldiers watch me, as I keep my hand completely steady. Then I nip off and apply some powder and rouge to my face to hide my cowardly grey, fearful complexion to give them further confidence. Then I wait at the bottom of the ladder with my watch in my hand, trying to look calm and casual, blow the whistle at the appointed time, and go over the top first.'

Both men had tears in their eyes. Hugh knew for the first time, the lonely vulnerability he and his brother were sharing, always having to go over the top first. It deepened their love for each other. They embraced and wished each other well, and hoped for a future meeting, God willing.

At the Somme, the battle commenced on the first of July, 1916. The guns were heard in Poole and in many other coastal areas as the Allies bombarded the German trenches for seven days and then sent 100,000 men over the top to attack the German lines. It was a disaster for the British as the Germans had endured the British artillery fire in deep trenches and emerged largely unscathed. On the First of July, as the confident British advanced, they were mown down by German machine guns and rifle fire. 19,240 British soldiers lost their lives. It was the bloodiest day in the history of the British army.

At dawn on the 14 July, despite morale being at rock bottom, the Seaforth Highlanders successfully attacked Bazentine Ridge, a subsidary part of the Battle of the Somme which lasted four days. However they were unable to capture Logueval and parts of Delville Wood. The British cavalry eventually attacked east of the wood and overran German infantry hiding in standing crops, inflicting about 100 casualties for a loss of eight troopers. The strength of this British-French offensive on the Somme which followed the earlier failure of the British attack on the first of July surprised the Germans, who suffered many casualties and lost a lot of their artillery. Hugh, armed with his bagpipes and the traditional sgian-dubh, or "black knife" in his sock, led a suicidal charge into machine-gun fire to reach the enemy trenches. He just played anything that came into his head, as loudly as he could. Hearing the pipes encouraged the men. The ground was very uneven, and he was worried about tripping. His own men were falling all around him under the deadly enemy guns. His bagpipes were shot to pieces and so was his left leg. He fell to the ground in a faint. Darkness fell over the battlefield, and he drifted in and out of consciousness. He had lost a lot of blood.

Overhead, during the heat of the battle, British aircraft fought bravely, destroying many German aircraft, gaining mastery of the skies. Deprived of the support of their own aircraft, the German troops were more vulnerable, dependent solely on artillery-fire. The German guns were exposed to the British planes as their navigators could see the German muzzle-flashes below, giving away their positions. On landing, they reported back to the artillery officers.

On the first day of the Battle of the Somme an estimated 60,000 men of the British Army died. It was mass slaughter. When the firing began to cease, the bugles of each company played the mournful last post, a tribute to those who were dead, defining the end of the day's battle, and providing a directional call for those men who had lost their bearings on the battlefield, and were trying to get back to their companies.

For Hugh and Jock, the Somme was the end of their war. During the initial advance Jock was shot in the right leg, but though in extreme pain he somehow continued to lead his men and captured an enemy trench. He assembled soldiers from another company who had lost their officer, and together they encountered a German machine gun attack. He was wounded again, in his left arm, but continued to control the situation. With just ten men standing, he ordered them to advance to the German Machine gun nest whilst he provided covering fire with his pistol. He was killed, but the machine gun emplacement was destroyed by his men with a Mills bomb. The average life expectancy for a young infantry subaltern at the Front was generally only a few months.

Hugh

Chapter Twenty

Hugh had a serious leg wound and was lucky to survive. He lay on the ground in 'no man's land' for many hours. During the night stretcher bearers from both sides were doing something that would be impossible to attempt in daylight. They were working stealthily, trying to sort out the living from the dead. The smell of blood and death was all around. There was no further enemy aggression. Both sides were exhausted, and both sides had many wounded to be recovered. A stretcher bearer team tripped over Hugh, who had lost a lot of blood and was lying as if he was dead, and he groaned. He was so very fortunate to be one of the ones to be found. Emergency field dressings were applied, and as he was strapped to the stretcher, he managed to say 'I need to see the Butch' (doctor). He thought that he would definitely lose his leg. They slipped a morphine tablet under his tongue. There were six bearers, and they worked as a team, taking turns to carry the heavy wooden stretcher, and managing a group of 'walking wounded' to whom they had applied bandages and slings. There had been careful planning for this almighty 'Push' against the enemy. Close to 'the front' there were emergency 'Dressing Stations' where the walking wounded, who might be able to return to the conflict were patched up and rested. The medic at the dressing station gave Hugh a morphine injection, and stemmed the bleeding.

He was put in a motor ambulance and carried further back to the emergency tented 'Casualty Clearing Station', which was quite literally rows and rows of white tents in the middle of nowhere for casualties to be 'triaged' so that the urgency of their wounds and illnesses could be assessed. Shelling continued around them. The nurses stripped off the shreds of his uniform clothing, and washed him all over, quickly and expertly. An Australian Medical Officer examined him. He was fighting to save all the lives he could. Hugh was facing two possibilities: immediate amputation to prevent sepsis or fast removal to a base hospital for intensive irrigation of his leg wound, in hope of saving both his life and his limb. He was put into a hospital gown and someone covered his stretcher with a brown blanket. He wasn't aware of a nurse inserting a tube into his bum and pouring in a magic mixture of warm saline, brandy and coffee into his bowel. Close to the 'Clearing Station,' railway tracks had been laid for hospital trains. His stretcher was placed amongst lines of others, and he was fortunate that there was a place for him. Hugh's wound was 'a Blighty one'. He would need intensive treatment in a base hospital to stabilize his wound. Once he was taken back to Britain, further lengthy hospital treatment would be required to promote healing. He would be unlikely to be fit for any further war service.

He was vaguely aware of being loaded into a waiting train in pouring rain as part of a 'push load' of 246 patients and he lay on a wall mounted train stretcher, the middle man in a tier of three. The train rocked as shells fell nearby. There was a halt somewhere to take on a second 'push load' of patients. A little later, the train partially de-railed, couplings snapped and the patients feared that the train had been hit. The sisters went from one patient to another, trying to calm them down. Everyone on the affected carriage had to be unloaded and their stretchers were laid on the track side. The orderlies unloaded everything from the carriage that was not a fixture, and to the encouragement and cheers of the nurses, managed to get the two affected carriage wheels back on line and temporarily fix the coupling.

One of the orderlies, Ossian, a really kind 'Conscientious Objector' sustained a serious injury to his right hand in the process. The nurses were very concerned when he said 'I'm a time served print setter in Civvy Street. I don't know how I'll manage now. As a non-combatant, I wouldn't have minded getting killed to save others, but losing the use of my right hand won't help me to make a living back home.'

The journey continued, without further stops or mishaps. It wasn't too bad. The train was well stocked with food. Hot drinks were distributed regularly. The nurses were very kind. One of Hugh's first memories during this painful journey was being given, along with his comrades, a clean white handkerchief. When you have lived in filth for weeks, such a gift seems like real luxury. The nurses regularly gave out sweets as well, which their kind friends had sent from home.

At about 6am, on the 19th July 1916, Hugh was stretchered into a temporary hospital. Most of the patients who had been in the hospital had been evacuated by train on the afternoon of the previous day. The nurses had been up at five, getting the hospital ready to take further 'push loads' from the Somme. He was thoroughly washed all over again, to ensure that no battlefield filth remained, and his wounds could now be properly cleaned and dressed with less risk of further infections. Nurse McGrath chatted away to Hugh. When he was washed clean to her satisfaction, she prepared a Carrell Dakin irrigation which involved careful mixing of two solutions. Doctor Campbell commenced the new treatment which involved putting a number of little tubes into Hugh's wound. These tubes were then connected to the irrigation solution, which slowly 'dripped' into his leg, disinfecting it, in the hope of saving both his life and his leg. At the same time, other doctors and nurses were heavily involved in the makeshift operating theatre, where many of the lads were having limbs removed and abdominal operations.

By 6pm on the same evening, most of the patients, including Hugh, were being loaded on to Number 16 Ambulance Train, bound for the Base Hospital at Boulogne. Train travel was extremely arduous and one of the orderlies told him 'this train is carrying 480 sick and wounded, most of them on stretchers'. Hugh felt very sorry for the few slightly injured men at the end of the carriage, who were 'sitters', and would continue to be sitters, day and night, until the train was blasted off the line by an enemy shell, or they reached their coastal destination. The men were on the train for three days. They were initially delayed eighteen hours, very close to enemy shell fire. Some of the very sick men were terrified, thinking they were back on the battlefield. Later on, the train got going again, but there was a further delay of six hours, due to lack of water for the engine –the station had been shelled. The final delays were as a result of having to be sidelined to allow troop and munitions to pass them on their way up to the front. The nurses kept cheerful throughout, supplying plenty of tea, cigarettes and snacks. The men had no doubt at all that the poor dear nurses must have been absolutely exhausted by the time the train finally reached Boulogne. Hugh asked Sister MacMaudie 'how do you ladies manage to keep going day and night?

'Well,' she replied, 'there are three tiny cabins on this train where we can take it in turns to have a lie down. Secondly, don't forget, we're army nurses. Most of us cut our teeth in the Boer Wars, dear'.

The train was unloaded, and patients taken to the General Hospital in Boulogne. During his first night, Hugh was chatting to one of the Queen Alexandra nurses who was irrigating his leg.

'What has happened to the lovely nurses who looked after us so devotedly on the train?' he asked.

'Simple', she replied. 'The orderlies have made up stretcher beds with brown blankets and pillows for them in the operating theatre. There's a big notice hanging on the theatre doorknob – OPERATION. Our nurses will have a sound sleep.' (Surgery was not carried out at night due to inadequate lighting at the time. Theatres had many windows to capture as much daylight as possible).

Now that the men were at a Base Hospital, they all had a reasonable chance of survival. Some of them would stay there until they were fit for duty again. The men who needed further treatment or convalescence in the United Kingdom were said to have '*A Blighty One*'. The Boulogne Hospital was capable of accommodating 1,040 patients and was well staffed. Hugh enjoyed five days rest from travelling. He knew it would be a long time before he would be able to move from a bed or stretcher, due to the continuous irrigation of his leg wound. He had seen his leg. A lot of skin and leg tissue had died and sloughed away leaving much of his shin bone exposed. The nurses were kept very busy attending to him and the other patients.

Men who were allowed out of bed did everything they could to help look after each other. The nurses were very kind and cheerful, but all working desperately hard. It was common to see some of the 'walking wounded' in the ward helping men who had no use of their arms, to smoke a cigarette, removing the cigarette, then putting it back between the man's lips. Particularly tragic were a pair of soldiers who had become very close friends in the trenches, Neil and Colin. Neil had very serious gas burns that couldn't be bandaged or touched and was covered with a tent of moist, propped-up sheets. Gas burns were the most agonizing, completely beyond endurance and Neil couldn't help crying out; he was clearly dying. At the end, Colin held the now silent Neil in his arms until his last breath, regardless of his blistered, stinking, weeping body. When he died, Colin kissed him twice on the forehead. Later Colin told Hugh that he kissed Neil once for his mother and that the other kiss was 'for myself'.

Hugh had a very long journey home ahead of him. He was ill from the infection in his leg that was barely under control with the continuous irrigation. A lot of nursing attention day and night meant that he had little sleep, and his temperature was up. He knew that tomorrow he would be starting his journey home in a hospital ship to Dover. He was completely unaware that a great muddle was unfolding. Before enlisting, he had been working as an electrician, staying in a rented room in Dingwall, Rosshire. His Scottish parents lived in Poole, and his wife was back with her parents in Bedford. Throughout the long journey, he drifted in and out of delirium. He knew that he had been stretchered in and out of a boat at some stage. He was carried from one ambulance train to another, often being left on chilly platforms for ages, waiting for yet another delayed train.

In one station he vaguely remembered seeing a chap on a stretcher next to him with gross facial injuries. There were some good women with a tea trolley giving cups of tea to the wounded. The man with the facial injuries couldn't drink from the cup offered to him. Hugh watched, with tears running down his face. A very kind lady appeared with a small teapot filled with milky, sugary tea, raised and supported the man's head and helped him to drink. Hugh watched, and tears of sympathy ran down his face. When the kind lady had finished giving the poor chap plenty to drink, she went over to Hugh, and wiped his tears with her own dainty little handkerchief.

When Hugh finally got home, it was to the *Dingwall* area. He was aware that he wasn't travelling like a piece of baggage any more (though he did have a cardboard label tied round his wrist with string). There were plenty of kind Scottish women's voices around him, and a great feeling of peace. He asked where he was. 'You're in Strathpeffer, in the Spa building. It's a hospital now.' It wasn't what he had expected at all. He managed to get a message to his former landlady Mrs McPhail, who came to see him. Clearly the army had, unsurprisingly made a mix up. There was a war on after all! She sent Mrs Dorothy Ross a telegram to tell her that her husband was in hospital in Strathpeffer. The eighteen years old Dorothy embarked on the train journey of her lifetime, travelling from her home in Bedford to Strathpeffer in packed troop trains to be with her husband. Over the following years, she told the journey of her own epic journey many times. She admitted that she never really knew just how she managed to get there, and claimed that she made the journey with a luggage label tied round her neck!

Essie

Chapter Twenty-one

By December 1914 as many as 10% of British officers and 4% of enlisted men were suffering from 'nervous and mental shock'. It was early 1917. Essie was working in the Monte Dore hotel, now a military hospital, where many of the relatively lightly wounded were being cared for. Initially she loved working in the operating theatre best, saying to her friends that she enjoyed *'the cut and thrust'* of the work. It was definitely the *drama* of the theatre that she loved. Most of the surgeons were a bit like highly spirited racehorses, and thought that they as individuals were 'the main event' rather than part of a team. Two of the doctors she worked with had been sent back to Britain to work, as they had been under extreme duress working at The Front. These poor chaps could be very temperamental if surgery didn't go as planned, and even burst into tears at times. The younger inexperienced doctors had little understanding of the organization of the theatre, which involved teamwork by everyone, rather than virtuoso performances.

Initially the doctors heartily disliked Staff Nurse Negus, as she had funny little ways. If she wasn't careful and took her eyes off *'the boys'*, the doctors would do a sloppy scrub up of their hands, to *'get on with the job fast.'* They seemed to think that they, and not she were in charge. They tried to snatch instruments before she was ready to assist them. She quickly learned to hide the scalpels and scissors and wouldn't issue them until she was completely ready for the surgeons to start, having counted all the instruments, swabs and needles, and ensured that they were correctly chalked up on the theatre blackboard by the orderly. At the operating table, any man brave enough to try to snatch instruments received a harsh rap over the knuckles with a sponge holder. This was followed with a charming *'Oh, I'm sooooh sorry doctor dear, I wasn't expecting to find your hand across my trolley!'* The doctors who loathed her initially grew to love her. They teased her for being so small that she had to stand on a wooden box during the operations.

Relaxing in a deckchair in the Bournemouth Gardens one warm summer evening, Essie was very sad to notice the numbers of men who had symptoms of a nervous condition known medically as neurasthenia, but commonly called 'shell-shock.' She perceived that these men, although said by their doctors to only be suffering from '*mild neurasthenia*' were actually in a very bad way. She had heard that quite a lot of men had ended up in locked wards around the country, as they had no grip on reality, thought they were still on the battlefield, and could be suddenly and unexpectedly violent. Those men would probably never be well again.

Having given the matter deep thought, three weeks later, on her next full day off in Poole, she had a long conversation with her father. The Negus Joinery and Funeral business was making a lot of money. Charles Negus was now making plans to build houses once peace returned. Essie explained that she wanted to help people with mild neurasthenic shock, as nobody else seemed to be helping. She felt particularly concerned about the officers who were getting bed and board as convalescents beside the seaside in Bournemouth, and whilst some appeared to get better and went either back into the war, or were discharged from service, others made exceedingly slow progress.

'Why on earth do *you* think you can help?' asked her father snottily.

'I'm a woman and a nurse,' she said. 'I've had a lot of experience at talking things out with men. Some of our surgeons at the Monte Dore are themselves psychologically as well as physically scarred by the war, and have been brought home to easier pastures. *Women are not threatening....*'

'Humph!' he replied, 'you and your mother can be quite lethal at times. Anyway, what on earth do *you* think you could do?'

'I would start by listening to them' she said. 'I could talk to them and reason with them. I could encourage them in gentle activities and perhaps some suitable work could be found to make the lives of these miserable souls a little easier. There are already said to be 80,000 of these poor souls in mental hospitals in this country you know. People are often unkind about them, accusing them of being malingering cowards. There are a lot of officers being treated in the Bournemouth and Boscombe war hospitals for physical injuries who are suffering very severely from shell-shock as well. Their emotions are so damaged that they can't see any future for themselves. In fact,' she went on 'I've noticed that this so called shellshock sometimes happens to men who had never come under fire, or even been within hearing range of exploding shells. The Nursing Times is beginning to describe it as neurasthenia, as it has a lot to do with chronic fatigue, anxiety and what I can only describe as a strange form of deeply depressive listlessness.'

Essie asked her father if he would give her financial security and some funds for social activities, as what she proposed would mean leaving her operating theatre work and moving back into the family home in Poole.

'Essie', he said heavily, 'the good citizens of Bournemouth are already funding free cafes, entertainments, and goodness only knows what else for these men, British and Belgian, what on earth do you want me to give you money for?'

She took a deep breath. 'I don't envisage helping a mob of just any injured men, British or Belgian, back from the war with bad legs or arms or neurasthenia. I will be looking at spending time with two or three officers per day, regular groups on different days, within a normal social setting. Natural conversation and sharing of experiences will be helpful. I would favour using a tennis court quite a lot, and would be looking for a wealthy household, probably in the Westbourne area, who would allow me to use one of their reception rooms for five days a week. Ideally such a household might also have a tennis court. If there is no tennis court, then I might be able to borrow the court at the Royal Victoria Hospital. Of course, I would have to come back home and live with you all again.'

'Oh, go on with you then,' he said. 'You and your sisters will bankrupt me with the way you're carrying on.'

Essie worked a month's notice and then moved back home to her family in Poole. She had approached Mrs Melville, a doctor's widow, who lived at The Pines, a large house with extensive grounds in Portarlington Road, Westbourne. They had a long talk.

'What is this 'shellshock' that we keep hearing about' asked Mrs Melville.

'It is not well understood, and there hasn't been much sympathy for those suffering from it' answered Essie. 'It is a catastrophe of this terrible war, and it comes on gradually, as the men slowly become traumatised beyond human endurance. At first the doctors thought it was a result of exposure to the noise of heavy artillery and gunfire. There has been little official sympathy for those suffering from it. They believe it to be a result of lack of moral fibre or some sort of degenerative disease. The military hierarchy are refusing to treat the victims as disabled, in spite of their devastating mental trauma. I have heard from some of the officers and soldiers that I've been caring for at the Monte Dore war hospital that in France and Belgium some of the men suffering from it have been shot for malingering and cowardice. Officers who suffer from it are speedily identified and brought home quickly, otherwise their illness would have a serious effect on their men's morale.

The worst affected chaps have to be brought back from the front in locked ambulance trains as they have gone completely mad and need to be locked in mental hospitals. Some victims of this awful illness, officers and men, are even reported to be suffering from hysterical paralysis, loss of vision, deafness, painfully contracted limbs and mutism. They hate going to sleep, to dream of blood, bleeding wounds, corpses again and again. Many walk around in daylight nightmares, and there is no ease for them, day or night.

The doctors at the Mont Dore hospital have told me that government statistics are showing that Officers are suffering four times more frequently than other ranks from dreadful nightmares, insomnia, heart palpitations, dizziness, depression and disorientation. Their positions have required them to continually stifle their own emotions in order to set a brave example to their men. They don't get much help. Would you believe it, a British General was quoted in The Times only this week as saying that '*there can be no doubt that the frequency of shell-shock in any unit is an index of its lack of discipline and loyalty. Such men should be shot for malingering and cowardice.*' Essie's gentle eyes filled with tears.

'Oh my dear,' exclaimed Mrs Melville quietly, putting a hand on Essie's shoulder. She had three sons, currently serving as officers. She was a widow, in very comfortable financial circumstances, and had initially offered the use of a very large room, which had often been used for dances when her husband was still alive. During their conversation, Essie stressed the importance instead, of a small, quiet, comfortable room, with easy access to the back garden for the meetings that would be held. The grounds included a tennis court. Mrs Melville agreed to help by acting as a quiet and gentle hostess. She knew there was little sympathy for shellshock victims. Domestic help was a problem in her large house, with so many women now involved in war work. Nonetheless, she insisted that a light lunch and afternoon tea would be served to the weekday visitors.

Essie

Chapter Twenty-Two

Fifteen men attended at 'The Pines' every week, three at a time on their assigned day. Each day contained a number of elements. At some stage there would be a little walk down to the West Cliff seaside. Tennis and croquet would be played. If it was very wet there were board games. The men were encouraged to talk about themselves and their families. Essie was convinced that if they would begin to put their memories and fears into words, they could gain some control of their repressed experiences and begin to feel better within themselves.

Essie encouraged them to 'tell me your stories' every time they met and eventually, after several weeks, they began, within the comfort of their borrowed room, the back garden and the tennis court to talk about their war experiences and their current fears and nightmares. They cried. They talked about wanting to hide. Wanting to die. Dreaming about what had happened to them was unendurable. They were frightened to sleep. Sometimes they woke up screaming. Essie found it was awful to listen to. She came to understand what she had already suspected, that the functional problems such as partial memory loss, insomnia and physical symptoms resulted from the men unconsciously distancing themselves from memories of their traumatic experiences. Their poor brains were constantly struggling to avoid the reality of their recent suffering. They were worried about other people perceiving them as cowards. They felt rejected, secretly wanting to die, hide, and not be seen. They felt so inadequate and flawed that they believed that they could never be of any use again.

Slowly, as the men began to talk about themselves and what had happened to them in more depth, they began as individuals, to recognize why some of their symptoms had begun to occur. Often the symptoms had begun after a final, deeply traumatic emotional experience such as the tragic loss of another officer who was a particular friend or the loss of men with whom they had served for long periods at the front. Sometimes it was a near death experience that jettisoned an experienced officer into neurasthenic illness. There was no doubt about it, these men were very ill. Instinctively, Essie was very good at being kind and sympathetic, but was never emotionally sloppy. She stressed that their problems were not unusual given the stresses they had been under. They were just normal people, and just like other normal people, they were bound to have been deeply affected by the experiences they had endured. She told them that she didn't believe that their sad memories would go away, but she did believe that they would be able to come to terms with them and that one day they would start to feel better. She insisted that talking about it, as often as they wanted to and in as much detail as they wished, was good for them. It was like lancing a boil – painful – sometimes difficult to heal, but with the right treatment it could become a scar, ever present as a reminder, but finally free from pain. They began to feel more confidence in the presence of this little bantam of a woman. Not least, she was an amazing tennis player! The games were hard fought, and the exercise and fresh air when it wasn't raining (much) was very good.

So began Essie's new work. On moving back home, she had made it clear from the start that her work was completely confidential, and she would not be talking about any aspect of it. It was hard emotional labour for her, but she did go round to the Albatross Pharmacy every Friday evening, where she and Phemie had about two hours together behind the locked door of the dispensary, talking confidentially about her week's work, sometimes they both cried at what Essie described as 'the pity of it all'. They discussed ways of dealing with some of the men who were still completely 'stuck' with returning memories of horrors.

Phemie enquired 'What about asking Mr Negus and your brother John if there could be a rota for any of the men you are helping who are well enough to come down to Poole on the tram. They could watch and maybe even participate in some woodwork in his joinery business? It would take them out of the company of other damaged combatants and back into something friendly and normal?'

Mr Negus was grumpily unimpressed with the suggestion, as the joinery was struggling, with most of his skilled men away from home on war service of various types (or even dead), and he didn't think that his remaining elderly foreman and two not very experienced men could manage having unbalanced and possibly unpredictable *officers* in his work premises. To add to the potential problems, they were likely to be well spoken and used to giving orders. He only reluctantly agreed to a 'trial', and stipulated that there wouldn't be any pay for having these officers '*mucking about*' and '*generally getting in the way*' on his premises. As a wartime builder, joiner, furniture-maker and undertaker, Charles Negus was a frantically busy man, and his son John was similarly over occupied. However after the month's 'trial', he and John drank a couple of beers together at 'The Grapes' on the High Street. Comments they'd overheard from the officers were :

'I'm learning new skills.'

'I like helping Mr Negus and his old men. They've taught me a lot'

'I think I'm beginning to develop a sense of my own competence again.'

'I was so miserable......this is a real help.'

'I'm hoping to be trained to use the lathe soon.'

'I'm not very practical, but I make myself useful unloading wood, helping with deliveries, tidying up, sweeping up and that sort of thing.'

'I'm finding it easier to talk to other people now.'

'We are helping each other to feel better.'

'I really look forward to my day at the joinery.'

'Now I'm working a bit I'm sleeping better.'

Mr Negus and John never thanked Phemie for her helpful suggestion regarding helping these very damaged men, but she heard a lot of positive stories about them from Mrs Negus, who reported that the one job Mr Negus did not permit any of the poorly officers to have any involvement with at all was, unsurprisingly, making coffins.

Essie's own work would have been far harder had it not been for the tram ride home from the stop outside the Royal Victoria Hospital, Westbourne. She always caught the same tram, which was usually quite full, and a strikingly handsome dark haired young man always smiled and gave up his seat for her. She liked him very much, but he was shy and silent. They began to smile at each other.

Eventually after a few weeks he said 'The weather is not bad for the time of year.'

She replied 'no, indeed.'

Their conversations improved. Then one evening she got on the tram, and could see immediately that he had been quite severely 'beaten up'.

'*My goodness!*' she said, in complete shock '*what on earth has happened to you.*'

'It's not the first time' he replied. 'People keep giving me white feathers and beating me up, calling me a slacker and a loafer. It's because I'm not in the army or anything.'

'Oh,' she replied. Shocked.

'I've signed up several times, but the military won't have me.'

'Why not?' She asked, thinking that most of the young men she knew were in uniform and serving in distant parts.

'Have you a medical problem? My brother Jack hasn't been able to sign up either, due to a severe skin problem all over his back.'

'No, it's because of my job.'

'Pardon?'

'I'm an accountant, and I work for the banking system, it's what the government call '*a starred occupation*'. I've tried and tried to join the army, but I'm not allowed to join. Seemingly I have a rare talent for dealing with figures – highly complex calculations- and the government insist that I cannot be released from my national obligations in terms of helping to work out the finances of this beastly war. I suppose somebody has to do it. I've been given this badge to wear' he said, pointing to his lapel. 'People still beat me up in the streets though'.

'Oh my goodness, you poor thing' she replied.

They exchanged names, and he got off the tram at Longfleet, Poole.

For men like George, life continued to be very hard. An anonymous person had a very threatening letter published in

To the Women of England

You have read what the Germans have done in Belgium. Have you thought what you would do if they invaded this country?

Do you realise that the safety of your home and children depends on our getting more men now?

Do you realize that the one word 'Go' from you may send another man to fight for our king and country?

When the war is over and someone asks your husband or son what he did in the Great War, is he to hang his head because you would not let him go? Won't you help to send a man to join the army today?

the local newspaper. It was just a copy of something that had been 'doing the rounds', but placed him in more danger:

Essie was very taken with George, and thereafter they tried to take the same trams to work, morning and evening.

Neither of them was able to discuss their work with each other, so conversation was limited to the weather, the lack of food, growing vegetables, impending food rationing and what was being printed in the newspapers, which was frankly dire. She obtained permission from her parents to invite him to afternoon tea on Sunday. Her father was a bit cagey about the nature of her friendship, but when he met George, they got on like a house on fire. 'I wish to propose marriage to your daughter' he announced to Charles Negus one evening when they were doing a bit of vegetable gardening together in the Negus back garden.

'I'll have to think about it....' replied Charles cautiously. 'Are you in a position to support her properly? I think I will have to run this proposal past my wife. We will definitely have to meet your parents as well.'

A very discreet engagement was arranged. There was no ring – instead George gave Essie a little locket with his picture inside. 'We'll get married when the war is over' he said.

The Ross Family

Chapter Twenty-Three

Isa felt very grateful to her sister Phemie for 'taking her in' at a very low spot in her life. When she arrived at the station in Poole, at seven o'clock on Saturday evening, her brother in law Alec was there to meet her. He and Phemie had been taking it in turns to sit there every day after lunch, watching for London trains, waiting for her. The travel had taken her three days, as there was so much troop movement. They had been extremely concerned about her for a long time, and periodically sent her money. Alec immediately recognised her. She was very poorly dressed, and emaciated from lack of food, hard work, exhaustion and insidious illness. He folded her into his kind arms, saying 'Aw hen, we're that glad tae have ye here.' He took her cloth bag, containing all that she had, and put her into a cab, in spite of the tiny distance from station to pharmacy.

After a quick wash, a cup of tea and a slice of bread and butter, 'Auntie Isa' went straight to the room formerly occupied by Hugh and Jock, who were at the War. She was completely exhausted and the next morning, Sunday, she said 'I've slept the clock round, and feel a bit better and brighter.' She didn't eat much breakfast, just a small helping of porridge. 'I'm just no able for it', she said, but accepted another two cups of tea and went back to bed for another couple of hours. By Monday she was feeling a lot better. She spoke to her sister Phemie:

'I can't live on family charity, I'll need to see about getting a job'.

'Not today, you'll not.'

'How no?'

'You're not fit.'

'I am.'

'No you're not. You need some decent clothes, and we need to see a deal more flesh on you first. Eat your porridge and have some toast and put some of this homemade blackcurrant jam on it.'

Isa consented to 'take it easy' and have some 'holiday time' over the week, but made it clear that she would soon be earning wages and paying her keep. She did accept a small loan from her sister Phemie to purchase some 'decent clothes' and true to her word, by Friday morning she had found a job as a counter assistant at 'World's Stores' on the High Street, to commence on Monday. On returning to the 'Albatross' (Albert Ross) pharmacy after closing time on Saturday, the whole family, except Agnes, who was a midwife and was *'doing a delivery'*, were assembled to greet and congratulate her on obtaining a new job. A great Scottish style high tea had been prepared despite all the vicissitudes of food shortages. The long, green painted kitchen table, covered with oil cloth was belching, Scottish style, with plates of girdle scones, little pancakes, white bread, and butter in the best dish. The finest homemade jam – a pot of blackcurrant - had been breached and emptied into a cut glass dish. There was a Victoria sponge cake, seed cake and even *fruit slices* as well. Morag immediately set to, preparing the hot dish – being Poole, it was going to be baked fish, potatoes and cabbage, whilst Isa was cheered on to eat as much as she possibly could with her burgeoning appetite.

On Sunday, Isa, feeling enormously better, went to the Methodist Church, and met a lady of similar age, Miss Liza Loader, and they seemed to form an immediate bond. They had a good chat together at the end of the service although there was a fair bit of language difficulty given Isa's strong Scottish accent and Liza's Darzet diction (Dorset ways of speaking).

They concluded that if they were to be friends, Liza would have to revert to *Elizabeth* and Isa should be called *Isabel*.

Elizabeth confided to her new friend that she had recently taken a 'live in' job at a villa in St Mary's Road, Longfleet. It was talked up to be very good. Madam was apparently pleasant, to begin with, and had stated that her household was '*seriously needing help*'. Elizabeth let all the unpleasant details out, namely that '*Madam*' was seriously lazy, had a very large house, was untidy and dirty in her ways, and expected Elizabeth to do absolutely everything.

She explained to Isabel that she had been employed to be a 'tweenie', the same job as she'd had before in a household in Wimborne. 'I had the same split responsibilities in Wimborne as what I got now. I done the kitchen an' cooking things. I also done all the cleanin and tidyin up in every room in the house. Difference was that in Wimborne Missis Mathews, the lady of the house knowed I couldn't do it all. The Missis could do the jobs round the house herself. I was paid to do the work, but as it was too much for one person, the Missis always helped with cleaning and tidying the reception rooms and living areas in the mornings. She always served out the refreshments herself at afternoon tea, and this give me the time what I needed for cookin an' servin dinner. If there was anythin special happenin' with several guests, or spring cleanin' or summat, she got another wumman in for a day or two to help. This Mrs Bollom what I got now is terrible dirty and untidy in her ways. I cassn't stand 'er laziness no more.'

On Monday, Elizabeth (*formerly known as 'Liza'*) started her new job at 'World's Stores.' It was a beautiful, modern grocery store with mahogany framed windows and doors, and a marble mosaic floor. The manager, Mr. Alwright, had fair hair, ruddy cheeks and sparkling blue eyes. Isabel had to 'make the tea' for the shop assistants mid-morning, lunchtime and mid-afternoon. Initially he set Isabel to work 'receiving the deliveries'. Each item in terms of pots of jam or tinned meat etcetera had to be stored in the back of the shop on the correct shelves. They were slowly 'brought forward' as required when items from the front of the shop were sold out. Mr Alright didn't want the shop to look well-stocked, as he was trying very hard to get people to buy *'just for the day'*, in the expectation that everybody would get some food, and the hope that the wholesalers would deliver something the following day. Basic food items were difficult to obtain and women and children queued daily outside shops, trying to get anything that was edible and available. The war had taken men and horses away from farm work. Farmers had difficulty obtaining nitrate fertilizers for their crops. The difficulties on farms and their low output forced vegetable prices up and richer people were hoarding packets of sugar, flour and suchlike.

Halfway through the week Mr Alwright took Isabel into his little glass cabin at the back of the store and showed her the 'Ready Reckoner' book, which provided calculations as he had noticed she was a bit slow on numbers. It was information she needed, to prepare herself for serving behind the counter. The war in France became ever more real to the citizens of Poole. Early on Friday morning, a regular customer came into the shop with her little boy, Frank. Her eyes were red raw. Frank was sobbing. Jenny, one of the women counter assistants came around the counter to the child, and cuddled him.

'Whatever is it?' she asked.

The mother answered 'We've come from the station where the casualty lists are pasted up. His daddy is dead.'

'Now you will have to be a brave soldier, just like your Daddy, and look after your mummy' Jenny said.

Mr Allwright took Frank and his mother into the stockroom, sat them on boxes and made them a cup of tea. He gave the little boy a biscuit to eat now, and a precious poke of sweets for later. Mr and Mrs Allwright had never been able to have children of their own. He was a very kind employer, although he teased Isabel a lot about her Scottish accent and some of the strange words she used. On Friday he asked her if she knew anyone who was looking for a job, as one of the men who worked behind the counter had signed up to join the Dorsetshire regiment.

'I think I might know another reliable woman like myself who would be willing to work here' she said.

Work at The World's Store was just what Elizabeth needed. She went for an interview on Saturday, and began work a week later. She was 'made for the job'. Phemie and the Methodist Minister both wrote references for her. Mrs Bollom had refused her a reference, made her work out a week's notice and then refused to give her the final week's pay. This was swiftly sorted out by the Methodist Minister, who made a short personal visit to Mrs Bollom. Elizabeth was thus without a home to go to, and Phemie invited her to be the second temporary occupant of what was actually Jock and Hugh's bedroom above the Pharmacy.

Alec Ross went to Poole station early, every morning, to buy a paper so that he could check the names on the casualty lists. (Poor people couldn't afford daily newspapers, so a porter pasted the daily lists on the station's tiled walls) On the sixteenth of July he went into the back room of the pharmacy carrying his paper. His face, completely expressionless, was white and grey and running with cold sweat.

Phemie looked at him. Colour drained from her face

'Jock' he said. 'Jock.'

'Sandy, oh Sandy' she croaked.

Sandy slithered off his stool behind the dispensary counter, alarmed, and limped into the back room.

'It's Jock...'

The family continued to work in the pharmacy that day, somehow.

Alec and Phemie received a Post Office Telegraph delivery later on the same day, stating

---

' *+Lieutenant Jock Ross died of wounds on June 28th +*

+Field Marshal Haig expresses his sympathy+.'

His parents were distraught.

Two months later the citation for his posthumous Victoria Cross stated: '*The gallantry and devotion to duty of this officer are beyond all praise*'. The family also received 'The Dead Man's Penny' a heavy copper disc, four and three quarter inches in diameter, cast with his name and iconic images of Britannia and the British Lion. It was inscribed 'He died for freedom and honour.' Phemie put it in a drawer underneath the clean tablecloths. It stayed there.

Chapter Twenty-Four

The events of that day and the days following changed everything relatively quickly. Jock was dead, and for a while no-one knew whether his brother Hugh was alive or dead. Hugh was listed as wounded, but no-one knew where he was. Eventually Dorothy, his very young wife sent a postcard to the Albatross Pharmacy. He was alive, and currently being nursed in a temporary war hospital at Strathpeffer. At eighteen years old, she had travelled on troop trains all the way to the little station at Strathpeffer in Scotland, to be with him. With the shortage of men to work in the tiny village, she quickly found both a job and a room at the Co-Op grocery shop, within sight of the Spa Pavilion where her husband lay sick. She visited him every day, and their relationship which had been put under great pressure from the war, began to flourish again.

At Poole, life at The Albatross descended into a quiet desperation. Alec, who had suffered from periodic mental problems did not cope with the death of his son Jock at all well, and for several days the military people, usually so efficient, had no idea where Hugh was and whether he was alive or dead. Phemie had Alec lying in her arms for most of that first night. They made love. Perhaps it helped a bit, but Alec began to lose himself completely by the end of the week. Phemie coped. She always coped with everything. The doctor advised her to send him to Herrison Hospital (the Dorset Lunatic Asylum). It wouldn't have been Alec's first visit to the hospital, and it had helped him in the past. Instead, she went to see Lydia, who had temporarily abandoned living in the house named 'The Poop Deck' on the harbour side, and was now spending most of her time helping out Mistress Caroline and Victor at Blake Hill

Farm. She asked the three of them if Alec could stay there, away from pressures and worries.

Phemie was sorry Alec was away, but it was the best thing as later events unfolded. He would be back when he was better. She prayed that the war would soon be over, and that her youngest son, Douglas, who was now fourteen would not have to go. Douglas was a proud member of the Boy Scouts, one of the first boys' organizations to provide practical assistance to the British war effort. He was always busy, doing his bit guarding the local telephone exchange and helping to unload casualty trains at the local railway station. Douglas knew that Baden-Powell sent telegrams to Scouts who did heroic deeds during the war and was hoping to be a hero himself!

It was Douglas who accepted the bulky brown paper wrapped parcel from the postman, addressed to his father. Parcels were unusual, and it had come from the military as far as he could tell from the markings on it. His mother was over-busy, so the parcel was not considered until the family had eaten their meal and cleared away. It was put on the kitchen table. Fortunately Phemie decided to open it herself in Alec's absence at Blake Hill. A sharp kitchen knife dispensed with the string and sealing wax, and the well wrapped parcel fell open to reveal its stinking contents. There had been no warning of what it contained….. Jock's officer's uniform which he had purchased himself, was inside, soaked with dried blood and stinking mud.

'Oh my bonnie lad, my dear, dear boy,' she said again and again. 'I always wondered why you were aye asking for nice perfume and talcum powder. Now I know. Thank God your father is not here just now. This would kill him.'

Isabel and Sandy took charge. They went through the pockets. Those who had collected and dispatched the uniform had taken everything. His watch, signet ring, pocket knife, cash, everything was gone, no keepsakes for the Ross family. Just this filthy memory. They took the parcel and its contents into the back yard, drenched it with paraffin and put a match to it. The loss of much loved Jock made the whole family feel very bitter. Phemie left a whole week before she felt able to visit Parkstone Farm. She broke the news of Jock's death, but never told Alec about the parcel, and the family at home were sworn to secrecy.

A few days later Jock's Colonel sent a letter of condolence:

Dear Mr and Mrs Ross
        On behalf of the Officers and men your son served with, I offer you my sincere sympathy in the bereavement you have sustained in the death of your son Jock. I feel that you would like to know that your son was a very brave and fine officer, greatly respected by the men he led. The loss of Jock was felt with deep sorrow by the Company. During the initial advance Jock was shot in the right leg, and despite extreme pain managed to lead his men to capture an enemy trench. Together with other men who had lost their officer, he encountered a German machine gun attack, was wounded again, in his left arm, but continued to control the situation. He ordered his remaining ten men standing, to advance to the German Machine gun nest whilst providing covering fire with his pistol. He was killed, but the machine gun emplacement was destroyed by his men with a Mills bomb. If it is any comfort to you, he died almost immediately and I am sure that he suffered no further pain. If there is anything you would like to know

or that I can do to help you, I shall be only too pleased to do so.
Yours sincerely
Robert J. E. Hamilton, Capt. Seaforth Highland 2nd Division

War is a maddening experience. People tend to react instinctively 'in the moment', without considering the consequences at all. They can act very well, with great courage and compassion sometimes, and other times they appear to act stupidly. After Jock's death and Hugh's serious wound, Isabel and Elizabeth decided to leave 'The World's Stores' and do something positive in defence of British freedom. Isabel had heard from a friend that a large munitions factory had been built in Clackmannanshire at the back of Culross Moor and the pair were determined to go and work there.

Meanwhile, as a midwife, Agnes Ross knew all about how babies are made, and how during a war, people often look for comfort. Shortly after the news of Jock's death and Hugh's serious wound, she met a very pleasant young army captain who was just back on leave. 'Call me Tony' he said, and they began to meet whenever Agnes was between delivering babies. They grew very fond of each other, but didn't want to marry in a hurry. However, matters proceeded between them, and on the last evening prior to Tony's departure back to France, they were walking in Poole Park. There were a lot of young couples in the bushes. Agnes and Tony noticed a couple exiting from under the generous cover of a mature willow tree and they dived under the foliage themselves, where they 'did the deed' in what Agnes described later as 'a complete moment of madness.'

'The moving finger writes,
And having writ moves on
Nor all thy piety nor wit,
Shall lure it back to cancel half a line
Nor all thy tears wash out a word of it.'

Agnes had acted on an impulse. Despite her considerable experience as a midwife, she had no thought in her head that she might get pregnant. She just wanted Tony to know before he left, that she really loved him. Such random acts were common amongst the poor and ignorant people of Poole, particularly as there was a war on. There was indeed a big increase in the numbers of 'war babies' being born 'legitimately' to soldiers' wives, following leave. However, a second kind of 'war baby' also existed, outside marriage. Some (understandably) lonely women 'accommodated' men rather freely. Some of the young mothers were very young girls. Indeed, the problem of 'illegitimate' war babies was endemic in Britain, due to the establishment of military camps all over the country. Poole had already established a maternity home and the Guardians of the Poor were building a maternity wing to the workhouse expressly for these mothers, many of whom just walked away and abandoned their unwanted offspring.

As soon as Tony was away, Agnes asked her Auntie Isabel and her friend Elizabeth if she had any objections to them going to Scotland, to work in the new munitions factory near Peppermill Dam. Phemie was very upset.

'You'll be such a loss to me, with Alec no weel up at Blake Hill, Mistress Caroline fit to drop, and Morag and Sandy being so busy here. I rely on the help you can give me domestically, and you will be such a loss to the town, where a great many babies are being generated. I suppose it's because there's a war on, and the men want to be sure of leaving something behind them. Why on earth don't you go to the Royal Navy place on Holton Heath?'

'Ma, I can't do other than to go and do my part to help win this terrible war. I've never seen Scotland, and it would be a great opportunity to see the country you and father left all those years ago.'

Chapter Twenty-Five

Life in and around Alloa

Isabel, Elizabeth and Agnes set off from Poole on the tremendous journey up to Scotland by the earliest train, on a dismal, mizzling rainy morning. There was quite a long stop in Southampton for coal and water to be replenished, and the trio opened the carriage window and bought a newspaper and cups of tea from the catering trolley. Their newspaper reported two unprecedented and lethal Zeppelin raids on London early the previous evening. The attacks were from such a height that the British fighter planes were unable to climb to the defence. The girls felt very nervous when they got out of the train at Waterloo, and Agnes was feeling a bit nauseous with the excitement. They were even more nervous finding their way from Waterloo to Kings Cross via the tube train, although Isa had bravely made a similar journey before.

They were to leave at 10am on 'The Flying Scotsman.' The journey was really impressive, opening with a run without a pause, from Kings' Cross to Grantham in Lincolnshire. The guard told the passengers it was a distance of 105 miles!! There was just a six minute stop, and then the mighty Scotsman took wings for York, flying 189 miles as fast as ever, completing it in three hours and fifty five minutes. Then the train entered the handsomest station in England, that of the North Eastern Company at York. Half an hour was allowed for the excited passengers to get out of the train at York to stretch their legs, use the lavatory and find some refreshments. A run of 84 miles to Newcastle, a five minutes stop, and then The Scotsman tore off to Berwick on Tweed, finally running into Waverley Station, Edinburgh, at 7pm.

By great good luck, the women were able to find cheap overnight accommodation in a nearby tenement room, bundling themselves and all their possessions into the cramped space. They were exhausted, and weren't looking forward to their journey to Alloa, which would involve several changes, but there was one highlight – the ride across the famous Forth Rail Bridge!!!

Early the following morning, the exhausted women, with Agnes still feeling sick, took two more trains to arrive in Alloa at twelve fifteen, seeking accommodation. The station porter at Alloa kindly undertook to look after their luggage, whilst they searched around for accommodation. They were finally able to find an old woman who was willing to take them in, Mrs Elspeth Ford, who lived in a room and kitchen in a run-down house in Main Street. Agnes remembered her mother Phemie talking about her late mother's shared cottage in the same street. It was a strange turnaround, to land up in almost the same place her mother had started at. They determined to find themselves a better place to live as soon as possible.

At the outset of the war, Britain's munitions industry had difficulty producing the quantities of weapons and ammunition required by the country's armed forces. The Ministry of Munitions was created in July 1915 to regulate pay, working hours and employment conditions in munitions factories. It forced the factories to admit more women as employees as so many men were fighting in the war that male labour was in short supply. By June 1917, roughly 80% of the weaponry and ammunition used by the British army during World War I was being made by 'munitionettes'. Sadly, the women were on average, paid less than half of what the men were paid.

The new, secret munitions factory near Kincardine was started in late 1914-15 in response to two problems. The first was the actual shortage of shells with which to bombard the enemy, due to a lack of manufacturing capability. The second and far worse problem was the extremely poor quality of munitions produced by private engineering companies who were more interested in profiteering than producing effective weapons of war. In the early days Mills bombs and artillery shells were often filled with inadequate amounts of explosive and topped up with rubbish such as wood shavings, and dust. The casings were so poorly machined, that the shells didn't 'fly true' and then they failed to explode at all, or if they did, were not capable of producing much real damage. This was attributed to fraud by greedy private firms who were charging high prices for poorly made products, which even included soldiers' guns and boots with cardboard soles. The 'Shell Crisis' in 1915 caused the British government to pass an act to increase government oversight and regulation of wartime industries.

Elizabeth and Isabel applied for work at the new secret Royal Naval Factory and were delighted to find that women's wage-rates in the munitions industry were higher than in Paton's Mill. By 1918, the average male weekly wage in the munitions industry was £4-6s-6d but for women it was only £2-2s-4d. However the munitions pay was far better than women could find elsewhere. They took the Dunfermline train from Alloa, along with their fellow 'munitionettes' and changed train at Kincardine, to take a dedicated 'works' train on a new line, near to the munitions site. The train from Alloa was usually packed with people. The porters knew that the women were all working on munitions, so they'd say, 'Go on, hen, hop in there,' and they used to open the first class carriages, for the munitions workers, and there'd be officers sitting there, looking at the women as if they were insects. Other officers used to look at each other and mutter, 'Oh well, they're doing their bit.' The workers felt very embarrassed about their clothes, because the chemicals from their work, in spite of the factory clothing supplied, seeped from their skins into their everyday clothing.

An old steam train took the workers from Kincardine a little further. For safety's sake, there was still a considerable walk from the train to the factory, which was hidden in a large disused quarry near Peppermill Dam. It had been hurriedly built by the Ministry of Munitions in early 1915, and was making shells for the navy. The buildings were new, but looked old and dirty. It must have been as a result of all the chemicals being used. Elizabeth and Isabel went to the main gate of the factory where they were eyeballed by a silent sentry, and they went inside. A skinny little man announced the pay rates and hours to the girls and told them where to find Mr Syme, who signed them up to work immediately.

The plant was being run by a handful of male supervisors, who didn't want to show the new women workers how the work should be done. However, almost all of the manual work was done by the women. Mr Syme, who was in overall charge of the work, said to Elizabeth, 'If you have any difficulty with the men you're working with, come to me.' When she passed this information on to Isabel she replied 'I should cocoa!' The person who was really in over all charge was a regular army officer, Major Buchanan, a very pleasant older gentleman, who had a small unit of armed soldiers to keep the factory secure.

Manufacturing was being carried out in small isolated buildings, well-spaced out, with brick walls and earth banks around them. Everyone was on their feet all day except for 'breaks', but Agnes said resignedly that it was probably better than she had endured when she was in service, and at least she wasn't emptying other peoples' disgusting chamber pots any more. The women were all glad to be doing their bit to win the war! In spite of being paid so much less than the men, their wages were still far higher than they were used to, but there were other factors of course....One woman, married to a very violent man who was now at the Front, said philosophically ' I expect he'll last out to the end. Others who will be sorely missed will be taken, for that's the way of things…' The work was generally unpleasant, uncomfortable and exceedingly dangerous. Accidents, explosions, or poisoning from handling chemical explosives were relatively commonplace. The women 'munitionettes', had very little protection from the toxic chemicals they were in contact with.

At the end of the fourth day, when Elizabeth and Isabel returned to their dirty little lodging in Main Street, Agnes was still not looking well, but had been out around the town, had shopped and best of all, had met up with one of the two professional Alloa midwives at the Co-Op grocery. Her name was Shona Duncanson; she was a qualified midwife, and lived in a large house, in a street called Ludgate. Shona was also out for messages, and invited Agnes back to her house for a cup of tea. She couldn't leave the house for long, just in case there was a 'call.' There were no calls that morning, and the pair enjoyed a right good 'getting to know you' chat.

Agnes was very impressed with the grandeur of the houses all around. Shona said that 'her house' actually belonged to her parents. They had moved into a hotel in Stirling for the duration of the war, as it was impossible to employ good servants, most people being fully occupied with 'war work.' Her parents said that the hotel costs were very reasonable. Shona said there were spare rooms in the house, and it was likely that the friends could move in for a reasonable rent if they wished, and if her fellow midwife Deoiridh was agreeable to the arrangement.

Agnes returned 'home' to prepare a good meal for her exhausted friends, who arrived back at 7pm, well-scrubbed at the public baths, but yellower than ever. Agnes had finally realized that she was pregnant, as her period was seriously overdue and her breasts were becoming very tender. Elizabeth and Isobel couldn't get over how an intelligent, well experienced midwife like Agnes could have been such an idiot! However they were much older than Agnes and their mental and physical feelings no longer ran so hot.

Shona and her midwife friend Deoiridh went round to see Agnes and were very sympathetic.

'We would have married' Agnes elaborated, 'but we had left *everything* too late. I didn't intend to do what I did, but our blood ran so hot, and if Tony doesn't come home, I hope that at least I shall have something of him left for me to love....' She sobbed. Shona pulled a beautiful handkerchief out of her bag and handed it to her. Shona put her arms round Agnes and rocked her in her great distress, saying

'You're certainly not the only one around here to be in trouble. A baby is a great comfort to a woman when the man she loves is away... Everything will work out. You'll see...' Unfortunately Agnes was unable to work temporarily as a midwife in Alloa (*English trained!*), and as a result of her 'condition' had to take work in town, at the local pharmacy. Her family background and the fact that she had often helped out at 'The Albatross' Pharmacy, was very helpful. She was completely honest with her employer about her 'condition'.

'I mind your Faither' said Mr Hamilton. 'I was just a laddie then. Is he keeping well these days?

'Aye, never better' she lied. 'Helping his ancient mother in law on her farm at the moment'

'Left the Pharmacy business then?'

'Och no. Ma maw and an assistant work mostly in the front of shop, and brother Sandy and faither do the dispensing. Our business is good, and sometimes faither takes some time off'.

Mr Hamilton said he was glad to take her on anyway, knowing that she had grown up in a pharmacy and had often helped her parents and brother with their work. His male assistant had perished at Gallipoli. Mr Hamilton wrote to Sandy Ross in Poole for a reference 'just for the record'.

Chapter Twenty-Six

Elizabeth and Isabel found their work very difficult. When they went to work on the first day, they were issued with special clothes. All workers had to hand in all their jewellery, cigarettes, matches and metallic items before they could pass through the door keepers' lobby. They were issued with special 'cream' to protect their faces, necks and hands from the TNT that filled the very air they were breathing. There was a big room with a partition down the middle, one side was 'clean' and the other 'dirty'. When the girls went to their work, they had to take their coats and clothes off and put them in a kit bag that was called 'dirty'. They had to remove hairpins, and anything else metallic and wrap their hair in khaki 'turbans'. They were issued with rubber plimsolls with 'War Department' stamped on them, then they stepped over a low barrier across the middle of the room, to the 'clean' side. They put a factory overall on, which had a bit of cloth stitched to the back, with their individual number and 'War Department' sewn on it, and a mob cap. Despite their cotton face masks and overalls they still went yellow *all over*....

The women had little time to enjoy themselves. They started work at 6am, and it'd be 7 o'clock before they got home, having had a shower before they left the factory. They ate the meal prepared for them by Agnes, and went to bed as they had to be up at 4 o'clock to be at Alloa station for the train at 5. Their lives just became bed and work. A lot of Trinitrotoluene (TNT), a yellow chemical mixture was used as at the factory, as an explosive material with convenient handling properties - it doesn't spontaneously detonate, allowing it to be poured or safely combined with other explosives. It doesn't absorb or dissolve in water, so can be used effectively in wet environments. Perfect for the Western

Front. The women workers did a lot of physical labour, which was both back-breaking and extremely risky from all the chemicals they were being exposed to. They were also involved in operating machinery. The night shifts were exhausting and everyone found difficulty staying alert when working. Nasty accidents were more likely in the small hours.

It wasn't long before the citizens of Alloa started to call the munitions workers *'The Canaries'* due to their bright yellow appearance. They were actually suffering from TNT poisoning - Trinitrotoluene – an explosive which turned the skin of those who regularly came into contact with it yellow. The older workers, men and women didn't mind too much, but the younger ones were unable during their time off to go out looking 'normal', as the colour stubbornly remained despite any amount of washing and everyone knew what their work was. Some of the munitions workers were very rude and rough in their ways. They took offence very easily, and were willing to fight. However suspension from work (although they were seriously needed for the war work) and the withholding of wages brought them into line eventually.

There were three women at the factory who spoke very *'pan loaf'* as they were accustomed to being waited on at home by servants. However, there were precious few servants now, and they were in their own words 'having to do for ourselves.' Two were officers' 'war widows' and the other was the wife of a captain who was on the western front. One lady was from Claremont, another from Grange Road and the third lived at Bedford Place.

Being 'upper class' these women were very spirited, but got 'taken down a peg' during their first week. Mrs Urquhart was accustomed to being waited on at home. One of the shifts was sitting in the works canteen during the night for the main meal that was supplied. Workers picked up plates and cutlery from a large trolley before sitting on benches, and the cooks banged a few dishes of unappetising fare down on the table for the hungry workers. People normally stretched across their neighbours to grab what they wanted. Mrs Urquhart said loudly and firmly to Betty 'Would you be kind enough to pass down the potato dish please?' There was no response. Mrs Urquhart repeated her request.

Isabel replied quietly 'you jist say gie us the totties hen!' Mrs Urquhart did as she was told. Everyone laughed, and the ice was broken. The working women were very glad when they found it was quite possible to have a laugh with the hitherto despised upper classes. In fact, Mrs Urquhart, Mrs Murray and Captain Black's wife were soon well accepted by the other workers. Mrs Murray, who initially worked in the TNT hut where she poured chemicals into shell cases, was spotted by Mr Abercrombie, her foreman, as being exceptionally useful and he arranged for her to be taught to use the mighty 7ft McNaughton lathe in the same hut as her friends. She took to it straight away and enjoyed plenty of job satisfaction although some foremen disregarded women who did skilled tasks. At home she had often been lonely and bored, with her husband serving overseas. She confessed to being glad to leap out of bed at 5.15 on frosty mornings to make her way down to the Alloa station, almost dancing along the road. Some of the munitions women had never met the upper classes before, and had strange ideas about them.

The 'useful women' from all classes began to really appreciate the leadership Mr Carruthers demonstrated in his section of the factory. He and the other women had accepted the three posh rich women well, and he made sure that everyone worked hard. He was always willing to help women with an aptitude for engineering develop many more useful skills. Everyone at the factory was yellow, all over. To make matters worse Isabel and Elizabeth both had greying hair which became practically green! Despite their careful washing, the yellow and green just didn't budge. A doctor came round occasionally to have a look at the men and women in the factory. He pulled their eyelids down and looked at their teeth. Elizabeth was embarrassed, as she didn't have many teeth anyway, due to poor diet and alcohol problems in her youth. To the younger women the doctor said 'Half of you girls will never have babies.' The women supposed the doctor thought they were pulling their innards to bits with all the heavy lifting! They never thought about the long term effects of the powder being used to fill the shells getting into their stomachs, often causing bad pains.

An older woman called *Iona Mackintosh* (her married name!) told the young cheeky ones that they had poor stomachs because they didn't keep their mouths shut and were always talking. Many of the women didn't realize the danger they were in, handling dangerous chemicals. They were all given milk to drink, to neutralize the poison in their insides. The younger women used to say 'we don't mind dying for our country!' Liza and Isa just looked on. The girls were young and stupid, they didn't realise. Another problem was cigarettes - almost everyone smoked. Their cigarettes and matches were taken from them when they checked in for work. They weren't allowed to 'light up' until they were on the train home. They got very irritable without their cigarettes.

The canteen wasn't too bad. When they were working 'days', the women got a quarter of an hour for morning coffee, and an hour for lunch, but sometimes this was cut to half an hour if there was a desperate need for shells on the front lines. They'd get a ten minute tea break for the afternoon cup of tea – more often than not, Liza and Isa made their own. They went to the end of the room where hot water was available to make tea. It was quicker than going up to the canteen, lining up and waiting.

They were very careful, and followed the factory rules. There were occasional little work accidents. You had to be very careful when you were soldering bullets. One went off bang! Murdo, the supervisor took a big fright when this happened to one of the women. She was very bad after it, couldn't use her arm, and had it in a sling. For six weeks she had to go to work every day *even though she couldn't do anything*, to get her wages because she wasn't allowed to stay at home and claim. The munitions work continued seven days a week, twenty four hours a day, but the workers did get two days a week off, because of their long hours and exposure to malicious chemicals.

Security was very tight. There were always armed police guarding the works, *'to prevent any possible malevolent attempts by enemies of the state'* as described by the police. Everyone in the wider area knew there was a secret factory, but no-one mentioned it openly, and it was rare for anyone to mention the numbers of yellow people around the local towns.

During Elizabeth and Isabel's second month at work, there was a problem in F block No.14 shell stores. A woman was just picking a shell up to put the fuse on, when there was a tremendous explosion. The woman and a lot of other people were killed in the explosion. Lisa and Isa had just got to the factory for the night shift; they went on from 10pm until 6am. Fortunately they were both in 'D' block at the time, and the block that went up in the explosion was across from there, but the explosion was limited by the thick brick and earth walls surrounding each small production hut and storage hut. It was terrifying. Four people were killed outright. The whole place had to be evacuated immediately.

Five women and a man who were outside at the time were injured. Two of the women were so seriously injured that they died within minutes. Major Buchanan and his small unit of soldiers got the fire under control quickly with the help of trained volunteer fire fighters from Kincardine. The wounded were treated and the dead bodies covered. All the workers were taken down to the town where the YMCA rendered aid to minor wounds, and offered sandwiches and tea to warm up the survivors, who were very shocked. The plant was shut down for thirty six hours whilst investigations were conducted and the damage was rapidly repaired. The cause of the explosion was never fully identified, but privately the Major suspected that some idiot had tried to have a crafty cigarette. Other people suspected that chemicals might have combusted spontaneously. There was no hint of sabotage.

Chapter Twenty-Seven

Back in Alloa the 'munitionettes' were enjoying some unpaid hours off following the explosion at the plant. Being reasonably well paid, as it was Saturday, some of them turned up at the local pubs, and drank a lot more than was good for them. It didn't help their stomachs which were already sore due to their chemical exposure. Elizabeth, Isabel and Agnes decided that they would go to church together on Sunday morning, as until this time, their working hours had precluded church attendance. Isabel highly recommended 'The Greenside Mission Chapel' in terms of excellent preaching, friendly people and good singing. The trio went along at the appropriate hour. It was only a short walk. She introduced her friends to a few acquaintances, and was told that the old minister had died, and there was a lovely new one. The trio sat down in the middle seats in the hall with Isabel in the middle. A woman was paddling her feet on the bellows to play a hymn on the harmonium. It was another lovely nostalgic moment for Isabel.

When it was time for the service to commence, a door at the back of the church opened, and half a dozen serious looking men came in and took their seats at the front, facing the congregation. The congregation rose to their feet, and the minister, walking with a stick in each hand, walked slowly up the aisle, dragging his poor clubbed feet with every painful step. Isabel was so surprised and shocked that she suddenly felt all her strength drain from her, and she had to sit down immediately and put her head between her knees. Her friends sat either side of her, supporting her, wondering if she had developed some illness associated with the munitions work. An old lady passed over her smelling bottle, which seemed to help a little. Elizabeth and Agnes were whispering in her ear that they would take her home. Meantime, the Minister, who had noted what was happening in the pews had been on his feet, announced the first hymn with a radiant smile, joined in the singing of it and had intoned a lengthy and actually quite interesting prayer. Isabel was at last getting over her shock at seeing Pastor Ewan McKenzie, the love of her life again.

Her friends were mightily relieved to see Isabel raise her yellow face again, and were still periodically whispering 'Shall we take you home?' They were obviously worried that Isabel had developed one of the strange illnesses associated with the munitions work.

'I'm alright now' she stated firmly, 'but I think I'll stay seated.'

At the end of the service, still seated, she was in no hurry to leave. The minister limped out first, to sit in an armchair by the door, shaking hands with people and speaking briefly with some of them. His congregation obviously loved him. Isabel and her friends were the last to leave. When he saw them coming, he struggled to his feet, put his arms round her, and said 'You were so very long coming... How about coming to visit me for a cup of tea this afternoon? I live on the premises as it's easier for my work.'

Isabel looked into his beautiful face. His eyes were filled with tears. She was blushing very hot, causing her yellow skin to look worse than ever.

Isabel only picked at the Sunday lunch that the midwives, Shona and Deoiridh had made for them all between their midwifery 'calls' to 'newly delivered' mothers. Her new friends were intrigued to hear that Isabel had met up with what they described as 'an old flame' (*at her age!!*). Elizabeth and Agnes attested to the facts that the minister was remarkably good looking, obviously very intelligent in a down to earth sort of way, and seemed really kind and friendly to his congregation. Then Elizabeth said seven very serious words: *'it's a pity about his crippled legs.'*

After lunch Isabel walked back to the Greenside Mission on her own. Seemingly the minister lived in a separate part of the building with its own door on to the street. Her heart was beating rapidly as she knocked the door firmly, then waited a while for Euan to open it. He opened the door, unsteadily, with a beaming smile.

'My darling…..At last! Come in, come in!'

She followed him, as he shuffled in to a very large cosy room. It was a study, a dining room and a place to sit in a cosy couch in front of the fire.

'After saying goodbye to you that day in Glasgow, I have prayed every day for this! You know how much I love you, but I wanted our Lord to set his definitive seal on our union with a small miracle.'

He transferred both his sticks into one hand, and laid them carefully on the table, putting his other arm on her shoulder before miraculously managing to keep his balance, and giving her an amazing, tender, long kiss. Her whole body was filled with the warmth of her desire for him. They lay together on the couch, and kissed and caressed, and he explained that he had asked God to show him that without doubt, Isabel was the woman for him.

Isabel was both pleased that things had finally worked out between them, and very annoyed at all the time Ewan had wasted, when they could have been together. They had always loved each other. For her, on the very first time she saw him, it had been a bit like Rachael meeting Jacob at the well, a life-changing experience. Then he had gone off and left her.

'*Why*?' she asked.

'I suppose that unsurprisingly a lot of my life has been about my feet. Remember what I said to the class in the Glasgow Missionary Home on the day I met you. '*How beautiful upon the mountains are the feet of him that bringeth good tidings, that publisheth peace; that bringeth good tidings of good, that publisheth salvation.* ' I had to be sure that if I married you, I would remain faithful to God's calling, and that we could live together happily doing His work. I am so limited with my disability. I have to pay Bruce McBride to wheel me out to visit the sick and Mrs Syme to manage my home here and daily needs. Will you marry me? It's a huge undertaking on your part. I wouldn't want you to feel that you had become an unhappy and unpaid drudge. I will carry on employing Mrs Syme.'

'Oh you silly, silly boy', she said. 'What a lot of time you have wasted. When can we get wed and get on with life?'

'I'll fix it up tomorrow', he said brightly. 'Sooner the better. Would this week suit us both? I can send a note to the registrar and ask him to come round on Wednesday morning?'

'WAIT, don't rush me' she said. 'I only intend to get married the once and I want to enjoy it. I'll need at least three weeks. I have to give my employer a week's notice. I need a further two weeks to try and get rid of some of this yellow on my skin. And I'll need to get a nice dress made. We must discuss where we will have the marriage ceremony, and you'll need to arrange for the Registrar to attend in person. You'll need to pay him a pound for the Wedding Certificate, and sixpence a mile for travel.'

'How do you know all this?'

'What do you think we girls speak about in the canteen at work?'

Isabel was very glad that she would be leaving her job in munitions. Whilst she was working her notice, she heard that one of her work friends, had died from toxic jaundice, due to chemical exposure after only a short illness, and was very concerned. She was getting really excited about her forthcoming marriage to Euan. Her friend Shona the midwife turned out to be an absolute whizz with *a modern sewing machine*, and measured Isabel very carefully, made a brown paper pattern, cut up an old bedsheet and sewed the bits together. She then tried 'the experimental garment' on Isa, and made some amendments. Finally, she found a length of blue satin belonging to her mother, which she said had 'been lying about for ever, and would never be missed.' There was no lining for the dress – Shona commented 'There's a war on, one can't expect to have everything.' The former modified bedsheet became a petticoat under the satin dress.

Meantime Elizabeth continued working at the Factory. Her friends noticed that she was really quite poorly and spoke to Mr Abercrombie their foreman, who arranged for her to see the doctor at the plant that afternoon. The doctor accused her of being under the influence of alcohol because she was falling about the place, and told her not to come back until she was sober.

'I used to drink, but I don't drink no more. Not for thirty years I haven't touched a drop' she protested.

'Well, I think you do' he replied.

Her friends got Elizabeth home at the end of the working day. She'd had to wait for them in the cold, empty canteen, her top half sprawled over a table. They got her back home with great difficulty and laid her on her bed. Unfortunately Shona and Deoiridh were both away from home. When they got home they took a good look at her. Deoiridh gently pressed her hand under the ribs on Elizabeth's right side. It caused pain. She said 'I think it might be your liver playing up, dear. All that yellow dye you've been absorbing must have been masking jaundice. You must go straight to bed, and I'll get you properly sorted in the morning.'

In the morning Deoiridh called in Dr McNulty, a highly intelligent young Irish doctor that she was very partial to, despite the fact that he was a catholic. He examined Elizabeth gently and thoroughly.

'Yes my dear, you were quite correct, your friend here has an enlarged and painful liver. Would you like me to arrange for you to go into the County Hospital Miss Loader?'

'No, I can't pay.'

Shona, who had a 'private income' in addition to her midwifery work had paid Dr McNulty for his visit. She was never short of a 'bawbee' and immediately said 'You have no need to worry about that. I will sort it out for you.'

In the event, Elizabeth was in hospital for two weeks rest, and missed Isabel's wedding. Isabel apologised. 'I've been waiting so long for that darned man that I needed to get on with things.'

Note

Munitions workers did twelve hour shifts with a half an hour break at midnight on the night shift, and a full hour's lunchbreak on the day shift. These were the only breaks; there were no cups of tea in the morning or afternoon and lavatory visits were frowned on by the supervisors. The work was exhausting. If the women worked with shells, the empty case *weighed 72 pounds, and they needed male help. It was heavy going, and initially the women were not allowed to join trade unions.*

The work was vital. When the war started, for every British shell fired, the Germans fired twelve. The problem was raised in Parliament. All the restrictions on women's labour were removed. If the Government hadn't done this, Britain would have been in even worse trouble.

Elizabeth (Liza)

Chapter Twenty-Eight

On her discharge from hospital, Elizabeth Loader's state of health remained very fragile. This was partly because of her malnutrition and alcoholism as a young woman, and from her short time in the munitions factory. Pastor Ewan McKenzie visited her at the Midwives' home in The Ludgate every week, hurled over the cobbles at speed in his wheeled chair by the elderly but extremely fit Bruce McBride, his 'odd job man' and general church helper. Very slowly, Elizabeth began to gain some strength, and was able to help around the house a bit. Avoidance of fatty foods was of paramount importance for her.

Many of the former 'servant classes' were continuing to earn good wages and obtaining bad health in the munitions factory. Elizabeth was seriously irked that she couldn't contribute anything more tangible to the household other than light housework. It was Isabel who finally came up with a good suggestion. Eggs were in short supply, and the hospitals were using them to feed the wounded, following a national campaign by Frederick Carl, the editor of Poultry World to 'donate eggs to hospitals'. Most of the neighbours in Ludgate had large gardens and their own backyard hens and quite a few people had decided to keep what they called 'a soldier's hen'. The eggs 'the soldier's hens' laid were dedicated to the war effort. They were donated to local hospitals, to be given to the wounded soldiers as they were considered to be 'easily digestible'.

Shona and Deoiridh were enthusiastic when Elizabeth floated the idea of having some hens. However, given the problems Elizabeth had with her liver, they pointed out that it would be better if she never ate eggs herself. She spoke to Bruce McBride, who kindly agreed to make a henhouse and a 'run' out of odds and ends of timber for the proposed new occupants. Feeding the hens adequately proved to be a problem initially. Eventually all food scraps were saved and chopped up for the hens, and these included bacon rind, meat fat, the odd very stale bread crust, potato peelings, outside leaves from vegetables. All these were boiled up in a galvanized bucket on the kitchen range and when cool, bran from the dried food shop was added and the mixture was thrown into the chicken run and gobbled up by the sixteen grateful hens. They were given corn as well.

Most of the eggs donated by the women of Alloa were sent into Europe for the soldiers. The hen keepers often pencilled messages of defiance on the shells of their eggs. '*Send the Kaiser where he belongs*' and so on, but generally the messages were gentle: '*I hope that you feel better today*' and '*I hope a Heilan sodger gets this one.*' It was a lovely thing for the women to do. The Alloa Advertiser was pleased to record that 27,600 Scottish eggs had been sent to France since the egg appeal had begun. It meant a lot of self-sacrifice by the hen owners, as eggs had become more expensive as the war progressed. When soldiers returned on leave they often visited their former schools and churches to thank the people at home for all that they were doing to help, and especially for the eggs.

Meantime Agnes's pregnancy was progressing, and she wrote her mother a letter, admitting her pregnancy. She was dreading the reply. Phemie's reply was brief and kind and very surprising.

Dearest Agnes,
I too was pregnant before marriage, by your father, Alec. Unfortunately I suffered a miscarriage. These things tend to happen when we are young and there are very strong feelings. Don't worry about it. Just come home please! We will all look after you and your baby will be a joy to us all in these dark times. We love you and miss you so much. Sandy is overworked in the pharmacy, and your father is suffering again at the moment, with the loss of Jock, and is having to spend most of his time at Parkstone Farm. He seems to be able to cope better when he is there.
Much love,
Mother

Jason and Victor

Chapter Twenty-Nine

Jason continued his work on the ambulance train until mid-January 1916, and then went back to work in and around the trenches. One morning in May that year, he returned to the British lines at daybreak, exhausted from a night spent in 'no man's land' attending to the dying wounded, and working with the stretcher parties, carrying to the First Aid Post those who had a chance of survival. An official letter was waiting for him. It was a summons to return to Poole and appear at the Military Tribunal Court under the terms of the Military Service Act which had been passed on 27 January 1916. All voluntary enlistment was stopped. All British males, married or single were now deemed to have enlisted on 2 March 1916 - that is, they were *conscripted* - if they were aged between 19 and 41 and resided in Great Britain. Only the medically unfit, clergymen, some teachers and certain classes of industrial workers were exempted.

The letter Jason received made it crystal clear that he would have to return to Poole immediately, and appear at a tribunal, as he had failed to sign up for service with the British Military. The situation Jason was in was 'Hobson's Choice', join the army or be put in prison. Before his travel arrangements were made, he sent a note to Lieutenant Colonel Mayhew, to whom he was 'attached' as an unpaid volunteer, explaining the situation, as he knew that he would have to go to prison for refusing to fight on the grounds of conscience. On Tuesday the 29th March, he made his appearance at the Poole Town Military Tribunal. There were a lot of other men in the queue to be dealt with summarily before his turn came. Jason was more scared about being put in prison than being killed trying to save others at the Front. The magistrate, George Payne, a highly unpleasant person, refused to exempt Mr Davis, a widower who was living with and supporting sick elderly parents and six young children. The magistrate gave the widower two weeks grace, and said that if nothing better could be arranged, the remaining family would all have to go into the workhouse to be looked after whilst their son/father was away.

Suddenly the door at the back of the court was flung open wide and noisily, as a large and powerfully built army lieutenant colonel accompanied by a major and a captain clumped in. They sat down heavily in empty seats at the front of the court. They sat there until Jason's full name was called out, and he stood before the tribunal, white and sweating. He didn't know what to think.

Magistrate Payne began his verbal examination:

'Name, address, occupation'?

'My name is Jason Lovejoy. As a former fisherman and lifeboat man I hold two Bronze Medals and one Silver Medal from the Royal Humane Society for saving lives. I am Qualified in Army First Aid and hold the Red Cross Male Nursing Certificate. Since the outbreak of war, I have worked full time for the British Army as an unpaid first aider. My work has involved me in driving a Red Cross Ambulance and working as a male nurse on ambulance trains. I am currently a stretcher bearer on the Western Front. At night I go out with a team of other men, primarily to bring our wounded back behind the British lines. Those we can't save we comfort with morphine, cigarettes and a prayer if they want one.'

Magistrate Payne: Why have you not joined the army?

Jason Lovejoy: I have no intention of joining the army as I will not take human life.

Magistrate Payne: Then you will be imprisoned for the duration of the war.

It was at this stage that Lieutenant Colonel Mayhew stood up, and said 'We have left an important meeting to be here. My colleagues and I appear on behalf of Mr. Jason Lovejoy, who has served unpaid alongside my troops as a qualified First Aider for the duration of the war thus far. He is an exemplary person who has saved many, many British soldiers' lives in various ways. With permission your worship, I would like to ask Mr. Lovejoy to strip to the waist.'

Jason removed his jacket and shirt with some difficulty. Those present in the courtroom gasped.

'Now turn your back to the court Mr. Lovejoy'.

Jason did so, and turned his back to the magistrate and then to the public. There was complete silence. He was so emaciated that his ribs, front and back were clearly visible. His arms and upper body were covered with old scars and newer scars that were at various stages of healing. Some of the lesions were suppurating.

Lieutenant Colonel Mayhew boomed out 'This man is no longer fit to serve his country. He has completely sacrificed his health in service to his fellow men, saving many, many lives and is an unacknowledged local hero.'

The Lieutenant Colonel sat down. He and his colleagues stared unblinkingly at the magistrate. The court was packed with local people who got to their feet and were suddenly, and bravely, vociferous: 'Quite right too.' 'e'es not a coward,' 'man deserves a medal!!!...'

'Order, Order' shouted the red-faced magistrate, hammering and hammering with his gavel.

The result was that the magistrate, grumpily and reluctantly had to register Jason as 'unfit to serve' in His Majesty's forces. Jason, who would have preferred to go to prison rather than don a soldier's uniform and be required to kill his fellow human beings, felt humbly grateful for the decision. The army trio, having given a 'show of force' to save the life of a very brave man marched off to the station to get the next train back to Southampton.

Jason walked slowly back to Teagues' Grocery store and Wesley's wife gave him a cup of tea (unsugared of course) and a thin slice of toast. Food was getting very scarce. He rested a while in the back room, caught the next train back to Parkstone, and walked up to Blake Hill Farm. He was completely spent, physically and emotionally. Mistress Caroline was sitting in the kitchen, taking a rare break, with her glasses on the end of her nose, peering at the newspaper.

'Allo my love', she said in surprise. 'Didn't know you was comin ome.'

'I didn't either' he said in a voice that spoke of flat exhaustion. 'I'm home to stay.'

'Thank Christ!' she said. Then as an after-thought 'I'll ave to feed you up by the looks of you.'

The old lady, still remarkably fit, rapidly beat up three eggs that she said were '*hot from the hens backsides*' with milk, vanilla, nutmeg and plenty of brandy. While he drank it, she buttered two thick slices of homemade bread for him. Jason stank. He was still carrying the filth of the dead from the soil of the battlefields. She spread an old sheet over the chesterfield and told him to go to sleep. She fetched a grubby old horse-blanket and threw that over him. 'No sense in makin unnecessary washin' she said to herself.

When Jason woke up, it was late afternoon. Mistress Caroline talked to him about how, at her great age, the work at Blake Hill Farm was very hard for her and Victor, despite the help that was being given by Alec Ross and Lydia. Her mare Julie, had produced another healthy foal the previous week, which they called Venus. George, the colt from the now dead gypsy mare was doing well, but she and Victor were desperately worried that in the fullness of time, both would be taken by the military. Indeed Caroline was most worried about Julie, as the military were taking mares now as well. 'How will our horses ever be replaced if they take our mares as well?' she asked. She told Jason that Victor had written a letter, published in the Poole and Dorset Herald about their concerns. Farmers would not be able to produce food without horses to plough the fields. During the first year of the war the British countryside was virtually emptied of horses, from the heavy draft horses such as the Shires through to the lighter riding ponies. Caroline had been really blessed so far in not having to give up Julie, as the last time 'the authorities' came round, they didn't want a mare, but had been visiting regularly to 'eye up' George, the colt. Julie was safe for the time being as she was feeding young Venus.

At dusk Victor, Alec and Lydia were still working. Lydia and Mrs Stone were doing the milking, and Victor and Alec were in the fields.

'Alec seems better doing simple laboring work. He's been a real treasure to us here' Caroline observed to Jason who was up and about after his short sleep.

'I don't have to get called up for the army' Jason told her at last. 'They've declared me completely unfit.' He paused to brush tears from his eyes, remembering his fitness and strength before he went to war to care for the wounded. He was aware that not only had his body suffered an accumulation of injuries over the years, but his mind had too. He had seen, touched, smelled and heard many, many dreadful things. They re-appeared again and again in his dreams.

'You will get better' the old lady said firmly. 'Thur's nothin like the good clean air round yur. Yor mother an me will look after you an get you properly better.' The happiness of having Jason Lovejoy at Blake Hill Farm for rest, recuperation and light duties on Tuesday was quickly dashed when his brother Victor announced on Friday 'I'm joining the army to work with horses in France.' It wasn't a sudden decision on Victor's part. He had done a lot of soul searching about volunteering for the war in some capacity, and it was partly driven by grief at his friend Claude's death, but also in reaction to Mistress Caroline's deep love of horses. They had done as much as they could, fund raising for The Blue Cross animal charity. Now he wanted to do more. He discussed his plans with Lydia Lovejoy who was staying at Parkstone farm, but did not mention them to Alec who had suffered a mental breakdown after the death in action of his much loved son, Jock.

Victor

Chapter Thirty

Victor began work in France and Belgium with horses and mules in late 1916. Although he had spent most of his life with his grandmother at Blake Hill Farm he wasn't very partial to hens, cows and pigs, but he was very, very good at working with his horses. In France, he was chosen to lead horse-drawn supply convoys, pulling loads of food and armaments for the troops from Ypres, along the infamous, deadly, Menin road which traversed the Ypres salient. The horses were better for pulling loaded wagons through the rough, rutted muddy roads than mechanized vehicles which had frequent breakdowns. The job of the transport section was to carry everything the battalion they were supplying needed, food, medical supplies and tools. They traveled over horrific terrain, sometimes moving at night, so that the German troops wouldn't detect them and shell them.

Victor wasn't interested in the causes of war at all. He vehemently hated any malicious damage to people or animals. 'In his head' he had signed up to help his fellow Britons and all the completely innocent animals that were involved. He was completely unprepared for what he was going to encounter when he joined his first convoy of supply horses and mules struggling together with their drivers, pulling ammunition carts, food and equipment for the troops who were holding their thin line against the enemy. The army had given him a pistol, and he had been taught how to use it, but he was mentally ambivalent about whether he could ever kill a fellow human being. He tried to focus on the animals and what he was supposed to be doing.

As for the road he was travelling, it was flattering to call it 'the Menin Road'. Even to refer to it as 'a mud track' was a barefaced lie. It was a dangerous, sticky mess, despite army efforts to board over the mud. On either side, in what had formerly been ditches was the detritus of the long and dreadful war – stagnant water, shattered carts, dead horses and mules, all rotting. If a cart turned over, often their loads were irretrievable as they were broken up and steeped in filth. The very landscape stank of death. As far as Victor could see, only a few remnants of shattered trees remained, poking through the mud. There was not a bit of green on what had once been fertile fields, everything was brown and black. Enormous shell holes, filled with rain, mud, oil and rotting human remains were strewn across the ruined, rancid landscape. Rusting barbed wire and chunks of concrete clustered together. The stench of decay was obscene. Victor remembered reading a line in Shakespeare's 'The Tempest' : '*Hell is empty, and all the devils are here*' as the deep sound of heavy guns filled his very being with cold fear.

For four years, the main easterly access for the British Army to the Ypres Salient was by way of the twelve mile Ypres to Menin Road. Only about a mile out of Ypres, the Ypres-Roulers railway crossed this road, and German gunners and sharpshooters, overlooking the spot from high ground, found this well used intersection provided them with the perfect opportunity for shooting at British troops, supply trains and particularly their extremely vulnerable trucks which were packed with artillery. Early in the war, the Tommies had nicknamed the spot '*Hell Fire Corner*' and put up a notice board to warn others. The danger was so great that it became standard practice for troops to cross the area as fast as they could run, horses went at a gallop and lorry drivers right feet slammed their accelerators to the floor. By the time Victor had to cross it the British Army had erected canvas screens on either side of the road to conceal their movements, much of which took place in the darkness, when the junction was inundated with activity.

Fortunately many of the men on Victor's convoy, particularly those who had worked with horses as part of their normal civilian work bonded closely with their horses.

However, many of the men who had been enlisted for the war were from manufacturing cities, had no experience with horses at all and were seriously frightened of them. Victor and the experienced men who had worked with horses and mules back home had to teach 'the new boys' how to feed and groom them. Each man was assigned to care for specific animals, and all were taught how to approach their 'own' animals gently, speak to them softly, play with them, stroke and fondle their tails and manes. Cleaning and brushing the animals at least daily, to get rid of the clinging mud, particularly on the insides of their back legs was another essential part of bonding with them. Most of the men respected and loved their animals as if they were close friends. The animals were brave and did great work, helped and encouraged by their men. In the event of a horse or mule being seriously wounded and having to be euthanized, the man responsible for the animal often mourned almost as if he had lost a human comrade.

Everything about Victor's work was awful. He felt more sympathy for the innocent animals than he did for himself. He loved Tom, Dick and Harry, the horses he was responsible for; they were so patient, stubbornly determined, and such hard workers. The Germans threw nasty iron devices around where British horses and mules were likely to walk, which got stuck in the soft tissues of their feet, causing in most cases, such severe infection that the poor affected animals had to be euthanized. The animals were lugging heavy artillery and supplies along the road for many hours a day, in great hardship, mostly through deep, filthy festering mud, polluted by decaying animal droppings and further infected from the dead, decaying animals in the ditches.

Victor also worried a lot about insufficient feed for the animals. As with the men, the animal food was also rationed, and the barely adequate supply of hay and oats was an extra burden on the already overloaded transport services. The army tried to supply about twelve pounds of dried forage, seven pounds of grain and some bran per horse per week, around ten times as much food by weight as a human would have received at the time. It was *actually managing* far less than the horses needed, as the army organization was in great difficulty sourcing and supplying enough fodder and getting it through enemy fire. The horses often went hungry, and seldom had sufficient clean water either. It took a total of about five hours of the exhausted horses' and mules' time every day to chew up their oats and hay. In the winter, another problem was shelter for all the animals, who were tied up in open, cold, wet conditions, with their coats closely clipped (so that any skin diseases, lice and mange could be promptly detected and treated). They were shivering cold in the evenings and overnight. Victor quickly learned that the biggest killer of these faithful, essential animals was 'debility'. They reached a tipping point when exposure to the weather, hunger, illness and fear caused them to simply die. The men were not much better off, and sometimes slept with their animals, hoping to share shelter and warmth.

On many occasions the animals suffered severe injuries and had to be dealt with summarily. Victor carried the humane killer, which he used on a number of occasions. It was extremely difficult to euthanize a horse or mule that was in extreme pain and panic, constantly lashing out with its head and legs, particularly when everyone was under intense enemy fire. Victor was a very gentle man. He cried for the men who got killed, but he also cried for the poor, dumb, patient, loyal animals in their suffering. He was particularly fond of an enormous horse called Colossus, who would work for hours, apparently tirelessly, without ever making any fuss. He was always calm as a lamb even under the most terrifying conditions as the carts got closer to the Front. He had the brains and good manners of a thoroughbred horse, but his appearance was disgusting. He was hit by flying shrapnel, and bled out rapidly, showing no signs of panic. Victor was unable to save him.

Many of the men kissed him goodbye and the drivers and soldiers who regularly fed him openly cried. There were appalling horse and mule death rates due to shelling, front-line charges and exhaustion. Eventually Victor's expertise with animals was noted, and he was told that he was being transferred to the British Royal Army Veterinarian Corps 11th Veterinary Hospital, a 'Remount Centre' as these places were called. He was pleased that he would be helping in the care of sick and wounded horses.

Chapter Thirty-One

During WW1 horses were essential to pull heavy guns, convey weapons and supplies to the Front. The Army Veterinary Corps admitted 2.5 million 'unclassified' horses and mules of all types to its Remount Centres, of whom 80% were returned to duty. The numbers of horses and mules, in terms of the vital task of transporting food, equipment and weaponry, and the increasing difficulty of replacing them, was critical by 1917. By this time, about 450,000 were delivering supplies and around 100,000 horses were being used around the front lines to deliver food, ammunition and to bring the wounded from the trenches to hospitals. Mules were also very valuable, as they had great stamina in challenging weather and over difficult ground conditions. Victor was quite shocked the day he heard an officer say '*the loss of a horse is of greater strategic concern than the loss of a human soldier*'. The vulnerability of horses to shelling and machine gun fire meant that the losses of horses were appallingly high. Britain was losing one horse for every two men. Other factors had an influence on horses' health. Their riders (particularly the cavalry), frequently exhausted and stressed, had little time to care for their horses (who were also exhausted and stressed) thoroughly. Getting hold of sufficient oats and hay in battlefield conditions was also a serious problem.

Fortunately, most of the men Victor was working with at the Remount Centre (known to the men as the '*Horsepital*') had worked with horses as part of their normal civilian work, and were good at 'bonding' with their sick and wounded horses and mules. He was impressed that so deep is the British love of horses, that several retired former army veterinary officers from Britain and the colonies came to the Remount Centres at their own expense as volunteer helpers. The centres were set up like the temporary military hospitals, in tents. There were some 'walking wounded' horses, however many required horse ambulances to bring them to the centre. In fact, more horses and mules arrived than could be properly looked after, so most of the men working there were doing far more than they should, and were permanently overtired.

On arrival at the centre, all horses were carefully assessed by the army vets. Those deemed to have seriously broken legs were shot in the head with a 'humane killer.' Those with flesh wounds were usually successfully treated and rehabilitated. Those suffering from mange were isolated and chemically treated in the dipping vat and regularly brushed.

Many of the horses and mules that Victor was sent to help with had never actually been used on the battlefields, but had worked, like him, on the supply convoys. These average working animals greatly outnumbered the thoroughbreds used by the cavalry and the officers' personal mounts. In spite of all the care that Victor and his colleagues gave, sometimes the horses and mules that had been 'rescued' and brought to the Remount Centre for treatment 'just died.' They'd done their best, and suddenly, they'd just had enough. It was both strange and surprising just how much tasty horse meat was appearing in the local town and village butchers' shops, despite the fact that the Remount Centre had a policy of burning or burying all carcasses. Notwithstanding careful observation, Victor was never able to discover who was supplying the local 'Black Market,' but he did enjoy nourishing food a little more often.

Once he had been assessed as being '*a really helpful and competent man*', Victor took his turn to help with 'the horse ambulances', which were used to transport sick and wounded horses and mules to the increasing numbers of Remount Centres spread across the allied territories. Unfortunately, unlike human beings, it was impossible to pack half a dozen injured, frightened horses into a large truck. Generally speaking, they had to be brought to the hospital singly as they were usually quite traumatized. The only way they were able to express their feelings of pain, misery or terror was by means of making loud distress noises, and the use of their fast flying hoofs. As with the human hospitals, the number of 'horse ambulances' increased, and horses were being moved in and out of the depot frequently. Victor was delighted when a London horse charity sponsored the first motorized horse ambulance sent over to France, and it was sited at his place of work!

Victor really liked driving the largest horse ambulance, the sides of its canvas covering emblazoned with blue writing: 'Gift of the Children of Nova Scotia'. The ambulance trips were very challenging for the crews, as like the men they had been serving with, the horses were frequently suffering from 'shell shock.' It was extremely stressful and time consuming trying to entice a terrified wounded horse into the ambulance, so a lot of patting them down and stroking and gentle voices were used. Exotic treats were offered to help calm them, and 'make friends', such as a handful of grain mixed with molasses or peppermints and sometimes carrots and apples.

As a group, the rescued horses strongly detested any kind of interference with their bodies, and needed to be anaesthetized for surgery. They were operated on for their wounds, and just like the humans, strongly disliked having a nasty stinky mask placed over their faces and they would kick out and jerk their heads to try and escape the stink of the chloroform. Tragically, as with humans at that time, many horses just didn't survive the surgery. After surgery, some horses never really recovered and still had to be destroyed with the humane killer. Horses who had undergone surgery needed, like people, a suitable period of convalescence and rehabilitation.

All the horses and mules that lived needed feeding and watering. Tons and tons of forage were distributed to the Remount Centres, but their food rations, as for the men, were pitifully small. They could only be given about 75% of the food they desperately needed to get back to good health. Getting enough food for the four legged friends (and the men who looked after them) was a serious problem in war-torn Europe.

Local farmers and peasants had left acres and acres of the land where great battles had been fought. Absolutely nothing was left, no trees, crops, grass. Where numbers of giant underground bombs had been exploded, the very hills and streams on the landscape had been changed. There was nothing left except devastation – shell holes and stinking mud. Bodies of friends and foes were waiting to be found amongst the mud, shell casings and rusting armory.

In late November 1917 Victor received a letter from Jason to say that he had been notified that two of Victor's close friends, William Rose the hairdresser and George Travers the gardener had both been killed at Passchendaele (3rd Battle of Ypres). Jason had included a cut out statement from Lloyd George that had been printed in the Poole and Dorset Herald 'Passchendaele was indeed one of the greatest disasters of the war. No soldier of any intelligence now defends this senseless campaign.'

The battle of Passchendaele lasted from the 31 July to the 10th November 1917. The Allies from the British Empire and the United States of America lost 325,000 men compared to the loss of 260,000 Germans. 54,391 British men had no known graves. In later years, when peace came, their names were recorded on the Menin Gate. Victor sat down and sobbed and sobbed, 'the waste, the rotten waste of it all.'

Passschendaele

The little village of Passchendaele lay on a ridge east of Ypres, 5 miles from a railway junction that was vital for supplying the German 4th Division. British attacks took place in appalling conditions there from October to early November. At home, *the Daily Mail newspaper* reported -

'Floods of rain and a blanket of mist have doused and cloaked the Flanders plain. Recent shell-holes, already half-filled with water, are now flooded to the brim. Moving heavy material is almost impossible and the men can scarcely walk in full equipment, much less dig. Every man is soaked through and standing or sleeping in a marsh. It is difficult to keep a rifle in a state fit to use.'

A junior officer wrote to a newspaper to say 'The living conditions in our camp are sordid beyond belief. The cookhouse is flooded, most of the food uneatable, nothing but sodden biscuits and cold stew. The men are complaining that their food smells like dead men.'

Passchendaele was finally liberated by British and Canadian infantry, with crippling numbers of casualties. General Haig was criticized for continuing attacks long after his plan had no strategic value. The 'high heid yins' were out of touch with the regimental officers and troops. They lived in comfort, which became more comfortable as the distance from their headquarters behind the battle lines increased as the allies pressed forward. The staff officers seldom spoke to the troops (who felt neglected), and the reports detailing appalling numbers of deaths and casualties at Passchendaele Ridge didn't seem to cause the heid yins much concern. Passchendaele became infamous not just for the massive scale of casualties, but also for the mud, which caused many deaths. General Haig eventually went to see the battlefield and when he finally saw the quagmire and the ghastly conditions where so many allied soldiers fought and died, he was very upset. He was reported as saying '*Do you mean to tell me that our soldiers had to fight under such conditions? Why was I never told about this before?*'

Marie

Chapter Thirty-Two

Marie, the daughter of Elizabeth (Liza) had trained to be a nurse at St Thomas' Hospital in London. Much to her stepmother Miss Langley's pride and delight, she had qualified to be a well-respected Staff Nurse there. In mid-1916, the reported deaths and casualties were so high that she applied to go to work at the British Hospital in Etaples. The 'Land of Hospitals' as it was called by the local people covered six square kilometers and could accommodate 6,500 patients. It was composed almost entirely of tents and was known by those living and working there as 'Hospital City'. The various individual 'hospitals' were funded and staffed by many different humanitarian organizations. The hospitals at Etaples were just part of a vast casualty evacuation chain, stretching back from the Base Hospitals to the Field Hospitals right back to the Casualty Clearing Stations. The Clearing Stations were close to the front, manned by troops of the Royal Army Medical Corps. Nearest to the Front were the First Aid posts, where slightly wounded men could be 'patched up' and continue fighting or sent further back behind the lines if they were more seriously injured.

The large site at Etaples was composed of many reasonably sized hospitals, run by British, American, and Australian people for their soldiers. They were all located close to a railway line, to facilitate the unloading of casualties close to the various hospitals. The large site had been deliberately located at Etaples as it was a channel port. This was important too, so that men with the worst injuries could be evacuated for longer-term treatment in Britain.

On coming ashore, Marie, carrying all her personal luggage, went to meet the Matron of no 12 Field Hospital, a mature and beautiful woman with a pale face and tired blue eyes. Matron Parker said she had perused Marie's excellent reference from her training hospital and said 'Under the prevailing circumstances here, I am minded to offer you an immediate position as a ward sister. Do you think that you would be able to take on this responsibility?'

Marie wasn't a shy person, or a 'show off', but she knew her own strengths and weaknesses, and thought it not unreasonable to say 'Yes Matron, I am a very steady person and believe that I would be able to carry this load with confidence and dignity.'

'Excellent' said Matron Parker with a smile. 'You will be in charge of Ward 60. It's for men with fractures.' She called out 'Tidy!'

A very large, well busted and muscular woman with a determined set to her jaw, a large well pinned reddish-brown bun at the back of her head, and an immaculate lacy cap, clumped in heavily on her big feet.

'Sister Tidy, would you take Sister Langley to her accommodation and sort her out please.'

Sister Tidy grunted and picked up more than half of Marie's baggage. Marie quickly noticed that Tidy's grunting was the major part of her communication with others. On what little evidence she had seen thus far, she assumed that Tidy was some kind of military style nurse-bat-woman who attended on Matron. In fact Sister Tidy was one of the three Assistant Matrons.

It was a chilly, moist October day, and Marie followed Tidy, who despite being heavily laden was doing a very fast military style march across the enormous area of ground, mostly covered by large marquee style white tents with big red crosses painted over them. The hospital was on one side of the road. They had to cross over to get to the Officers and Sisters' quarters. The path to the sisters' quarters was marked for new people like her, by white wooden pegs which had their tops coloured with different paint colours. Tidy led the way, following the *red pegs*, and eventually the pair reached a large group of huts and tents. The tents were all marked with large red crosses, presumably to deter enemy aircraft from bombing.

'Sisters' Accommodation' announced Tidy. 'Supper at eighteen hundred hours'. She dropped the items she had been carrying outside a tent numbered '12', barked 'Carry on Langley!', and marched off briskly. Marie was grateful for the red pegs, as she had felt too strange and panicky to take too much notice of the route by which she had come. She went into the tent, which was for three sisters, but one of the bed spaces was unoccupied. There was a pile of bedding, what looked like a new ceramic hot water bottle and three clean, but slightly worn sisters' uniforms on her folding green canvas bed. Beside her bed there was an open wooden box thing that looked rather like an orange box stood up on its end, but was taller. This was the place for her to hang her uniforms.

She felt both excited and frightened. She made her bed, unpacked her few belongings, and decided to make a brief visit to 'her' new ward. She put on her sister's uniform for the first time. It took a long time, as her hands were shaking with nervousness, and every item had been so well starched, so that the button holes took a lot of work to open.

'What will the nurses, the patients, the doctors, think of me' she wondered as she wrapped her cloak around her. 'Have I the confidence to take on this great responsibility? I hope I won't let anyone down.'

Marie had to walk over what felt like miles of duckboards, following blue pegs to find 'her' ward, which was somewhere in the area occupied by No 23 General Hospital. On arriving in the vicinity, there were no more pegs, and she had to ask directions twice, so large was the site, and all of the tented wards were white. Eventually a male orderly steered her to her new domain. Staff Nurse Chaffey, a Somerset lass, was the qualified nurse in charge.

'You are most welcome Sister Langley' she said with hearty relief. 'We run this ward with VADs and orderlies' she explained rather breathlessly. 'Hardly any of these poor men can move independently, and then only with sticks and crutches. We have a lot of men on Carell Daykin infusions and together with everything else, particularly all these men strung up on Thomas's splints, we're on the run most of the time. Everything has been made worse since our last Sister got pneumonia and had to go back home to Wales. We're so busy. Would you mind awfully if I ask VAD Barraclough to show you around?'

Sister Marie Langley was so terrified when she realized the size and scope of her new responsibilities that she didn't smile at anyone from that moment on.

'*Oh my goodness, oh my goodness, however will I manage to handle all of this?*' she wondered secretly, clamping her teeth together to stop them chattering and compressing her lips, hoping that nobody would notice that she was shaking all over. It was then that Nurse Chaffey, who had a strong Somerset accent started referring to Marie as 'The Bath Gorgon' behind her back.

The next morning, Marie went on duty earlier than necessary. She wanted to 'get a grip' on how the staff managed the wounded men. Her ward comprised sixty men in two huge marquee tents. Most of them had fractured femurs. One of the tents was constantly referred to by the staff as 'The Bad End.' Those patients were very ill, often with open wounds, and the most likely to die. Marie knew that she would have to concentrate hard on what ailed each patient in her charge. She needed to thoroughly get to know her nurses, their strengths and weaknesses. She would be ordering supplies, making sure that her patients had enough to eat and drink and were conscientiously nursed. She had to learn about the new treatments being tried out. Most difficult of all, she would have to find the best ways of managing the army doctors, many of whom were only recently trained themselves and thought they knew everything. Marie continued to develop an impassive 'stone face', and a lot of courage. She got on with her new job. At the end of her first week as Ward Sister she heard one of the VADs saying to another 'Well, the new sister certainly works very hard. She's very scary, and she won't let anyone get away with anything! I've just been seriously told off for referring to the other half of the ward as 'the Bad End' (*because most of the patients were likely to die*), and they needed a lot of care. We are to call it Rose Cottage instead.' She sniggered.

What the VADs didn't know, and they would have split their sides laughing if they had, was that Sister Langley had already been in serious trouble. She was working so hard, and was getting so tired that she was leaving her area in the bell tent she slept in very untidy indeed. Because of this, she wasn't very popular with her fellow sisters either. What no-one had told her was that the infamous Sister Tidy regularly carried out tent inspections in her particular fiefdom - *the nursing staff quarters*. Poor tired Marie was nearly late for work one morning, and left her possessions even more untidily distributed than usual. Sister Tidy was making her flatfooted inspection tour, and spotted the mess, which in truth was most inconsiderate to the other two ladies Marie shared with. She wasted no time in making it even more untidy. A note was left on Marie's bed:

'*This area is a disgrace. See me! You are very fortunate that I didn't bring Matron to look at this. B.Tidy.*'

Poor tired Marie had to humbly apologize. Tidy had to try very, very hard not to laugh.

Chapter Thirty-Three

The Étaples Camp was the largest overseas Army Base ever created by the British. It was a base for British, Canadian, Scottish and Australian forces. It was built alongside the railway line by the town. Networks of railways, canals, and roads connected the camp to the southern and eastern battlefields in France and to the ships which carried troops, supplies, guns, equipment, and thousands of men and women across the English Channel. On her walks around the Etaples hospital site Marie passed by the massive training camps for Australian, New Zealand, English and Scottish troops. Thousands of men were marching on the roads through Etaples every day. Day after day the local residents were calling 'Adieu' and 'Bon chance' to men laden with full kit on their backs, towards that well known place known as 'UP THE LINE'. Every day, from very early morning, the town was filled with the incessant noise of men tramping all day long. Every morning just after breakfast, hundreds of 'new' soldiers tramped to the 'Bull Ring' for drill, usually headed by an Australian Army band.

On her first day off (one a month) Marie went out for a walk. She kept well away from the motor ambulance depot which was known as 'Thumbs Up Corner' and away from the Land of Hospitals where the tents covered six kilometers of ground. She desperately needed to relax her body and her brain. She walked through the village, along past some farms, under a railway bridge and towards the village of Etaples. In the town itself Marie was struck by the effluvium of the streets, where animal waste of every kind and decaying fruit and vegetables lined the filthy dirty narrow, slippery, pokey little streets. There was no sign of decent drainage. One of her friends had warned her '*Try not to take more than two sniffs when going through 'Paradise Alley', it's enough to choke anyone.*' Marie noticed the slovenliness of the unkempt looking housewives. They weren't a bit fussy and Marie had to dodge basins of rubbish and pails of water all the time, because the local residents had the habit of just opening their front doors and flinging all kinds of rubbish out into the street.

Many of the side streets were so narrow that Marie could touch the walls on either side. In the centre of the town the shops were facing onto a square and nearby she found an old stone building. Marie spoke good 'English school' French, and a local woman told her Napoleon had once stayed there. It was currently a wine and spirits store, doing good business. If her day off was on a Tuesday or Friday morning, there was an interesting street market where local people could buy almost anything, from a sewing needle to a chair. Barrows and stalls were laden with fruit, fish, vegetables and clothing of all descriptions. Customers queued up to purchase pigeons and rabbits which were taken home live to be eaten when required. More sensitive customers had them killed while they waited.

By mid-October Etaples was becoming decidedly chilly. Marie was enjoying her much needed day off. She could see the fishing fleet going out to sea, with the sun shining low in the sky, the water still and mirror like and the little boats with their brown sails clearly reflected. It was such a refreshing, beautiful calm compared with dealing with crises and dashing from one patient to another, and having the Damocles sword of having to write and submit the Ward Report to Sister Tidy most evenings. (Tidy was sometimes very critical). Marie realized that she would have to manage herself better if she wanted to remain a Ward Sister, as with great opportunity and responsibility there is always the possibility of failure.

She looked at the water which was now dazzling in the light of the October sun and realized that she must learn to carry the calm of those few moments back with her to the hospital and remember them always. She accepted the need to learn to deal more patiently with herself and with her tired staff through the turmoil of the long days and wearying nights in the ward.

Sister Marie Langley, after a clumsy start was at last going from strength to strength. She had lost her initial 'nerves', smiled and was genuinely cheerful and much liked by her staff. She dealt with paperwork smartly and efficiently. She and Sister Emily Lethbridge were soon, with Matron's permission, working interchangeably between nursing in the orthopaedic ward and working as surgeons' assistants in the operating theatre. This had been a particular help to Sister Lethbridge as she had been on duty most days from early morning until very late at night and sometimes late into the following morning! Between them they alternated for 'on call' orthopaedic emergency theatre calls every other night, usually as a result of haemorrhage –caused by sutures giving way or sepsis causing wounds to re-open. On one day poor Marie had to assist the surgeon at ten amputations. The gas gangrene was the worst. Oh, the stink of those ghastly wounds!

Just a single monthly day off felt like a life saver. It gave Marie a chance to lie longer in bed, and not to put a uniform on. After a late breakfast there was the possibility of walking in the fresh air and feeling the cleansing power of the wind rustling through her clothes. She and other 'off duty' nurses could walk up the slope from the hospital, stop and look at the river Canche and its verdant meandering landscape of calm waters, marshes, meadows and small woods. Now and then they could go past the railway siding and into the sand dunes and see the mouth of the River Canche widening out into the sea and beyond. Sometimes the sky was gin blue and the sunshine on the water could be dazzling. It gave a sense of calm in the middle of a desperate war. But the guns could still be heard.. .

In June 1917 the military hospitals in Etaples were severely bombed by German warplanes during the night. The majority of the staff had presumed that the hospitals would be safe from enemy attack as there were red crosses painted on some of the tents which were brightly lit inside, so that they could nurse their patients. Surgeons were still operating on casualties. There was a sound of approaching aircraft, hand-bells were rung loudly in the tented wards and lights dimmed as a precaution. The enemy demonstrated their hatred. Bombs were falling, whistling through the air. A British Sister was killed and seven nurses wounded, plus many patients and other personnel. Damage was spread over the huge hospitals site. The Canadian General Hospital had no nursing staff casualties but three doctors were wounded and some patients killed. The Nurses' Club was wrecked. At the British Hospital where Marie was working, there were minor casualties among the nursing staff. Sister Tidy remained apparently rock solid, but her nervousness was more visible to Marie. At the time of the raid she was having a severe conversation with Marie about *the untidiness of her ward.* She suffered a slight head wound and had to be admitted to hospital herself for overnight observation. One of Marie's patients was killed. Parts of the British Sisters' quarters were wrecked.

In one of the neighbouring hospitals a VAD was so severely shell-shocked that she had to be sent home to Blighty within the week. At 56 General Hospital a staff nurse was wounded in the eye. The remaining nursing staff were emotionally shaken but physically fine. At the time of the raid, three Ambulance Trains were waiting in the hospital siding to be unloaded. The train was bomb damaged and some patients were further wounded. Four similar attacks had already been carried out in May 1916, using incendiary bombs directed against the various hospital sites on the French coast.

Marie was swimming strongly in the waves of war. She felt resilient enough to take anything the Germans threw at her. However, she had very logical worries. The Germans had visited and they were likely to come back. The 'authorities' had arranged for slit trenches to be dug around the perimeter of the site with the view of using them to shelter patients in the event of bombing. Any possibility of a direct hit on her orthopaedic ward would mean that patients and possibly nurses would be in deadly danger as there were no 'walking wounded' in her ward. As soon as the men showed positive signs of recovery they were shipped back to Britain, on stretchers. Marie managed to get the bad thoughts out of her head most of the time. She thought about her next day off (*if it wasn't cancelled*).

In spite of her initial feelings about the grubby town of Etaples, Marie was very impressed by the numbers of local women who volunteered to help part-time in the hospital wards. Some local people such as the cooks worked on a regular basis, and were paid. Other people arrived to help as and when their home and family obligations allowed.

Then it happened. It was a hard winter, and the hitherto strong and healthy Marie suddenly became very poorly. She developed a chest infection, and felt as if she had flu. She herself became a hospital patient, and was put in a staff isolation tent. Matron Parker visited her, noted that her condition was deteriorating and was most concerned. She told her that 'I have arranged for you to go back home and be nursed in a local hospital'.

Chapter Thirty-Four

Strapped to a stretcher, Marie was loaded into a cabin on a troopship bound for Dover. On landing she was then 'entrained' as it is described and finally fetched up at Alderney Hospital, just outside of Poole. It was a new, temporary hospital, where war casualties could be cared for close to their families. The wards were basically huts. She was very poorly indeed by the time she was tucked into bed in Ward 17. '17' was an isolation ward, and all the patients lay in glass cubicles to prevent their infections from travelling to their neighbours. The nurses could safely observe their patients from the corridor. If Marie rang for assistance the nurse had to put a special mob cap, tie on a mask, enter her room and carefully don a white gown with a small red cross on the outside, which hung by the door, with its outside aspect to the room. Then she could attend to her patient. Any fluids or solids emanating from the patient were tipped into a lidded bucket containing Lysol. There was another huge tub of Lysol for sheets and clothing to be soaked in.

Marie's adoptive mother, Miss Langley received a cross Channel telegram from Matron Parker, saying: '*Sister Marie Langley quite ill. Being repatriated to Poole.*' She and her sister were beside themselves with worry. As with many soldiers' families, no-one had the slightest inkling of where or when their loved one would turn up. Crossing the Channel could be protracted and difficult in terms of weather and enemy activity. As the United Kingdom was at war, no port had been mentioned or any date or time of sailing. As it happened, Marie was placed in a troop ship bound for Dover, with almost equal proportions of sick and wounded soldiers and nurses as troops going home for a short leave.

Marie was indeed very poorly. Her last address had been the London Hospital where she had worked prior to leaving for France. Miss Langley had no idea when or if Marie would be sent back to Poole. Communications on such matters were extremely poor. The most common comments passed when anything went wrong tended to be 'there is a war on you know.' She wondered if she should do what other relatives did – go and wait at Poole Station for the hospital trains to arrive? She felt sick with worry. Finally, at last! A telegram arrived care of an annoying young show off boy, who skidded his motor-bike (with a lot of disgusting blue smoke) up to St Faith's doorway, disturbing the gravel drive. *'Sister Marie Langley arrived at Alderney Hospital yesterday. Ward 17'.* Miss Langley burst into tears of relief and handed the telegram to her sister, who was by her side.

She rang Canon Dugmore, who had been praying for Marie. Although there was a war on, he now had a *motor-car* and chauffeur. 'I'm so sorry to trouble you, but I was wondering whether it might be possible for me to be conveyed urgently to the new hospital at Alderney. I have just had a telegram to say that Marie arrived there yesterday, and is very poorly.'

She felt guilty for asking, but felt the situation to be something of an emergency. Marie might die.

The Canon said 'My dear, I'll organize my chauffeur to call for you at 2pm. would you like me to come as well?'

'I'd be so very glad, Canon.'

Miss Langley had never ridden in a motor-car before, but took no notice of the car or the journey. She didn't even speak to the Canon, she was just full of concern for her beloved adopted daughter. She had packed a small bag of things she felt Marie might need whilst in hospital, plus a slice of sponge cake, some biscuits and two fresh eggs. When the car pulled up in the driveway to the hospital, the Canon helped her out of the car and took her arm. In his free hand he carried the little case he used when making *really serious sick visits.* The ward was a large, long wooden erection. They went in the front door, and knocked the Ward Sister's door. It was a very tiny room. Under her desk was a black cat sleeping in its basket.

Sister O'Connor was very Irish, and had an abundance of very rebellious curly red hair. She spoke quietly, throwing her words out at such an amazing speed, that it made it very difficult for those unused to such torrents of information supplied with a strong Irish brogue to understand or even remember. It also gave the impression that she was very busy and didn't have much time for hanging around.

'This ward is an Isolation Ward. Troops have been picking up all sorts of infections we've never come across before. Then of course, there are the civilians with diphtheria, salmonella, polio, tuberculosis, cholera, typhoid, typhus and many others. All our patients are in single cubicles, and are being barrier nursed so that they don't share any infections with other patients or pass them on to the doctors and nurses. All washable items are soaked in Sudol, excrement is similarly treated. Only medical and nursing staff can enter the cubicles, and must don protective clothing. You will only be able to view your daughter from the corridor, through the glass panel Mrs Langley. Food rations are very short with there being a war on. Thank you very much for the eggs, cake and biscuits. I will see that she eats them. We will have to build up her strength.'

Marie was lying in bed, extremely pale, and sleeping. The Canon had been hoping to be allowed to administer the Sacraments for the Sick, but wasn't allowed in either. A nurse carried two wooden chairs along the corridor, so that they could sit and watch in case Marie woke. After about an hour she stirred, and opened her eyes. She didn't look well at all, but they tapped on the window, and when she saw her visitors, she gave a radiant smile. The Canon said a prayer for her, made the sign of the cross to the window and Miss Langley, weeping with joy waved. Marie quickly went back to sleep again, so her visitors went to ask Sister O'Connor what ailed her.

'Its called PUO, Pyrexia of Unknown Origin. She's certainly very run-down, seems a little bit chesty and has a slight cough. She clearly hasn't had the time to eat properly, she's been so busy. She did mutter something about sleeping in a bell tent at the base hospital. *In this weather*! I can't tell you any more until Dr Grenfell, the doctor in charge comes to see her. I do promise you both that she will have the best of care here. She MUST REST. Visiting days here are generous, Monday, Wednesday and Saturdays, from 3-4 pm.'

Canon Dugmore was very kind. He regularly sent his car to St Faith's Orphanage on Mondays and Saturdays to collect Miss Langley to see her daughter. Miss Langley walked up to Alderney Hospital on Wednesdays. In four weeks, with plenty of rest, Marie was improving rapidly. After six weeks in Isolation, Marie was brought home to St Faith's in Canon Dugmore's car. Most of the children already knew her, as she had grown up at St Faith's. They were desperate to have some sort of celebration. Miss Langley had to explain to her orphans that Marie had been very poorly, and wouldn't be able to play with them for some time, as she was still very weak and needed rest and quiet. The children had been told that she was a very brave lady, and had been looking after poorly soldiers at the war. So they made little cards and presents for her. Christmas at St Faith's was much quieter than usual.

Slowly Marie's strength came back. She spent short periods with the teenie-tinies, worked in the kitchen a little bit and did some light dusting. One bright day she decided to walk down to the Vicarage to visit her invalid friend, Lady Louise Dugmore. Lady Louise's poor mis-shapen hands were slowly and determinedly knitting. Marie was most impressed. Lady Dugmore explained:

'I started knitting for the first time in my life when we heard about how cold our poor troops were getting in the trenches during that first winter of the war. It was all in the papers, Lord Kitchener went to ask the formidable Queen

Mary if she could do anything to help keep our troops warm whilst they were in the trenches. As a result Queen Mary is leading the movement to keep our troops warm during winter in the trenches. Apparently Lord Kitchener asked her to undertake the huge task of providing 30,000 pairs of socks for our brave lads. I had to ask young Fanny Snell to come round to teach me to knit. Fanny says knitting is 'useful work for anxious fingers'.

'I'm slow, because of my illness, but I've got used to it now. All the patterns are standardized, grey wool is mainly used, but we knit coloured stripes in at the top of each sock, as there are three different sizes. Small socks have a white stripe at the top and there's a blue stripe for Medium and a red stripe for Large. We don't just do socks, we do scarves as well. Some ladies also knit patches to hold dressings in place. Some *really clever ladies* also do balaclava helmets and large knitted belts to keep our mens' internal organs warm as well, but I find those too difficult with my disability. Like many women of my class, I have had to learn to knit late in life! We knitters usually slip little notes into our finished articles to show that we knitted these at home, with love for our men. Look, here is one' she said, handing a note to Marie. *'Into this sock I weave a prayer that God will keep you in His love and care.'*

Chapter Thirty-Five

Christmas 1917 at St Faith's Home came and went. It was so cold that the Poole and Dorset Herald reported that the wooden toilet seats had been stolen from South Road School. The reporter suggested that they had been taken to burn in the grate of a very poor household. There was also mention of the exceedingly high rate of illegitimate births during 1917, attributed to 'troop movements!' At St Faith's, the children seemed to be taking it in turns to be quite poorly with colds and coughs and bronchitis. Miss Langley was very concerned that Marie had taken on a lot of the care of these children. She didn't want her to be ill again!

By March Marie had decided to look for another nursing post. She was very attracted to the idea of going to help out at the little hospital at Swanage, if there was a post vacant, and wrote a letter to the Matron. There was a quick reply:

Dear Miss Langley,
Thank you for your letter and enclosed references. I was sorry to hear of your recent serious illness, and agree that a staff nurse's position would be more suitable for you at this present time. Our hospital is very small, with just fourteen regular beds, and ten more in a temporary wooden construction. I will be happy to employ you subject to a doctor's note to confirm that you are well enough to resume working.
Yours faithfully,
L.M. Bowler (Matron)

Marie was delighted, her stepmother less so. On the one hand, she adored having Marie around the place helping, but on the other hand she was terrified that working in a hospital would expose her to the possibility of another serious illness. Significantly too, St Faith's Home existed on the charity of the local people. Really, it was necessary for Marie to earn her own living. Her nurse's pay would be poor, but the hospital would feed and house her. Marie just wanted to get on with her life!

Canon Dugdale's chauffeur took Marie and her trunk to Poole Station and helped her aboard the train to Wareham. She had to change trains to continue her journey on the tiny branch line to Swanage. As ever, there were plenty of men in khaki moving around the country, on and off leave, so she had plenty of help with her trunk, and an old man with a horse and cart drove her to the hospital, which had just fourteen 'regular' beds, but a temporary hut with twelve beds had been erected for convalescing war casualties. It was just what Marie needed, with relatively little stress, and she easily settled down to her new work, as the Night Staff Nurse.

As spring came, and the days lengthened into Summer, she chose to use her 'off duty' to spend time either walking on the local hills or on the beach. Brenda, also known as 'Bin' (she had a very large unfussy appetite), one of the assistant nurses, passed on a knitting pattern for a bathing costume to her.

'If we can get time off together, I'll show you how to swim' she offered. 'I'm that bored with my husband being away at the war.'

With Brenda's help, Marie took to swimming, but was disinclined to 'go out of her depth.' However, eventually she was swimming quite strongly. One afternoon in early September 1918, she was 'caught by the tide', in Swanage Bay and got into difficulties quite a distance from shore. As luck would have it, Jason was out in his little fishing boat, still trying to get to grips with some of the turmoil inside his head, as well as catching fish to supplement the meagre quantities of food available in the local shops. He spotted what looked like a person in the water, and with quite a lot of difficulty managed to haul her into his boat. She was extremely cold, and he stripped off most of his own clothing to warm her up, and steered for the jetty.

'Have I caught a mermaid?' he asked her, but she was too cold to answer. She did however notice the appalling scarring on his back, arms and hands, now fully exposed.

Anyway, he got her ashore, and took her back to the hospital, where her nurse friends could look after her. He took his clothes back, and also got her full name: Marie Faith Langley.

Jason wrote letters to Marie and she replied. They met again in October, on her monthly day off, and spent a little while fishing from Jason's boat in the shallow water, but Marie got very cold. They shouldn't have been there at all really, but Captain James Lovejoy, Jason's father, was operating the paddle steamer 'The Bournemouth Queen' (*re-named for the war as HMS Bourne*) as a mine sweeper around the local coast, and he had a deliberate 'blind eye' for little fishing boats close to the coast. Food was very hard to come by, and Jason had a reputation for wooing nice young ladies with fishy gifts.

In November, the weather was cold and wet. Jason sent Marie return train tickets to travel from Swanage to Parkstone, praying that her day off wouldn't be cancelled. He wanted her to meet Mistress Caroline and see the farm. His aged grandmother was very worried about having a visitor who was a *'proper trained nurse.'*

'O my lor...', she said. 'We'll all need to get cleaned up a bit 'ere. Posh folks don't understand what farms are like what with animals an mud an all gettin walked about the house. I'll ave to imprison Napoleon (*her current most ferocious cockerel was always called Napoleon*) in the stable. E'won't like it. Give the girls (hens) the day off though.'

There was little to worry about really. Marie travelled from Swanage to Wareham, Wareham to Poole and Poole to Parkstone, where Jason was waiting for her. From Parkstone they travelled on the footplate of the tiny engine named

'George Jennings' which went up and down the line to the local pottery. From the pottery it was just a short walk to the farm, and there had been a heavy frost for the previous two days, so the muddy paths and general mud outside the farm were no problem.

It was a lovely visit. Mistress Caroline and Marie took to each other immediately.

'We doan get many visitors yur.' Caroline told her. 'You remind me of someone I seen yurs and yurs back. Young woman, down on 'er luck, and been a bit naughty *if you know what I do mean*' she said, touching her nose. 'I kep her yur furra night. Gave 'er money. Often wonder what 'appened to 'er. Went to the bad, most like.'

On the way back to Poole, Jason asked Marie to marry him.

'I don't rightly know what to say' she replied. 'This is all very sudden. Perhaps on my next day off we could meet again, and I could introduce you to my mother.'

Marie didn't give any more information. She felt perplexed and said 'I think I need to write to you before we next meet, to share some information about my personal circumstances.'

She wrote from Swanage:

'Dear Jason,
    I am a foundling. I have no idea at all who my real parents are. The only family history that I have is that I was deposited at the door of St Faith's Children's Home one evening. There was a note attached to the filthy rags I was clothed in. *'Her name is Marie.'* Miss Langley kept it for me. It was written extremely badly.
Miss Langley and her sister, who made their home into a refuge for unwanted children, took me in, although their home was already full. Very unusually, in spite of my obviously bad parentage, they decided to adopt me,

and Miss Langley senior is my mother.
With the financial help of Canon and Lady Dugmore I attended Parkstone Grammar School. I really wanted to be a nurse, and went to work in Mr Perret's grocery shop after leaving school at sixteen, so that I could pay for my nurse training in London. I was a staff nurse for a short period in St Thomas's Hospital, London.
In the hospital at Etaples I became a Ward Sister, and eventually Sister Emily Lethbridge and I took turns to work in the orthopaedic ward and as surgeons' assistants in the operating theatre. That way we were both able to get some sleep!
As you know so well yourself Jason, the circumstances in the battle areas were dire, with countless desperately injured young men, many haemorrhages caused by sutures giving way and sepsis. In this atmosphere of stinking infection I became very ill, and was sent home. I have to admit to you that I'm not the young woman that I once was. My health isn't great, and I feel safer in my current not very demanding work.
With best wishes,
Marie

Dear Marie,
I am delighted to hear that you were found, and are clearly a great treasure to your adoptive mother and aunt. You have had a golden upbringing compared with many of our local children, particularly in Poole Town. I feel that I understand what you are saying about your work and the stress and strain it put you under. I am just starting to recover a bit myself, having spent so much time in and around the Western Front. My little fishing boat and the farm are very helpful in terms of dealing with sudden awful flashback memories. Hopefully peace will come

soon.
If you weren't too put off by the farm, perhaps we could
alternate visits monthly, and see how things work out for
us?
Yours affectionately,
Jason.

Chapter Thirty-Six

In his past, Captain Harry Lovejoy had been a difficult, naughty boy, a teenage drinker, a street fighter and a young man who chased women, notably the highly attractive Liza Loader with whom he had enjoyed a very steamy full on sexual relationship. In order to bring his son 'to order', his late father, Captain James Lovejoy took him on as an apprentice. They sailed around the world together, until his Father's death in Alloa from heart failure. At the time of his father's death Harry Lovejoy was a fully competent First Mate. Unfortunately their sailing ship, 'The Daphne' wore out. The repairs were too costly for him to fund.

On his return, Harry Lovejoy settled down with his business on Poole Quay, buying and selling commodities just as he and his father had done during the time they sailed together. He lived with his beloved wife Lydia and their two sons, Victor and Jason. In spite of the Armistice, Victor was still serving in France, as were many other men. There was a lot of clearing up and organizing to do, and it was going to take a long time. However, Jason was desperately anxious to introduce his father to his fiancée.

'All right, my boy', said Harry. 'Can you arrange a date with your young lady to come along to 'The Poop Deck' (the Lovejoy family home on Poole harbour-side). It took a while for Marie to get her monthly day off. She finally arrived at Poole station on a Thursday morning, and was met at the station by Jason, who was now less jumpy at the sound of loud noises. Jason's father, Harry, immediately took to Marie. She had a familiar look to her, as if he had met her before. He wasn't too far wrong. As a young man he had got her mother 'into trouble,' and in just over an hour, he was going to remember all about it.

Lydia Lovejoy prepared a very nice lunch despite the wartime shortages. She had cadged some precious vegetables from the Ross family, as the Lovejoy seniors, living on the quay, had no proper garden. Generally they obtained their fruit and vegetables from Blake Hill Farm. There was plenty of fish, as Jason and Harry had caught a selection of plaice and red mullet in the harbour that morning.

After lunch, conversation by Harry and Lydia with Marie started to become deeper. Marie chattered about her work in France and Swanage, and how she had met up with Jason. Pleasant questions were asked by Harry and Lydia and more details slowly emerged. Marie was adopted and had a lovely stepmother and aunt.

'Is your stepfather no longer living?' asked Lydia with interest.

Marie went pink, and began to speak nervously. 'My stepmother and aunt run St Faith's Girls' Orphanage. Neither of them are married. They adopted me when I was very little. I have no clear memory of my parentage. I remember a person who might have been my mother. She wasn't kind. I have no awareness of ever having a father. I am a foundling. I was left outside St Faith's Orphanage in Upper Parkstone. There was a note to say 'her name is Marie.' Miss Langley and her sister took me in. I have some vague memories of my life before going to St Faith's. I lived in a filthy room, wasn't fed much and was often tied up to what I think now might have been a table leg. My mother was seldom home, I was hungry and cold most of the time. One day the woman I think was my mother walked and carried me up a lot of hills. She left me in the cold outside a big house. I screamed and screamed. The people in the house, which was actually St Faith's Orphanage took me in and were very kind to me. Eventually I was legally adopted by Miss Langley who owns and runs the orphanage. She is the only mother I have ever known. Without St Faith's Home and the Langley sisters, I don't know what would have become of me.' Large tears rolled down her face.

Harry Lovejoy, who had been listening intently was slowly losing all colour from his face, which was now wet with perspiration. He slid sideways off his chair on to the floor. Marie and Jason were the first off their chairs to help him, and turned him on to his side.

'I can't find his pulse' said Marie, with tears in her eyes. She looked into Harry's eyes. His pupils were slowly dilating. Harry was dead. What a dreadful way for such a happy day to end! The doctor was sent for, confirmed death and wrote out a certificate. He said that like his father, Harry had died from a heart problem. Harry's youthful bad behavior had finally caught up with him.

After a suitable period of mourning for Harry Lovejoy, Jason and Marie were married at St James's Church in Poole. From their first meeting, the couple had a remarkably close relationship, and local people said that they looked like 'two peas in a pod.' Eventually two children were born to them, a boy and a girl, but sadly, they *'weren't right'*, and only lived for a few days. Jason and Marie looked after Mistress Caroline and Parkstone Farm until she died.

At long last, the terrible World War reached a *ceasefire* on the 11th of November 1918. This did not of course, mean that everyone involved could immediately come home. Thousands of men were needed to clear up armaments, move huge pieces of equipment, carts, tanks, horses and search for and bury bodies. There were still huge numbers of men in hospitals across the Empire. The Great War, as it became known, had included many other regions of conflict. Agnes's boyfriend Tony, died in the battle of Loos. His body was never found. Poor Victor had to stay in France long after the Armistice was declared, and was not released from his duties until late 1919. Unfortunately of the 10,000 Poole men who went to war, 1,000 never returned home after World War 1. Of the survivors, many had been in prisoner of war camps, been gassed, were shell shocked and suffered from a variety of injuries. Of those who were brought home, many died from their serious injuries. Some are buried in the churchyard of St Mary's Longfleet, beside the Cornelia Hospital. It took a long time for those returning home to adjust to home life again, as most of them had horrific flashbacks of the things they had endured. Throughout the United Kingdom, most of the original army regiments were decimated and in some towns whole streets and communities had become suddenly fatherless after single battles. Scotland had provided more men in proportion to population than any other part of Britain. Women had to make decisions that previously the men would have made, and if their men came home it was often difficult to go back to how things were.

There were two surprising sources of joy in Poole. In her fifties Phemie gave birth to a little girl! She was conceived on the night following the news of her son Jock's death. She and Alec named her Grace. The second celebration was Victor's return home to Poole in late 1919. He married Agnes, who had produced a red haired son, thanks to her dalliance with Tony. Victor and Agnes shared a special kind of love. He was an excellent husband for Agnes and stepfather to her son Graham. Victor never changed his ways, and was often discreetly 'out' in the evenings with friends.

Elizabeth (Liza) continued to live happily with the midwives in Alloa, and spent a lot of time with Pastor Ewan and his wife Isabel. Her health was never strong, and she died quietly one day, whilst feeding her hens. She was much missed by the Ludgate midwives, Shona and Deoiridh.

Appendix 1
Alloa - Paton's and WW1 knitting

Many clubs and social organizations either added knitting to their regular activities or raised funds to supply wool and needles for knitters, or to ship comfort packages to the troops. Social historians point to women's involvement in these fund-raising efforts as a way in which ordinary women gained experience in grassroots organizing. On the other hand, it has also been argued that the efforts of women who had been active in the women's suffrage movement before the War were now diverted into the war effort; organizations with substantial female leadership before the War gradually came under male leadership as regional organizations were consolidated provincially and nationally.

Women on the home front contributed to the war effort while also capturing the harsh realities of frontline trench warfare.

Unfortunately with all the nice middle class ladies knitting away, many working class women lost out on a valuable revenue stream. After a meeting with the Queen it was suggested that ladies from the upper echelons might buy the wool and pay the lower classes to knit the socks, keeping everyone happy.

Thousands of women and schoolchildren knitted throughout the war. Over 1.3 million pairs of socks were sent overseas – often with a small personal note inside the sock informing the digger who had knitted the garment along with a brief message.

One set of standardized patterns specified a colour-coded stripe at the top of each sock in order to indicate the size: a white stripe for Small, a blue stripe for Medium and a red stripe for Large.

Organizations assembling comfort packages included a label to show that it had been produced by their group rather than the government. Knitters sometimes tucked a message into the finished garment for the soldier who would receive it, to remind him that he was in their prayers. A typical note might read: *"Into this sock I weave a prayer, That God keep you in His love and care."* Many recipients wrote a thank you note, sometimes addressed to the local newspaper in the knitter's home town.